A Soldier's Quartet

COLIN BALDWIN

A Soldiers Quartet © 2021 by Colin Baldwin.

All rights reserved. No part of this book may be reproduced in any form or by any electronic or mechanical means including information storage and retrieval systems, without permission in writing from the author. The only exception is by a reviewer, who may quote short excerpts in a review.

This book is a work of fiction. Names, characters, places, and incidents either are products of the author's imagination or are used fictitiously. Any resemblance to actual persons, living or dead, events, or locales is entirely coincidental.

Printed in Australia

First Printing: September 2021

Shawline Publishing Group Pty Ltd

www.shawlinepublishing.com.au

Paperback ISBN - 9781922594341

Ebook ISBN - 9781922594334

Dedicated to my father.

I hope you enjoy my first novel.

Regards
Colin Baldwin

FEB 2022

Music comes to me more readily than words.
— Ludwig van Beethoven

Once you make a decision, the universe conspires to make it happen.
—Ralph Waldo Emerson

Inspired by true events.

Chapter 1

2018. April
Tasmania

Wolfgang Deppner… Wolf Deppner… Wolf…

Conrad Bentley sipped his morning coffee and examined a 1914 photo of Wolf Deppner with his two older brothers, Otto and Ernst, all three in uniform. Conrad had come to think of them in terms of their Christian names, intrigued by their faces, just as a letter written by their father in 1918, describing Wolf's death on the Western Front, had initially intrigued him. An unknown soldier had returned to Tasmania with the letter, a war souvenir, and it fell into Conrad's hands a century later.

The words in the letter, the grief of losing a son to war, immediately resounded in Conrad's mind and initiated a clarion call to bring past events into the present.

From that moment, just under a year ago, Conrad had felt Wolf's presence. It was something he struggled to fully understand, so he kept it to himself. Wolf had urged Conrad to search for his living relatives and let them know about the letter. Wolf had stood beside Conrad, shadowed him, and guided him as he undertook the quest.

Conrad's wife, Gretel, was at work, aware her husband was at home enjoying his third year in retirement. Although she accepted researching the letter was Conrad's new project, she was still bewildered at how much time he devoted to it. There were jobs around the house that had been pushed aside, planned tasks that were on Conrad's list of retirement activities. Only that morning, they laughed at his intention to repaint the balcony railings in the first year of retirement. Conrad had cited grounds for his procrastination— he looked after grandchildren, had joined a bushwalking club, crewed with three others in weekly yacht races, was a member of a German conversation group, regularly exchanged emails with German pen friends and, for extra enjoyment, attended German lectures at university. In addition, the rehearsals for his string quartet and amateur orchestra occupied two nights a week or more. His violin playing was particularly important to him. Music had been a source of great pleasure since his youth and Conrad's parents were proud that his musical talent had been passed down through the family: one of his great-grandfathers was a trumpet player, the other, a violinist.

Despite the excuses, Conrad conceded that the letter from the First World War, and now the photo, had dominated his time, his thoughts and most of his waking moments. Little had he known that the task of researching Wolf's fate would lead to a chain of events that succeeded in relegating everything else to a position of marginal importance.

Franz Deppner, the ninety-year-old grandson of Hermann Deppner who had written the letter back in 1918, had recently emailed the photo of the three brothers. When Conrad opened this image, he immediately felt his connection with the Deppner family, and with Wolf, strengthen. He needed to learn more about Wolf's life, his death. He needed to give Wolf a voice.

Conrad's own inner voice of doubt was hovering. You're obsessed, Bentley! It's just a photo. Stop wasting your time.

Despite his doubts, questions about the photo still preyed on his mind. And now here he was, studying it once again. It differed from the usual images splashed across the pages of history, black and white portraits taken in studios with stylised props and the soldiers aglow with patriotism, their eager faces often slightly turned to flatter their profiles. Conrad believed this was no typical image of tailored and handsome soldiers, their nationalities detectable only from their uniforms. This was a spontaneous, candid photograph taken in the open air. The men were standing in a private courtyard with rectangular garden beds enclosed by a tall, dark-stained paling fence. The lack of mature plants or flowers in full bloom implied it had been taken in autumn. Another hint, to the left of the picture, was a rose bush devoid of flowers and most of its leaves. Otto and Ernst Deppner were looking directly at the camera, their hands clasped behind their backs, left legs forward in an apparent confident pose. They were looking directly at the camera, but Conrad interpreted their expressions as somewhat apprehensive, perhaps even startled. In stark contrast, their younger brother appeared curiously nonchalant. Wolf's smile, or grin, looked incongruous when compared with the expressions beside him. He had tucked his left hand in a tunic pocket with his index finger pointing to the ground, which to Conrad, seemed a dramatic gesture. Wolf stood with his legs apart, a position that also seemed to Conrad awkward and peculiar when compared with the poses of his brothers.

Wolf, you seem to grin at the camera with an indefinable air. Is it happiness or contentment, or is it more of an overconfident and reckless disregard for the impending perils of war? Why do you appear to smirk while the expressions of your brothers exhibit a more circumspect understanding of war? What influenced your brothers to look apprehensive, and you audacious, mischievous?

Conrad closed his eyes to imagine the scene. Who took this shot a century ago? A family member? A friend? You were dressed in crisp, new uniforms. Were you on the eve of deployment? Was this a hasty farewell picture?

Again, Conrad focused on Wolf's face, his expression supposedly imbued with the moral high ground that war was a glorious necessity, a rallying call Für Kaiser und Vaterland—for king and country. He wondered if Wolf had contemplated the prospect that his war would turn out to be filled with incessant mud, water-filled trenches and agonised screams, or had he been oblivious to such horror, falling prey to the propaganda that his war would be won within months or, at most, a year.

Conrad's thoughts started to blur. He had domestic responsibilities and needed to get to the supermarket—they had invited their eldest daughter and her family to dinner. His inner voice told him to give up and go to the supermarket, but he ignored the advice. *How much time can I steal?*

The letter, a single piece of the puzzle, had provided some details that helped bring Wolf's fate into focus, but the remaining missing pieces frustrated Conrad.

Wolf, you were twenty-three when you were shot and killed in June, 1918, he recalled. *You died near a small village in France. What was the appearance of that village when you fell? Was its surrounding landscape fields of swaying wheat and bursts of red poppies, or was it already a scarred and burned wasteland like so many of the images we have seen of the Western Front? Your father wrote that you died a hero's death. Did you die instantly Wolf? Or did you suffer and cry out in pain? The letter named three comrades who helped bury you. Were you one of four good friends who fought together, looked after each other, patched each other's wounds and longed for home? What happened to your friends after the war?*

Conrad turned back to the photo. *I don't want your death to be in vain, Wolf. For you to have died without a voice. Too many young men died in this Great War, but it's your story that has fallen into my hands. Wolf, I'm still seeking answers…*

When he had finally made contact with Wolf's relatives in February, they had supplied details about the three brothers and their respective regiments, but Conrad wanted to know more. The Deppners were often bemused as to why he would continue to speculate on what might have transpired outside the known facts.

Conrad yawned and stretched. His shoulders were tense. Wolf's expression in the photograph was unsettling him. *Leave it, Bentley! You won't get the answers you're seeking. It's futile to try and reconstruct the past.*

He tried, unsuccessfully, to slow his thoughts. He wished his neighbour, Wally Archer, had not gone away for the weekend. Their decade of chatting over the boundary fence had become an essential ritual, and Wally was a willing collaborator in this war letter research. Conrad wanted to see if Wally could help shed more light on the brothers' disparate expressions. He had begun to think the elusive past would defeat him.

Conrad grabbed his shopping list and headed for the door. He brushed past his music stand and paused to glance at the open pages of the slow movement from Haydn's string quartet, the Emperor, one of the pieces chosen for the concert. Damn it! I should have done some violin practice before tomorrow night's rehearsal.

Conrad's string quartet was rehearsing for an upcoming concert and he felt behind in mastering those tricky passages and shifts up the fingerboard, such dexterity not often demanded of the second violin. The quartet's leader, Alan, had frequently reminded Conrad that the counter melodies and cross rhythms in good quartet writing were often treacherous for the second violin and viola, the middle voices, and that it was vital to devote extra time to learn them. Weeks ago, he had strategically placed the music on the stand as a constant reminder to practise it, but now accepted that his increasing fascination with Wolf's story had won the battle against taming the difficult passages in the Emperor…

As he drove to the supermarket, Conrad found it difficult to shake off the image of Wolf's puzzling expression. You're overthinking this, Bentley!

Chapter 2

2017. June
Tasmania

On a crisp, midwinter morning, Conrad met two friends from his German conversation group for coffee. Irene hailed from Cologne, Paul from the Black Forest area—the other regular members from all corners of Germany, territories of the former East Prussia and Switzerland. Conrad admired their post-war resilience and tenacity in building new lives on the other side of the world. He was grateful for their patience in helping him with correct pronunciation and grammar.

'Why German?' people had often asked, to which Conrad replied, most times unconvincingly, that learning French at high school, which to him had sounded flowery and unconvincing, came in a poor second to the robust and satisfying sound of the German language. As an adult, he had endeavoured to master German as a second language, yet piecemeal, until life in retirement offered him the opportunity to pursue this in earnest.

The German conversation group frequently met for coffee in a café after its formal sessions. However, receiving invitations to exclusive morning coffees with Irene and Paul had become a special event for Conrad, an additional opportunity to practise his German in a more intimate environment.

Irene—her name melodiously pronounced in German with three syllables—called out from her kitchen, 'Please help yourselves to cheese and biscuits. I'm just cutting the cake to serve with more coffee.'

Her house sat high on the slopes above the suburb of Sandy Bay. Its elevation offered uninterrupted views of the Derwent River and, from the wide lounge room window, Conrad gazed across the river to the Eastern Shore. He admired his suburb, Howrah, and its neighbour Bellerive, their sandy beaches seductively sparkling under the reflection of the winter sun.

Conrad was a crew member on a friend's yacht named Focus and familiar with the river's ever-changing moods. He scanned upriver and noticed a translucent full moon hovering high in the deep blue sky. For Conrad, a daytime moon was mystifying. It created a sense of unreality. He sometimes joked with his grandchildren that a daytime moon was avoiding sleep.

Paul had been absent for Conrad's first session with the conversation group but announced a week later, 'Oh, so you're the new member. I've heard a lot about you! Do you spell your name with the German K?'

Paul was pushing ninety, slim in build but not emaciated from illness or age—'I still do the Royal Canadian Air Force 5BX Fitness Exercises, you know!' Within weeks, Conrad had invited himself for coffee and chats, the start of a friendship, often in the guise of a teacher with his student, sometimes substituting the coffee for a glass of beer, but always with humour thrown in. Before long, Irene had joined them. Little by little, Paul offered insights into his life as a boy-come-teenager in the defeated Germany of 1945. He spoke of his eight-year apprenticeship onboard German, Norwegian and Swedish merchant vessels, eventually docking in Melbourne where he literally jumped ship and forged a new life in Australia. Members of the conversation group seldom raised the topic of the Second World War, and Conrad learned to curb his curiosity. Over time, and with increased trust, Paul's reticence softened and led to some veiled disclosures—'The end of World War Two was a difficult time for everyone, you know, and particularly difficult for teenage boys like me who were left behind as Germany's last defence against the Allies!'

Before the size of the conversation group increased, Irene had hosted a couple of Christmas lunches, spoiling her guests with lovingly prepared dishes accompanied by an abundance of wine. At such events, Conrad's friends would invariably break into song—'You Germans have a song or folk tune for everything!'

On one occasion, they had impressed Conrad by singing the chorale from Beethoven's Ninth Symphony, adopted more recently as the Anthem to Europe, and he felt confident enough to congratulate them. 'Beethoven's Ode to Joy. I love it!'

'Oh no, my dear Conrad,' corrected Paul. 'The music is certainly by Beethoven, but the text is from the famous ode by Schiller, An die Freude, which yes, the English have translated as Ode to Joy. Schiller's poem is all about the unity of mankind.'

Until that time, Conrad's appreciation of Beethoven's music had been superficial, but with his usual fervour, he set about researching the works of Schiller and collecting various recordings of Beethoven's Ninth. Over time, he resisted an urge to skip forward to the last choral movement and soon gained an appreciation for the grandeur of the entire work.

Paul was passionate about 18th and 19th Century European history and he regularly gave talks to the German group about key events and figures from those eras. He volunteered at the Army Museum of Tasmania where he catalogued artefacts and translated documents or letters, mostly from both world wars. He had arrived at the museum highly recommended, following similar work at the National Archives and Australian War Memorial in Canberra.

Paul's work at the museum fascinated Conrad, who regularly pestered him about a current task or project—'Just more military buttons to identify and catalogue, Conrad,' would often be the light-hearted reply.

Today, along with a bouquet for Irene, Paul had brought a surprise to the coffee morning—something for Conrad from the museum. While they engaged in pleasant small talk and admired the views, Paul waited for the most appropriate time to offer his gift. He had little doubt that what he was about to reveal would stir excitement. He knew that Conrad was less interested in historical events and more in how these events shaped the lives, hopes and desires of the people who lived through them—the human stories.

'I've got something for you, Conrad. It's a German letter I'm working on at the moment.'

As if it were something precious, Paul carefully removed the original letter from the plastic sleeve and passed it over.

Conrad experienced an eerie sensation, as though the handover was taking place in slow motion. He felt a distinct change in the room's atmosphere, an odd feeling he could not define.

'Read it to us, Conrad,' prompted Irene.

At the top of the letter, Conrad made out the word Cleve and a date, 17th June 1918, but the rest was indecipherable. 'I don't think I can. It's written in the old German script. What does it say, Paul?'

'It's written by a father to his son named Otto, who's fighting on the Western Front. He's letting Otto know that one of his two brothers, Wolf, has been killed. Wolf is short for Wolfgang.'

Conrad was aware his mouth was agape in child-like wonder. The mention of the brothers' names felt strangely intimate and not at all diminished by time. His head was awash with anticipation and, to avoid any confusion, he suspended his usual insistence on all things German and asked Paul to read out the letter in English.

Paul relaxed back in his chair and took a breath. He explained that the place name of Cleve had been officially changed to start with the letter K in 1935 as a result of the German language purification process. 'This is my translation.'

Cleve

17th June 1918

My dear Otto,

Please brace yourself as this letter brings terrible news of the death of your brother, Wolf.

As I write this letter to you, I am in pain and my heart is crushed under immense grief. We are deeply saddened and try to support each other, but we find it difficult to accept this war could be so cruel as to take away our beloved son.

Lieutenant Preiser, from 6th Company, Reserve Infantry Regiment 273, wrote to inform us that Wolf died a heroic death on the 3rd of June.

The lieutenant described a fierce battle to overrun the French on the crest of a hill near a small village on the outskirts of Licy-Clignon.

Wolf was wounded on the left foot and went back 50 metres to find shelter from enemy fire. It was there he suffered a second blow to the back, close to his heart, and died.

Our Wolf was not the only loss on this sad day. Two of his comrades from the regiment were also buried alongside him and our condolences go to their families.

Our sadness is somewhat lessened to know Wolf's dear friends, Wittmann, Klug and Wiese, were by his side when he was welcomed into heaven and then helped bury him the next day near Licy-Clignon.

My dear Otto, even the mention of this French village fills our thoughts with eternal pain.

Felix Wittmann also wrote to us, but his descriptions of Wolf's injury and death are too horrid to repeat.

Your mother and I cannot forget how Wolf and his three friends brightened our lives so much, as did you and Ernst. When you all return, we will see our Wolf reflected in your eyes and hearts, and we will be comforted.

We worry about your sister. Helga was young and innocent when the war began, but now she carries the heavy burden of losing her dear brother. Please write and console her. She weeps and has not left her bed for days.

I have penned this same letter to Ernst. For too long now, we have heard nothing from him, but we are grateful for the assistance of the Red Cross in trying to locate him in the East. We pray for news soon.

The mayor and Father Schilling ask after you. So do our neighbours, Herr and Frau Graf. They are anxious to receive news of their own son who is also on the Western Front. The war has affected us all.

As a grieving father, I beg of you Otto, be on your guard and take the greatest of care so that nothing will happen to you.

Come home safely. Only with you and Ernst back with us will our family, *the proud and loving family of *******, be able to recover from this dreadful war and rebuild our lives in the absence of Wolf.*

Return to us strong, so we can do this. We pray that God protects you.

Your father…

Paul looked up from the letter. There was silence. Conrad leaned forward in his chair, puzzled why Paul had withheld the surname from the letter. He felt his heart beat changing, not so much racing, but agitated, reacting to the evocative words penned a century ago. He felt as if he was leaning over a cliff face with only a headwind preventing him from toppling.

Irene and Paul knew Conrad would speak first. They waited.

'This letter is so sad!' Conrad was struggling with strong emotions. This brief account of one family's loss epitomised the senseless loss of so many young men in the so-called war to end all war, and it angered him. He tried to compose himself. 'What's the family's name, Paul?'

'I can't make it out. Maybe is says 'the family of Rettner', but I'm not sure.'

Conrad looked between Paul and Irene. 'This letter could have been written by any father from either side—English, French, Australian, Canadian, New Zealand, American. By any father who loses a son. It's heartbreaking.'

Conrad's words resonated around the room. Irene gently nodded and motioned to Conrad to continue.

'How did this letter end up in Tasmania, Paul?' he asked. 'How long has it been here? I don't understand.'

'There's a notation about that. Take a look.'

Conrad flipped and rotated the letter. He saw different handwriting in the margin before recognising it as a short English inscription. He glanced at Irene who, again, gave him an encouraging nod. He read aloud:

Keep as a souvenir. It's a German letter found on the morning of the big stunt, 8'8'18. I don't know what it's talking about.

'What does 'stunt' mean, Paul?'

'Fight, or battle.'

Conrad's mind flooded with images of battlefields and dead soldiers, scratchy black and white images often shown in war documentaries. He gathered his thoughts and anticipated researching this date—the 8th of August 1918—and any major battles that took place on that day.

Irene and Paul were accustomed to seeing Conrad's mind race, teeming with enthusiasm. They noticed he frowned, an almost painful expression. Paul readied himself for Conrad's questions.

In a slower, more deliberate voice, 'So, Paul, am I right in thinking that a Tasmanian soldier took this letter from a dead German soldier, I think you said his name was Otto, and kept it as a souvenir?'

He knew instantly that his question had been framed as a statement and was unreasonable, even naïve.

Paul was forgiving. 'That's how it was, Conrad. All sides took souvenirs. You know about my work at the museums, here and back in Canberra. I've been translating letters like this one, and looking at buttons, wallets and diaries, for a long time now, all things that were brought back as souvenirs. Ha! We even have a German cannon from the Great War, for goodness' sake!'

'You do such valuable work at the museum,' said Irene. Paul nodded with gratitude. He received praise from military personnel and further praise from Irene was encouraging. 'What a sad letter, indeed. I'll get us some more cake.'

Tactful of you Irene, thought Conrad as he struggled to quieten his mind. He looked at Paul. 'Does the family in Germany know about this letter? We need to find them! We need to let Wolf's family know the letter is here!'

Conrad was surprised how easily Wolf's name fell from his lips. Again, he felt something change in the room. At first, he was unsure, then he began to sense the presence of someone else—a young soldier. Conrad questioned the plausibility. Yet the odour of a damp and dirty uniform was unmistakable. The soldier's presence did not alarm him. He heard an unfamiliar, but pleasant voice.

'I applaud your plans to take action on my father's letter, Mr Bentley.'

Conrad's cynical inner voice interrupted. Really? You're hearing voices of dead soldiers now? Get a grip, Bentley!

Wolf retreated.

'Are you still with us, Conrad?'

'Yes. Yes, Paul. I was just thinking about how sad this is. Such a waste of a young life. I want Wolf's family to know the letter is here, in Tasmania. What are we going to do?'

'I agree it's sad, Conrad. I translate many similar letters, but I can't get involved in just one of them. I don't have the time… but I thought I'd bring it along to show you.'

Conrad frowned as he fought against saying, Really, Paul? If there are many similar letters, why this one? Why does this particular letter resonate with you? You must have known it would touch me and ignite something unstoppable.

'Here, Conrad. I've got a photocopy of the letter and my English translation for you.'

'Oh Paul, that's so nice of you,' said Irene. 'A new project for Conrad. That's what you intended, isn't it? That Conrad searches for the family?'

Out of the corner of his eye, Conrad saw the two smiling at one another. He speculated Irene had been complicit all along. He smiled to himself.

The three relaxed in their chairs and allowed time for reflection.

Conrad gazed out the window again and noticed the moon had finally left the daytime sky. His mind was racing forward. He imagined talking to his neighbour over the fence. You'll never guess what fell into my hands today, Wally! In his mind, Conrad was already calling it his 'war letter research project' and drafting communiques to the relevant German authorities to locate Wolf's family. He glanced around the room in search of the young soldier, wishing to reassure him. But the odour of the damp uniform had disappeared.

You fool, Bentley!

As she farewelled her guests, Irene gently touched Conrad's cheek, a graceful gesture that reminded him of the tenderness of his own mother's farewells. 'Good luck Conrad. You're going to have fun with this research.'

'I appreciate the lift home, Conrad,' said Paul. 'I hope you understand my time is precious at the museum and that I can't devote extra time on this letter.' He steered the conversation toward small talk. 'Remind me. What's the name of your string quartet again?'

'The Sage String Quartet. We're rehearsing the slow movement from Haydn's Emperor at the moment. Do you know it?'

'Conrad! Of course I do! The melody of Germany's national anthem. I must give you an essay I wrote about the original words, you know, Deutschland über alles… Those words were misunderstood or misconstrued, often manipulated for political reasons. They didn't mean Germany wished to take over the world.'

'Sound's very interesting, Paul. I'd love to read it. Is it in German?'

Arriving home, Conrad's mind was awash with plans for his new project. Re-reading the letter and its translation in more detail, he noticed Paul had recorded two possibilities for the obscured surname—Dettner and Rettner—but believed the indistinct letters more likely spelled Deppner.

He convinced himself that it was not too late to call over the fence to his neighbour, Wally. The afternoon had turned colder, but he knew they would manage a quick chat in extra layers of clothing.

Gretel saw him head for the backdoor. 'Oh, sweetie. You won't find Wally out there. Trish told me earlier they're off shopping and then going out for dinner. Isn't that nice for them… hint, hint!' Conrad's preoccupation with the letter ensured Gretel's hint fell on deaf ears. 'Trish wants us to come over tomorrow. She's keen to talk about getting the fence repaired.' Gretel knew her comments were futile. She recognised Conrad's excited, distracted expression and assumed something interesting had happened during his coffee morning. But she tried again anyway. 'So, do I take it that's a 'yes' from you?'

Conrad was unsure whether Gretel's throwaway line referred to the ongoing topic of a replacement fence, visiting the neighbours, or both. He knew a new fence was overdue, as some sections had succumbed to decay. He wanted to show Gretel that he could be positive about it, but his mind was still adrift with the war letter. Would Gretel be as fascinated with the letter as he was?

He took a gamble. 'Gretel, something really exciting happened today…'

Chapter 3

The Great War
The German Soldier's Story

As a ceasefire mercifully settled in on the afternoon of the 9th of May 1918, the men of Reserve Infantry Regiment 273, Wolf Deppner's regiment, bivouacked just northwest of the village of Jouaignes, northern France. The soldiers had time to enjoy the summer warmth, which intensified the fragrance of the swaying wildflowers and ripening corn in adjoining fields. Jouaignes had been spared the effects of war since the first wave of fighting nearly four years earlier and, at the height of summer, looked attractive in its modesty. As with preceding villages, the troops found it recently abandoned by its townsfolk. The fields and gardens were well tended and the kitchens and cellars adequately stocked, tell tale evidence of a hurried evacuation. Marching past open classroom windows, the soldiers could see lesson outlines still hanging on tripods which, to some soldiers, were painful reminders of their own children. It was here in Jouaignes that the men of RIR 273 enjoyed a long-overdue respite when even the wine was not limited to the officers.

Doing his rounds, Platoon Commander Lieutenant Preiser approached Wolf and his three friends. 'Here, men. A bottle of local wine for you. The quartet has earned it!'

Rarely did he utter the title of quartet, particularly in the presence of his sergeants, yet, on this evening, observing the group's jubilant mood, the title escaped him.

'Thank you, Sir,' replied Felix Wittmann, eagerly grabbing for the bottle.

'Like all the men, you four should be proud of yourselves. We've had a tough campaign lately and, now the Americans are mobilised on the Front, we need to rest when we can. Let's make the most of it.'

A collective 'Thank you, Sir,' sang out from the quartet.

Sergeant Armbruster observed his lieutenant moving amongst the squad and suspected he would linger longer with this group known as the quartet. He was unsure if the lieutenant had invented the title or the group brought it with them to the regiment. Either way, he thought of it as folly.

The lieutenant knew the four—Wolf, Felix, Bruno and Erich—wished to be alone. He respected their strong bond that would have been forged over many years in their hometown. He decided not to linger, but took a few moments to consider them before he moved off: Felix Wittmann, with his charming bravado and self-assured smile, who often returned a gaze with a slight tilt of the head and wink of an eye; Bruno Klug with his respectful and loyal temperament; Erich Wiese, the deep thinker who showed intuition for art and the aesthetics of nature; and Wolf Deppner, often seen as the light-hearted prankster of the group whose enthusiasm for life and laughter and his beaming smile, brought comfort to the others.

'Enjoy the wine, men!' urged the lieutenant as he moved away. 'Corporal Braun! Fetch me more bottles from the cellar.'

The quartet watched their lieutenant weave among the troops. He shook hands and gave a friendly clap on a shoulder whilst handing out the gift of wine, undoubtedly repeating the same encouraging words.

Lieutenant Preiser had commanded the platoon for the past two years. Sergeant Armbruster, a career soldier of more than twenty years, led Wolf's squad, Section A, with Sergeant Berg, a younger, but no less a competent soldier, assigned to Section B.

At six-foot two, the lieutenant towered above the rest of the platoon, the cut of his uniform showing his athletic build. His distinctive moustache and chiselled jawline were impressive and, to his men, he was the quintessential German officer. Stories of the lieutenant's past romances had circulated amongst the officers, but all banter and inquiry ceased when it became known that he had fully surrendered his heart to the beautiful Rosa. At their first meeting, Rosa had found her admirer irresistible in uniform and, upon meeting her, the lieutenant had known instantly that this new, but undeniable feeling of love had replaced his past fleeting experiences of romance.

To all appearances, Lieutenant Preiser dispensed his respect and attention evenly amongst his men. But, privately, he looked upon the quartet as something special. The four reminded him of his old university study groups that had bonded over discussions about philosophy and art, its members, on graduation, disbanded and dispersed throughout Germany in pursuit of work and marriage. He wondered if any of his old classmates, undoubtedly now all officers, would survive the war. He resolved to contact them, even arrange a reunion.

When assigned to the regiment, the lieutenant had immediately noticed the quartet was different from other cliques he observed among the troops, not because they doggedly stuck together, but because their collective form was arresting, poetic. Nobody, not even Lieutenant Preiser, could put it satisfactorily into words. Apart, they looked curiously awkward, but together, they were efficient and resourceful. He avoided splitting them up for missions or sending one off alone on an errand.

Again, this did not go unnoticed by the more critical Sergeant Armbruster, who resisted favouring any of his men and privately believed his superior was flouting military protocol. Nevertheless, he knew his rank and said nothing. On that evening in May 1918, whilst he watched his lieutenant move off from the quartet and offer the other men wine and words of encouragement, even Sergeant Armbruster could not help but feel a degree of admiration for him…

'Good God!' cried Felix. 'This wine tastes so good.'

Wolf laughed. 'All French wine tastes good!'

Bruno added, 'Ah, but not as good as my uncle's beer back home!'

Erich agreed.

The four settled themselves into a circle, a customary formation, and passed the bottle around whilst feasting on smoked ham and cheese, with the extra pickled artichoke hearts they had discovered in one of the abandoned kitchens of Jouaignes. The combination of the ceasefire, the aroma of the food and the smoothness of the red wine boosted the quartet's sense of togetherness, forged in their hometown of Cleve and made ever stronger after nearly four years on the battlefields.

Erich could not resist. 'Do you know what I was thinking about this morning?' More often than not, the others would have rolled their eyes and teased, 'Oh no. Here he goes again!', but on this occasion, they willingly surrendered to Erich's gift of storytelling. 'When we moved out of that town—what was it called again?'

'I think it was Cerseuil.' Ordinarily, Bruno was not the first to respond, but the wine had given him courage. 'But I'm not sure how to pronounce it correctly.'

'Oui, Monsieur Bruno. It was Cerseuil.' Erich pronounced it with a better French accent. 'Did you notice all those flowers along the roadside? They were something special.'

Erich had been charmed by the blooms. The flowers he spotted were particularly bright, yet surreal amongst the sounds and smell of battle; a swirling palette of pink clover, marguerites, blue sage, yellow daisies and intense, blood-red poppies. In other contexts, their colours would have clashed but, in their natural setting, kissed with sunlight and gently swaying, Erich thought they created a tapestry of beauty.

Felix was embarrassed that he had failed to notice the flowers, just cornfields and dirty soldiers, but the wine also gave him some courage. 'Wee, Monsieur Erich. They were beautiful.'

Wolf laughed. 'Here, Monsieur Felix, have another sip of the wine. It might help improve your French accent!'

Affected by the moment, Erich let his rhetoric rise above the distant sound of shelling as the bottle was passed around. 'The flowers reminded me of back home, in the field behind Herr Winkler's house. Remember?'

'Oui, Monsieur Erich!' Wolf threw him a wide smile. The others knew a smile was rarely absent from Wolf's face. 'Tell us more, Erich. I always applaud your imagination and use of clever words. And your French accent's not bad either!'

'We would jump Herr Winkler's fence and hear him yell out, 'Stop trespassing!', but we ignored him and stayed in his field for hours, looking up at the sky, drinking Klugshof beer and listening to Felix boast about his success in wooing girls. What does he call it again?'

'The blood sport of courtship!' chipped in Wolf, with another beaming smile.

The four easily recalled the scenes in Winkler's field and yearned for home.

'And we visited the field just days before our deployment,' continued Erich. 'Sporting our new uniforms, drinking and talking about all the adventures we were going to have in the Army.' There was a momentary silence as the quartet realised how the years of fighting had left dreadful marks on their uniforms, a visual mockery of how blindly idealistic they had been about what war would bring. 'And remember our farewell party that day, hosted by Wolf's neighbour, Herr Graf? We all got our pictures taken in his courtyard.'

'Wee, Monsieur Erich!' added Felix. 'I remember it well. Not only did we get drunk in old Winkler's field and miss church, but our antics also annoyed old man Graf until steam came out of his ears!'

Erich's thoughts turned to Frieda Graf and his vanquished love for her, before her image disappeared behind the disapproving face of her father, Herr Graf, the ill-tempered foundry manager of Cleve.

'I miss home,' sighed Wolf.

Anyone within earshot would have been mystified by something as bizarre as talk of flowers contrasted with the horrors of war. The other soldiers avoided intrusion but were often envious that they lacked the quartet's capacity to escape into a fantasy, a similar place where they could also escape the distant pounding of cannon fire.

Erich's own capacity to escape lay in his poetic sensibility and imagery. 'Ah, those blooms we saw this morning will soon bid farewell to this hot summer and be vanquished by autumn.'

His friends looked at him. They saw he was not present, that his mind had wandered off to a faraway place. They recognised his customary daydreaming gaze. The quartet was quiet. Erich's words and soft voice invited his friends to fall deeper into his imagery:

Yes, thought Felix. I remember those times in old Winkler's field. I took Lina there. My dear, lovely Lina. My fiancée. We lay in the grass out of sight and kissed. She picked flowers and said she was going to miss me.

Yes, remembered Bruno. I took an extra bottle of Klugshof's best brew on that day of our farewell. I hope my uncle will forgive me for pilfering his beer. And we talked about Frieda Graf who fell in love with our Erich; their secret romance and how they would need to run away to escape her father's disapproval.

Erich wondered whatever happened to the secret messages from his Frieda, messages that flourished in the first year of the war. My sweet Frieda. I miss you. Please wait for me...

Frieda's father, Herr Graf, had forbidden any correspondence between his daughter and 'that Wiese boy'. Yet in defiance, the best friends, Frieda and Lina, had devised a plan of subterfuge—Lina would write love letters to her fiancé, Felix, but also add Frieda's coded words intended for Erich, her banished beau.

Felix was complicit. During ceasefires, he showed Erich the relevant parts of her letters:

Cleve

23rd February 1915
My darling Felix and our dear members of the quartet, Frieda and I love you all. We talk about you constantly and our hearts ache thinking about your sweet faces. We miss you so much and long for the day when you return to us so we can shower you with kisses.
Frieda told me she had a dream last week. The war had ended and the quartet came home to Cleve. She hugged and kissed you all. Frieda loves you...

Over time, Lina's coded messages from Frieda disappeared. Although Felix longed to hear from his beloved Lina, he also began to dread Erich's eager eyes, so cruelly dashed when there was nothing to share. For a long time, the streets of Cleve remained untouched by the anti-war marches, worker's protests and the increasing revolutionary sentiment that had spread across Germany. Yet some of the townsfolk had begun to doubt the purpose of the war. Publicly, they feared voicing dissent, instead preferred their growing unrest to sing out, vicariously, from the anti-government rallies that were taking place in neighbouring cities. As such, Lina's letters became shorter. She described the bleakness descending on Cleve, the shortage of food and rising disorder. Her choice of words, or absence of words, were signs she was struggling to cope, and Felix chose to protect his friends by keeping most of her latest news to himself.

Wolf also mused about the field behind Herr Winkler's house, but his thoughts became uncharacteristically melancholy. We made a pact to protect each other in this war, he thought. We promised we would never be separated on the battlefield. I hope we can keep such promises.

He snapped out of his glumness. 'Yes, Monsieur Erich, I have fond memories of Herr Winkler's field, where you often told us about your plans to travel to the ends of the earth.'

Instantly, they recalled the geography lessons with Herr Stummhofer, their devoted teacher back home, his talks about his relatives in Australia and the pictures of Canada displayed on his classroom walls.

Their private musings were briefly interrupted by the realisation that the wine would soon run out. Erich relieved their disappointment by continuing his rhetoric on flowers and far-off places. He spoke about his boyhood holidays with his uncle in Heimbach, a small village tucked away on the northern fringe of the Eifel mountain range where he had learned to appreciate the beauty of nature. He transported the quartet back with him as he reminisced about hikes through the valleys, risking swims in the river that weaved through Heimbach and, as a reward for helping his uncle with house repairs, sitting at an outdoor café in the town centre and enjoying refreshing lemonade with cake. He described the green canopy of the forest and watching his uncle lift a leaf or flower up to his face. Erich's uncle was unfamiliar with the scientific names of the local flora and fauna, but his teachings on the landscape and the wildlife around Heimbach, through sight and touch instead of words, had been invaluable.

Erich finished with a sigh. 'I loved those hikes in the Eifel.'

The taste of wine lingered. The quartet was happy. Although distant shelling could still be heard, the sounds of combat and the acrid smell of their uniforms temporarily faded beneath Erich's sweet words. His words evoked wistful memories of their beloved Cleve. Surely they would be home soon…

Side by side, the quartet fell into a peaceful slumber, laying closer than other soldiers would have dared, whispering to each other, fondly punching each other's arms and making plans for their post-war Cleve.

Wolf was the last to fall asleep. He gazed up at the night sky and watched the bright, full moon drift out from behind her protective clouds. Forget your flowers and forests, my dear Erich. Look at the moon up there. What a beauty!

In the early hours of the next morning, any warmth and security of the previous night disappeared with the sound of Sergeant Armbruster yelling at close range: 'Wake up, you layabouts. We're moving out!'

As RIR 273 snaked its way southeast and passed through several small villages, Erich again examined the landscape. He slowly sensed the vegetation transform. He imagined the flowers becoming unfriendly, covertly leading the troops deeper into battle. The sensation confused him.

The skirmishes at Bonnesvalyn Forest and Monthiers were particularly intense, and Wolf's regiment needed to fight harder to take out the French machine-gun nests and other strongholds. Several homesteads and farms offered effective vantage points to the advancing Allied troops, whose once unfamiliar uniforms were now becoming commonplace.

On the evening of the 1st of June, exhausted and dishevelled, they reached the strategic position of Licy-Clignon. After assembling on the banks of the Clignon Brook, there was little time to repeat the rest and relaxation they had enjoyed two days earlier, although it was obvious the men craved it more. As usual, Lieutenant Preiser made his rounds to offer encouragement and comfort, this time without the tonic of wine. The men maintained their gratitude—he was their mentor; like a father, their protector.

Over the following days and nights, the fighting was relentless and bloody. The increasing intensity of combat and the ever-growing numbers of injured and fallen comrades alarmed the quartet.

A flurry of orders filtered down from the outlying command post listing various hills, creeks, and farms in and around the Licy-Clignon area as strategic targets. In Lieutenant Preiser's experience, the attack orders appeared to grow exponentially more demanding and desperate. Although outwardly he maintained a calm and reliable demeanour, as expected of his rank, inwardly the lieutenant had begun to feel rattled by the unfolding events.

As the 3rd of June 1918 dawned, a thick, malevolent fog hovered over the damp ground and created a trapped, claustrophobic atmosphere. When the sun's rays finally pushed through and saturated the landscape, the day became oppressively warmer and the soldiers were unnerved. The fragrance of the wildflowers was no longer sweet. After years of fighting, and often soaked by rain, their once handsome uniforms, immaculate when the soldiers had posed for studio portraits or during private farewells, were now tarnished with a noxious layer of perspiration, campfire smoke and cordite. The blood spatters, some from their comrades, some from the enemy, had become ingrained in the fabric and were now indiscernible from the overall grime.

Late in the afternoon, Lieutenant Preiser informed his men that the platoon was to lead an attack on Hill 165, just southwest of the neighbouring town of Bussiares. Following that, all immediate regiments would combine to take the next key target of La Mares Farm, currently held by American Marines. The concluding chilling reference in the orders for attack, 'at all costs', the lieutenant kept to himself.

The thrust through the outskirts of Licy-Clignon up to Bussiares severed communication between the regiment's units and, at the northern perimeter of Bussiares, Wolf's squad found itself separated from Sergeant Berg and Section B. The men hunkered beside a lime washed homestead at the fork in the road.

A scout reported the French had dug into a ridge just below the crest of the hill and a field map showed the strategic La Mares Farm lay just beyond its rear slopes. 'There's a small abandoned farmhouse in a thicket half-way up the rise, Sir. It offers good cover.'

Lieutenant Preiser considered his orders. The French will pick us off one by one if we don't take this hill successfully, he thought, but the words 'at all costs' kept ringing in his ears.

Further attempts to contact Sergeant Berg failed, and the lieutenant decided to push on alone.

Chapter 4

2018. January
Tasmania

'Conrad, sweetie. Wally's at the fence.'

'What! Already?'

Gretel heard Conrad fumbling for things in the bathroom as he rushed to get ready.

Conrad and Wally had not chatted for a few weeks. After the Christmas-New Year break, Wally and his wife, Patricia, had taken advantage of a warmer than usual January and headed off to the East Coast to renovate their shack.

The two men greeted each other with their customary nods. Conrad, in a light-hearted tone that had become indicative of their friendly banter, was the first to speak. 'It has come to my attention, that my neighbour, the upstanding Mr Wally Archer, who regularly brags about being a skilful sailor in his youth, can't take any time off work to come and sail with his mates on Wednesday afternoons, but, to everyone's surprise, can easily find time to shoot off to his love shack on the East Coast!'

'My word, Mr Bentley! What a posh speech, and delivered with such a serious tone. I feel the need to reply in the same, smart-arse manner.'

'I didn't know you could talk posh, Mr Archer!'

'Oh yes, Mr Bentley. It comes from living next door to a right royal smart arse!' They both grinned at each other. Wally took a sip of coffee and lifted his face to the bright sun. 'This weather's been good lately, eh mate?'

Declarations about climate change were creeping more and more into the Tasmanian vernacular.

'It's global warming, Wally. The Focus crew knows all about it. The weather's getting crazier than ever out on the river. Four seasons in one race!'

'How is old Captain Baz these days?'

'Same as ever. Great skipper, terrible at conversation!'

In their teens, Baz Simpson, Wally Archer and a mutual friend, Joe Furlani, had crewed on a Cole Traditional 30 named King Will, owned and skippered by Simpson senior. It was reported that the four could easily make their way around the deck blindfolded, and handle anything the often unpredictable Hobart weather could throw at them. In his youth, Baz's father had conquered three gruelling Sydney-to-Hobart races in the days before sat nav, maxi yachts and powered winches. His ability to beat other yachts over the line on the Derwent River had put a target on his back and exposed his younger crew to alcohol-fuelled disdain at the club bar. With Simpson senior at the helm, King Will enjoyed many years of successful racing before its crew disbanded.

Decades later, after finishing work in the industrial fibreglass industry on the mainland, Baz returned to Hobart and lost no time in purchasing his own racing yacht, repairing and modernising it to his exacting standards before setting out to find a competent crew. He approached Wally and Joe, but both declined to sail due to work and family commitments.

Baz met his substitute crew—Conrad, Martin and Chris—when he joined the Waratah Bushwalking Club, and it was through discussions on the track that he learned Conrad was Wally's neighbour. 'Say G'day to Wally from me, Conrad. You'll have to convince him to get back on the river!'

The four apprentice walkers had retired within months of each other and signed up to the bushwalking fraternity to maintain their health and help fill in their free days. They quickly developed an appreciation for the Tasmanian bush and formed a friendship on the track, where Baz covertly assessed their crew potential. Given Conrad and Chris had sailed before, they escaped heavy scrutiny. But Captain Baz harboured doubts about Martin, a complete novice. Following appeals from Chris, Martin's longtime friend, and promises of close supervision, Baz capitulated. The three recruits underwent simulated training in the marina before Baz was confident they were ready to sail. With the racing calendar fast approaching, Baz grinned as he handed Martin a copy of Sailing for Dummies and a list of conditions: 'Once you learn the difference between the bow and stern, and that the ropes onboard are called sheets or lines, can successfully attach the spinnaker pole to the mast for what we call 'goosewinging', when the wind comes directly from behind, then you will be a qualified crew member!' Sailing theory and motivational sessions also took place in the club bar where the three listened to Baz's stories about his time onboard King Will. 'Dad once told me that his crew of Joe Furlani, Conrad's neighbour, Wally Archer, and me was the best he ever had. So, you three have big shoes to fill!'

At the fence, Conrad accepted further attempts to convince Wally to join the Focus crew were futile. 'It's a shame you can't get time off work to join us, Wally. But I understand.'

'Tell Baz to hound Joe Furlani instead. He's still around here somewhere.' With a wink, 'Anyway, a crew of four is enough for a boat that size. You'll have to throw someone overboard to make room for me, mate!'

'And I suppose it's still a 'no' to bushwalking too, eh?'

'Shit, Conrad. You never give up! No way, mate. You've told me this bushwalking stuff is all about walking in circles on Mount Wellington and then searching for the nearest coffee shop! Thanks, but I think I'll leave the bushwalking and the… cafe lattes to you!'

Unlike their wives who had enjoyed immediate rapport, Conrad and Wally initially found their differences in taste, personality and background a source of awkwardness, but their neighbourly small talk gradually grew to more insightful discussions and, with that, came friendship.

Conrad saw his neighbour as the quintessential Tasmanian, a subjective impression he found difficult to explain. Wally was tanned with a round face, dark eyes and a mass of curly brown hair, its absence of grey a source of envy to many. Wally resisted defining anyone by ethnicity or race, which, combined with a frankness, were qualities Conrad admired in his neighbour.

'I'm a proud Tasmanian, Conrad, and love our way of life here. All this clean, fresh air would explain my handsome looks!'

In stark contrast, English-born Conrad had straight, mousy-coloured hair desperately defending itself from an aggressive attack of grey, pointed features with a fair complexion and blue-grey eyes. Initially, Wally had thought his neighbour was German, given his Christian name, an overly upright posture and interest in learning the language.

'No, Wally. I was born in England—in your language that would be Pommy-land. My parents emigrated when I was nine. My sister's tracing our family tree at the moment. Who knows? Maybe she'll find something interesting that would explain my handsome Scandinavian looks!'

'Ha!'

'I just like learning German, Wally. Simple as that. And I've heard it's good for the brain to learn a second language when you get to our age.'

'Steady on there, mate. I'm not as ancient as you, and I'm still workin' for a living. Anyway, it's all a mystery to me. What bloke is born in Pommy-land, but hates cricket, marries someone with a German background, prefers documentaries about Germany instead of England or Australia, and wants to visit Germany for his holidays? And to top it all off, has a German name! It just doesn't frickin' add up!'

They laughed out loud.

'All jokes aside, Wally, I guess my parents just liked the name Conrad.'

'We could make it sound a bit more… Australian by changing Conrad to Con?'

Conrad reflected on how he had disliked his name when it was shortened by his peers at school. 'Actually Wally, I'm not a fan of shortening names. Do you mind if we stick with Conrad?'

'No worries.'

'What about you, Wally? Do I call you Walter?'

'Shit no! My mum's the only one who called me that and she died over twenty years ago!'

With time, they had begun to look forward to their meetings, increasingly engaging in more stimulating discussions about their families, Australian history and world events. Wally frequently surprised Conrad with his always logical, occasionally sophisticated, responses. When Conrad's father died a few years earlier, in Conrad's mind heroically, released from his illness and pain, Wally was on hand to give subtle, yet invaluable support.

'I know you say your mum's doing okay, but what about you, mate?' Conrad had appreciated the enquiry. It gave rise to a candid discussion about grief, a topic often stifled by awkwardness, yet on that occasion Conrad was not afraid to admit that his father's death had robbed him of more than a parent.

Over the past six months, the German letter from the First World War had dominated their chats and Conrad was heartened that Wally remained his strongest supporter, in contrast to others who seemed disinterested or critical of his research. 'Even if you do find this German family, why would they be interested in something that happened a century ago?' they would say.

At times, Conrad would also question his own efforts. Is anybody going to care about events that took place in the Great War? Is all this research a waste of my time when I should be doing other things around the house? It was at such times of self-doubt that Wally's support had become essential for Conrad to sustain his motivation. 'So, are you ready to hear the latest on my war letter research, Wally?'

'Have I got any choice?'

'I'm not sure where I left off last time.'

'Bullshit! Don't give me that. We talked about it two weeks ago.'

'I see,' replied Conrad with raised eyebrows. 'Come on then, let's have a test to see if my trusty neighbour has really been listening all this time, eh?'

'So, you want me to give you a blow-by-blow description of what you've done and who you've been talkin' to about this German letter since June last year, do you?'

'Yes. Humour me.' Conrad was already impressed that Wally had remembered the month the letter fell into his hands.

Wally accepted the challenge. 'Okay then. Now, let me see…'

Conrad looked up and saw Wally grinning. 'I'm waiting, Mr Archer.'

'Once upon a time, there lived a man called Conrad Bentley from Howrah, in Tasmania. One day, a friend gave him a letter that was written in 1918. A German father wrote to his son, Otto, to let Otto know that one of his brothers had been shot and killed in France. The brother was called Wolf, said with a V, not a W, and, because Mr Bentley didn't like to shorten names, he preferred to call him by his full name, Wolfgang…'

'Ah, very witty Wally!' Conrad already felt at ease with the promise of Wally's amusing storytelling. 'Please go on.'

'Mr Bentley was sad. 'This letter could have been written by any father from either side of the war,' he cried. 'A Pommy or an Aussie father. The message is the same—death and destruction. But this time, it's a German father who wrote it.' With tears in his eyes, Mr Bentley called out to his patient and good-looking neighbour. 'It's an outrage, Mr Archer! One of our Tassie soldiers must have taken this letter from a fallen German.' Mr Bentley huffed and puffed. 'It's terrible to think this letter is still here, on the other side of the world. We need to get it back to Germany!' So, Mr Bentley believed he was clever enough to look for the German family. He thought by finding them, he could be a hero and give a voice to… all the soldiers who died in that war. But there was a problem. Mr Bentley didn't know the surname of the German family. The name was smudged in the letter. Had someone deliberately made it indecipherable? Conspiracy theories were rife! But nothing was going to stop Mr Bentley from workin' it all out…'

Conrad raised his eyebrows. 'Keep going, Mr Archer.'

'Shit! We could be out here for hours! I need another coffee!'

'No, Wally. We'll get coffee later. Keep going. That's an order!'

'For many months, the tenacious Mr Bentley from Tasmania… By the way, Conrad, I heard the word tenacious the other day and thought it describes you to a T!'

'Ha!'

'For months, Mr Tenacious from Tasmania showed the letter to anyone he could find. His sailing mates were too busy fighting the waves on the

Derwent River to give two hoots. The players in his violin band were too strung out to get involved.'

'Too strung out! Love it! Witty Wally strikes again!'

'He showed it to his wife but, by then, the poor thing was fed up with it all. But Mr Bentley wouldn't give up. And… lucky for him, he had a handsome-looking neighbour who could help him with the clues in the letter; there was the name of Wolf's hometown in Germany, the names of his brothers and sister, his regiment details and even the name of his lieutenant…' Wally paused.

Conrad's head was lowered, his eyes closed in concentration. He continued to marvel at Wally's account, but sensed the pause was an invitation for him to respond. 'Yeah, Wally. The lieutenant's name was Preiser. Lieutenant Preiser. And Wolf's siblings were Helga, Ernst and Otto. The hometown was Kleve, but in 1918 it was spelt with a C.'

'Okay, okay, Mr Bentley. You're such a details man! So, the story continues. Armed with the four Christian names—Helga, Otto, Ernst and Wolf from Cleve—today spelt with a K—the tenacious Conrad Bentley—that's Conrad spelt with a C, not K—wrote a thousand emails harassing poor public servants at the Kleve Births, Deaths and Marriage Office, begging them to search their database for a match. But sadly, they were unable to help him as no records of the family could be found there.' Wally started to quicken his voice, as if he were reading a fairy-tale to a child and getting to the exciting part of the story. He recounted how Conrad had trawled the internet in search of people in Germany who could help him solve the puzzle of the surname—a writing expert and a military enthusiast. 'Someone else suggested the annoying Mr Bentley should contact the Federal Military Archives in Freiburg. So of course, Mr Bentley didn't hesitate to do that.'

Conrad could not resist. 'What an impressive memory you have, Mr Archer. You're such a details man!'

'Ha! Anyway, some bloke from this Archives Office replied: 'Yes mate, you're in luck. We have a box in our basement that's full of stuff from your dead soldier's regiment…'

'Reserve Infantry Regiment 273.'

'Yep, that's the one. But this bloke also said: 'Dear Mr Bentley, please feel free to visit us in Freiburg and have a look at the documents. Unfortunately, we don't have the staff to do that for you.' Ha! To fly all the way from Tassie just to look in a bloody box? And to think people say the Germans don't have a sense of humour! But Mr Bentley's wife said, 'You're dreamin' if you think I'm letting you fly all the way over there just so you can look in a bloody box!' To which Mr Bentley grumbled, 'But I need to get my hands on the list of all the soldiers called Wolfgang from RIR 273. Then I can find my Wolf and hunt down his family.' Mrs Bentley said, 'Sorry, sweetie! No way.' And that's the end of story! Well, for now.'

The storyteller had a satisfied smile on his face.

There was a natural pause. The two took a few deep breaths as they examined each other's gardens.

'Nice native bushes, Mr Archer!'

'Thanks, Mr Bentley. Shame I can't say the same about your posh Pommy plants!' They laughed as they warmed their faces in the sunshine. 'All jokes aside,' said Wally, 'I've had fun watching you from my side of the fence, you know, runnin' around like a headless chook tryin' to work it all out.'

'I'm glad to hear I've entertained you!'

'Now Conrad! No doubt you've got an update on your research. You always do! How 'bout we get that coffee before we start stage two of this chat, eh?'

The two did an about turn and raced off…

Inside, Conrad surprised Gretel with a kiss. She took a step back. 'Have you finished out there already?'

'Not quite. Just getting a second cuppa.'

'What's Wally said about Andy?'

'What do you mean?'

'Conrad! Don't tell me you haven't asked Wally about his son! Andy's in some kind of strife over in Melbourne.'

Andrew Archer had recently moved to the mainland in search of a better life. He had achieved good results at school but failed to find his niche, often complaining about the small-town mentality of Hobart and wanting to experience what better opportunities the mainland could offer.

Patricia was troubled by the move and constantly worried about whether Andrew was happy, appropriately nourished and mixing with respectable friends, but Wally suspected his son was hiding the truth. Such ambiguity tore at him.

'Oh, Conrad. Have you just been bombarding poor Wally with your war letter and not even talked about anything else? For goodness' sake.' Gretel saw his brow crease, but she kept up the salvo. 'Trish and Wally are beside themselves with worry. It's a surprise Wally didn't say anything. You need to talk to him about it. Don't just peer over the fence and pester him about that letter!'

'Sure, sure.'

'Anyway, don't forget we're out for dinner tonight and didn't you say you were going to mow the lawns?'

Bravely: 'I have to do some violin practice before next week's string quartet rehearsal instead.'

'Huh! Anyway, Conrad, ask Wally if Trish has received the quote from our lovely fence builder. He's French, so he has a gorgeous accent and sexy legs!'

'What?'

'Trish and I have met with a fence builder with a French accent who wears shorts all-year-round. A lot goes on behind the scenes when you're off sailing or fiddling, you know sweetie!'

'You forgot to mention bushwalking and the German sessions… sweetie!'

'I'll ignore that. Anyway, once Trish gets the quote, we'll all get together and sort it out. The fence has to be fixed. It's practically falling down.' She looked at him closer. 'Did you hear me?'

'Loud and clear. I'll be meeting a Frenchman with short legs who's going to knock down our fence and build a stronger one to keep the neighbours out!'

'Very funny. Now, make sure you talk to Wally about Andy. That's an order! I'm off shopping, don't miss me.'

Wally had beaten Conrad back to the fence. 'So, let's have it, mate. What's the latest with the letter?'

'Before that, how's your Andrew going in Melbourne?'

'Oh, I understand, mate. You've been given orders!' Wally dipped his head. 'Yes, things are a little hairy at the moment. He won't answer our calls.' In a softer voice, 'Trish will always worry about him, that's what mums do. She really got upset when we saw a photo of all his mates with shaved heads, and she literally cried when Andy shaved his.'

Conrad flinched at the image of the handsome Andrew without his thick hair, a source of paternal pride for Wally.

'Trish wants to go over there and check it all out. Between you and me, she wants to go over there and drag Andy back. But shit, mate, he's over twenty!'

Wally took a moment to recall his little Andy, his adorable, playful boy of five years, bouncing on his knee and at risk of falling, affectionately stroking his father's face and laughing, 'Daddy, it feels like sandpaper!' Wally shuddered as the delightful image was replaced with Andrew as a grown man with a shaved head.

'We just need to hope it all works out for Andy over there. Come on, mate. Enough of this shit.'

Conrad took this as his cue to change the subject. 'So, I hear you and Patricia are planning to visit the shack a fair bit over summer.'

'Yep. Those are the orders! You and Gretel should come up some time.'

Similar polite invitations had been issued before, but Conrad was not disappointed that they were never seriously followed up. He respected the shack at Binalong Bay was the Archers' private escape. He and Gretel shared fond memories of camping trips to the East Coast and knew the area around Binalong Bay intimately. 'That sounds great, Wally.'

'We just need to finish off the renos before we can lay out the red carpet and invite royal guests!' Wally's empty coffee mug was a signal to swing the conversation back to the war letter. 'You've done your duty, mate. I really appreciate it.' He let the compliment sink in. 'Now, come on. What's the latest with your research?'

'Well, after I let that bloke from the Military Archives know that I couldn't just fly over to Freiburg to look in a—as you say—bloody box…' Wally tilted his head and gave Conrad a wink. '… he sent me a list of people who can do the search for me.'

'What, like a private investigator?'

'Yep! If a private investigator, or I think they call it researcher, can help me get clues to Wolf's identity, then bullseye!'

'Won't that cost you a packet?'

'To hire the private investigator? Um, yeah sure, there would be a service fee, but I don't think it'll be too much.' Conrad looked down and whispered, 'Maybe we shouldn't mention there's a fee at this stage. It could put me in a spot of bother.'

Wally matched Conrad's cautious tone. 'Trust me, mate. Mum's the word.'

'From the list, I've picked a bloke called Herr Steinhoff.'

'Ha! These German names crack me up sometimes. I love 'em!'

'Me too, Wally! If Herr Steinhoff can find a list of all the soldiers called Wolfgang who were enlisted in RIR 273, in 1918, then I'll be over the moon.'

'I can feel you're gettin' close to cracking it, Conrad. Once you get your teeth into something, you don't frickin' give up!' He was tempted to use the description 'tenacious' again.

Conrad breathed a sigh of relief. His inner voice of doubt had been raging lately, and Wally's reassurance came at a good time. 'Between you and me Wally, this letter stuff has taken its toll. I've let quite a bit slip. I haven't been on a bushwalk for a few weeks and Captain Baz got shitty with me last week because I wasn't focusing enough on the race. And let's not forget the jobs around the house.'

'Oh yeah, all those jobs you said you'd do when you retired what, three, four years ago now?'

'Thanks for reminding me… mate! And to top it all off, I've got a concert coming up with the string quartet—that's violin band in your language. I'm not pulling my weight in the rehearsals. My mind's always on the war letter.' He was tempted to tell Wally that he sees and hears Wolf Deppner, but resisted.

'What sort of gig, mate?'

'Another charity concert at the retirement village in Sandy Bay. They've invited us back again! It's later in the year, but we need all the practice we can get to put on a good show.' He adds the favourite one-liner from the leader, Alan, that despite all the hard work, the quartet would not be ready for Carnegie Hall.

'I have no idea what that means, mate, but it sounds like you'll be famous soon!'

'You and Patricia should come.'

Wally gave a frank response. 'Ah, I'm not sure your violin band's my cup of tea, sorry mate. What's the name of your violin band again?'

'The Sage String Quartet.'

'How did you come up with that name? Actually, shit no! Don't answer that! I don't have time for another Mr Bentley story!' The two laughed. 'That reminds me, Conrad, doesn't your friend Anke play the violin? How's she and that bloke of hers….'

'Pascal.'

'How's she and Pascal settling back in Germany?' The German couple had frequently chatted to Wally over the fence and warmed to his care-free nature.

'I think they're doing fine. Both very busy, as usual, so I try to leave them alone.'

Bullshit, laughed Wally to himself. 'Really, Conrad? That doesn't sound like you. I bet they get a tsunami of emails!'

Conrad had met Anke, an ecologist, through the Hobart music circles and she had offered him free German lessons when he retired. After the funding for her position at the University of Tasmania ended, she and Pascal reluctantly returned to their home in Hasenfeld, a small satellite suburb of Heimbach in North Rhine-Westphalia. Conrad and Gretel had visited Heimbach in 2016 and enjoyed meandering along its river bank and strolling through the adjacent national park.

'Say hello from me next time you email them, Conrad. I enjoyed chattin' to Anke about her research on those bloody feral cats and how they're killing off our native wildlife. And what about your German pen friend on the Swiss border? Do you still harass him?'

'Yes, Wally. I still exchange emails with my pen friend, and no Wally,

I don't harass him. He loves hearing about Tassie and getting all the beach photos. Same with my other pen friends in Berlin.'

'Shit! How many pen friends have you got? I don't know how you keep up with it all. No wonder you don't have time to mow the frickin' lawns!' They sensed the conversation was coming to its natural close. 'Well, I hope you have some luck with your… Herr Steinhoff.'

'Thanks, Wally. I'm hoping he's just as tenacious as I am.'

'Impossible!'

'Hey! Have you heard our wives have found a French builder to put up the new fence?'

'Yes, mate. Trish has been swooning over him for days. Apparently, he's got—'

'Wally!' came an excited cry from Patricia. 'I've finally got Andy on the phone!'

Wally turned to Conrad with raised eyebrows.

'Go, Wally!'

Chapter 5

1918
A German Soldier Falls

Lieutenant Preiser scanned the slope up to the summit of Hill 165 and assumed the French troops were at the ready, primed to defend their position. Before he gave the order to advance, he turned to look at his men. Behind them, he noticed the picturesque whitewashed buildings scattered around the village of Bussiares. He wondered how much longer the village would escape destruction.

Wolf and his comrades cautiously crossed the road to the ditch, fanned out just below the start of the slope and also raised their eyes to the summit, unable to see signs of their enemy but aware they were there, dug in well and taking aim. They inched up the slope in formation. An advance of ten metres, with no enemy fire, offered the squad a false sense of security. They reached the safety of a ramshackle empty farmhouse and crouched beside a stone wall, collapsed in part through lack of repair.

Again, Erich Wiese could not ignore the flowers scattered around the garden. This time, the fierce sun had tainted the blooms. He could taste something bitter.

They pushed on.

Within metres, there was a loud crack, and the men instinctively dipped their heads and hugged the ground.

'No!' cried Wolf.

Lieutenant Preiser looked to his rear. 'Are you hit, Deppner?'

'My foot!'

'Sergeant Armbruster! Pick one of the men to help Deppner retreat to the farmhouse.'

'No Sir! I can get there myself.'

The lieutenant hesitated. He made a quick mental calculation. 'Do it Deppner! Do it now!' Wolf nodded and moved off. 'Men! Keep advancing, but with a keen eye. They have us now.'

Wolf slid past a dense clump of wild sage, grown taller than usual. He could smell it. Honey, he thought. No, something sour. He was unsure. He shook off the distraction. His ankle knocked against a stone fallen from the wall. He suppressed a cry of pain and realised he was going to have difficulty putting weight on his foot. He reached down. It was wet. He leaned back and arched his neck in pain.

Lieutenant Preiser took another quick glance to the rear and saw Wolf was nearing the farm door. He was relieved the French were yet to spot him. 'Forward!'

Wolf heard the lieutenant's order in the distance just as he felt an explosion and something sharp hit him in the back. The young soldier fell to the ground. He was in pain and disoriented. His ears were ringing. He attempted to call out to his friends for help, but could not utter the words. He could taste blood in his mouth and lost consciousness...

When Wolf stirred, his left arm was numb and his jacket soaked in blood. He heard fierce fire coming from the slope behind him and hoped his friends were safe. He raised his head and saw the open door of the farmhouse and a voice inside of him yelled, Go!

There was an intense round of enemy fire. The sound was deafening, much louder than any in the squad could have expected. Bullets and exploding grenades threw up a blanket of dirt and the men instantly realised they had become dangerously exposed.

'Sir! They have us,' yelled Sergeant Armbruster. 'I don't think we can make it any further.'

Lieutenant Preiser gave the order to retreat. The slight undulations in the slope were in their favour and the French struggled to pick them off.

Felix was first to reach the stone wall and saw a blood spatter, and possibly a handprint. His heart skipped a beat. *Wolf will be fine. I know it.*

The French fired another volley but had not timed it correctly. The lieutenant joined the forward thrust of his soldiers, reaching for the safety of the farmyard. As they crouched behind the wall or beside the farm exterior, he hoped he was the only one who noticed a pool of blood on the courtyard cobblestones.

The enemy gunfire ceased.

Erich saw Felix and Bruno enter the farmhouse. He heard a sound and thought, did someone yell from inside? Was someone screaming? He was unsure. He convinced himself his mind was playing tricks. He followed his friends inside and saw an opened hatch to a cellar. He heard whimpering and raced down the stairs with the lieutenant at his heels. The intense sun's rays streamed in from a large basement window and merged with a reverse shaft of light falling from the hatch. It cast an eerie, theatrical glow over the scene. Nobody spoke. Dust was floating in and out of the columns of light. Erich struggled to adjust his vision. He felt as though everything was in slow motion. In other circumstances, he would have paused to admire the contrast of light and shadow. It took him several seconds to recognise the three intertwined figures on the floor. Felix was crouched behind Wolf, tenderly cradling his head in both hands. He had shaped his hands around Wolf's cheeks, his thumbs caressing them like a sculptor working clay. Bruno was beside Felix, his arm stretched over Felix's shoulder. They were unaware Lieutenant Preiser had entered. He remained on the staircase—respectful, silent. He assessed the situation and prepared himself emotionally for the turmoil that was to come.

The sound of soldiers jostling above them interrupted the stillness.

Erich and Lieutenant Preiser turned in unison. The light that streamed in from the opened hatch obscured the lieutenant's shape.

Sergeant Armbruster pushed his way through some of the men and yelled from the top of the stairs, 'Sir! The firing's stopped. We've all made it!' He squinted to get a better view into the cellar and realised this was not the case.

'Sergeant! Move the men back to the road. Make contact with Sergeant Berg.'

Erich heard faint sounds of voices around him but was oblivious to them. He turned back to his friends. Felix and Bruno were in a trance.

A couple of men peered over their sergeant's shoulder. They looked apprehensive. 'Is Deppner okay, Sarge?'

'You heard the lieutenant. To the road! On the double. Go!'

The lieutenant turned as Erich's rifle clattered to the floor. Erich flew to the others, crouched down, and placed both his hands gently on Wolf's chest. All four were now illuminated by the combined shafts of light.

The lieutenant shifted his position and momentarily disrupted the beam of light from the hatch, but the four remained unaware of his presence. Initially, the lieutenant believed Erich was trying to staunch a chest wound, but soon realised he was, instead, joining the others in their soothing embrace of Wolf. Once before, following one of many gruelling battles, Lieutenant Preiser had stumbled upon the quartet's ritual. He observed they had formed a circle, arms over shoulders, foreheads forward, their temples almost touching. He instantly recognised it as a private ceremony, akin to a fellowship, a pact. Before retreating with a knowing smile, he had paused to admire them. With a similar embrace now before him, he allowed his mind to wander as he tried to escape the war. There was time and silence to do so… He did not wish to disturb the group bonded on the floor. Not yet.

As a young man, the lieutenant had been fortunate to study fine art and painting in Paris, something his parents had arranged. The spirit and attractiveness of France had captured and overwhelmed him. He learned to appreciate the beauty of colour and brush strokes when painted with a sensitive and discerning eye, and often gasped at the evocative power of a masterpiece. His first love had been in France and together they visited art galleries, marvelled at the spectacle and agony laid bare on canvas, drank local wines, whispered declarations of love and danced in fields. He missed such splendour. Only a handful of his men, he had observed, shared his appreciation for landscape. At one time on the march, he noticed young Private Erich Wiese had slowed his pace to look at clumps of flowers and herbs that had sprung to life beside ditches. Sadly, the war had taken its toll. The lieutenant had begun to feel the flora was losing its appeal…

The scene of the quartet, absorbed in fear and impending loss, reminded the lieutenant of a painting, but he struggled to recall the artist. He wanted to recall it. He needed to recall it. There was still no sound or movement from the quartet, and this offered him an unspoken invitation to escape further into his thoughts. In silence, his mind drew aside the stiffened and grimy curtains of four years of fighting. He looked through a window to a brighter past. The painting was revealed—The Death of General Wolfe by Benjamin West. He recalled it intimately. The odd feeling that a death scene could depict such beauty. Three officers or adjutants comforting the dying general during the Battle of Quebec in 1759. They gathered around and propped up their commander, just as the three were now doing for Wolf. The painting's bright display of red and blue tunics, juxtaposed against the turbulent background of grey clouds, had always fascinated the lieutenant. He looked back at the quartet. He was humbled and strangely moved by the blending of the vividly remembered painting and the scene before him. Longingly, he wished himself away from war. He allowed himself a few moments to bathe in the imagery of visiting an art gallery in Paris or Vienna, holding Rosa's hand whilst pointing at a masterpiece and breathlessly explaining its symbolism. He imagined kissing Rosa as she smiled back at him. His mind travelled back to his agonisingly short home leave in the previous year, lying with Rosa as they made plans to start a family after the war.

Something stirred, and the lieutenant's attention snapped to the scene before him. Despite giving the quartet privacy, he now felt like an intruder, a voyeur.

Bruno lifted one of Wolf's hands and placed it gently on Erich's outstretched forearm, then put his own hand on Wolf's shoulder. He looked up at his friends with tears in his eyes.

Their embrace was complete.

The three waited for signs from Wolf, to hear him speak…

It came. 'I'm cold!'

Erich looked directly at Wolf's closed eyes, willing them to open. 'Wolf,' he whispered. Again, 'Wolf.' Although Erich's hands remained on Wolf's chest, he was alarmed at the lack of a discernible heartbeat. 'Wolfi!'

The other two were shocked. Never had anyone from the group uttered this pet name, reserved solely for Wolf's mother.

Erich would later reproach himself for allowing the pet name to escape him, believing his mind had flashed forward to hear Frau Deppner cry out in anguish, 'Wolfi! No! Not my Wolfi!'

Erich's mind doggedly tried to avoid the word death, but he was powerless to stop its malevolent, insidious intrusion. He felt nauseous.

Wolf opened his eyes. He whimpered, 'Please hold me.'

The three looked at each other, alarmed at Wolf's lack of awareness.

Erich moved his face closer to Wolf's and whispered, 'We're here, Wolf. We are holding you now. You're safe.'

Wolf convulsed. 'Oh, God. It hurts.' His face mirrored his pain.

Bruno sobbed. He released his hand from Wolf's shoulder and wrapped both his arms around Felix. 'Do something, Felix. Please save him.'

Felix felt utterly powerless and was brought to tears.

The three waited.

Wolf began to writhe in pain. 'Make it stop… Erich, please. For God's sake, make it stop. Tell me something, Erich… Anything. Please.' The urgency in Wolf's voice was unmistakable.

Erich closed his eyes and took a breath. He was unsure why he chose the story that followed. He had an array of stories, memories, daydreams. Some his friends already knew, some he kept private. The story chose him. As if he were reading a fairy-tale to a child, but with pathos, pausing after each sentence to stress its importance, he began: 'This is something I've told you all before… It's something that's always been very special to me. I want to tell it to you again.'

Felix and Bruno looked at him, eager for him to continue.

'There is an island called Tasmania. It's part of Australia… We learned about it in Herr Stummhofer's geography class. Do you remember? He had relatives there and talked a lot about it. Nobody had heard of this island before… We felt Herr Stummhofer had let us in on a grand secret.'

Felix and Bruno longed to escape and be transported to this place. They remembered how Wolf had laughed at the reaction of his family when he told them about this extraordinary, far-off island. Seated around the dining table, the Deppners had listened with wonder and curiosity. None of them had heard of Tasmania before, and they were equally bewildered at learning German immigrants had settled there.

'Wolf, do you remember?' continued Erich. 'Your father was amazed that the German immigrants named their town Bismarck.' Erich's voice faltered. 'After the war, I'm going there.' He opened his eyes, hoping Wolf would do the same. 'I'm going to Tasmania! I'm going to get as far away from France…' he hesitated, 'and as far from Germany as I can go.'

Lieutenant Preiser was unfamiliar with this island, Tasmania, but he was spellbound by Erich's story. The words drew him in. He heard Felix and Bruno crying.

Erich paused. He had no tears.

Wolf moaned and the sense of urgency intensified.

Erich quickened his speech. 'Can you believe it? Germans living on the other side of the world… as far away as you can go… in a place called Bismarck. It must have rolling hills, mountains, just like the Alps!' He paused again. The sound of Felix and Bruno weeping was comforting. Erich felt oddly calm.

Lieutenant Preiser inadvertently scuffed his boot on the wooden steps. The sound finally alerted the three to his presence. They looked up at him. Their faces conveyed a sense of gratitude that their platoon leader was supporting them. He cleared his throat, a deliberate sound that invited the story to continue. The lieutenant knew Erich was running out of time.

'You can come with me, Wolf… to Tasmania!' Erich became anxious. Wolf had not opened his eyes. 'We will all go! You, me, Felix and Bruno. The quartet will go to the ends of the earth together!'

Wolf's chest heaved. 'Yes. I want to go with you!' His words gave his friends a brief, cruel reprieve before his mouth erupted with a flash of red. Felix felt the warm blood on his hands as Wolf writhed and shook his head.

Silence…

Suddenly, Wolf opened his eyes. For a moment, his friends noticed that his look of pain had disappeared. Wolf had accepted his fate.

Lieutenant Preiser shifted his posture. He knew Wolf's pain would return.

The pain returned. 'Oh, God!' Tears streamed down Wolf's face.

Silence. Everyone was breathless.

Lieutenant Preiser lowered his head. He had witnessed immense misery, pain, and death. This scene was different. It was harder to bear. His rank discouraged, even prohibited, emotion. He must remain stoic and strong for his men. He knew he would shed private tears. Maybe not tonight, but in the days to come. Maybe in a month. Maybe when the war was over. He knew this death of young Wolf Deppner would haunt him and make him question the war. The lieutenant had grown tired of the coarseness of battle, the smell and company of men. Inside his head, he heard pounding and felt pain. Oh, this endless, damned war! He longed to return to his wife. Smell her. Touch her softness. He longed to sink into her beauty. Oh, how I love you, my beautiful Rosa…

Lieutenant Preiser raised his head.

Wolf died, held by the friends who cared for him so dearly.

There was silence.

Wolf's hand, now lifeless, remained on Erich's forearm, whose mind was still wandering off to Bismarck in Tasmania, pointing out the hills and mountains to his three friends.

Coldness entered the room and Felix felt a change in the texture of Wolf's skin.

Wolf's hand fell to the side.

Erich gasped. Now his tears fell.

Something stirred the dust. The beams of light across the cellar floor had shifted. They had previously resembled pillars of light in a cathedral, but now there was no grandeur to them. The dust resembled snowflakes whirling in circles on a breeze, but it was not a joyous display. Lieutenant Preiser noticed it too. He waited.

The lieutenant alighted the stairs and looked at his three men. 'We will need to move Deppner back to Licy-Clignon.' His voice was measured and reassuring. 'Cover him up. We will take him back soon.' The friends understood this meant for burial. 'Before that, we must regain contact with Sergeant Berg and work out our next move to take this hill. Private Deppner will be safe down here for a while.' In a more formal tone, 'I want you to fall out to the yard and report back to Sergeant Armbruster. Men! I want you to do that now.' Lieutenant Preiser exhaled. He was relieved to hear no immediate resistance. He was immeasurably proud of his men, his boys.

Felix wiped the blood from Wolf's face with his tunic sleeve. He gently rested Wolf's lifeless head on the floor. The three friends released their embrace, stood to attention, and wiped away their tears. For a moment, they looked down at their friend. Wolf's body did not resemble the many ghoulish corpses they had seen on the battlefields, the mutilated figures left in unnatural forms. Wolf's limbs had fallen gracefully into a dignified pose. His mouth was not agape. He looked young and handsome.

Felix searched for a covering and found a tablecloth draped over stored preserved fruit and jams. Lieutenant Preiser noticed someone had randomly decorated the fabric with hand-embroidered flowers, lovingly crafted over many hours of conversation and sisterhood. Despite their intended charm, the flowers failed to evoke the usual response of joy. Instead, they appeared hostile.

The trio turned to their lieutenant.

'Men. Report to your sergeant, but be mindful of the snipers out there. We foiled them by reaching this farm, but it won't last long, so be on your guard. Stay focussed.' They nodded, still numb, but dutifully responded to his order. They knew their lieutenant was protecting them. 'I will arrange for a couple of your comrades to stretcher Private Deppner back to Licy-Clignon.'

His plan to shake them from their trance worked. 'No, Sir!' cried Felix. 'Please! This is a job for us. We will take Wolf… we will take Private Deppner back.'

'Of course, Private Wittmann. Of course. After we knock out the French on this blasted hill, you can arrange it. Either way, we will fall back to the Clignon Brook. Make sure you are ready with a stretcher.'

All three nodded. Lieutenant Preiser's orders gave them brief purpose. They understood that reminiscing about Wolf and more weeping would return later. First, they must re-join their squad. The trio exited into the bright sunshine and remained vigilant of the French snipers, just as their lieutenant had ordered.

Now alone, Lieutenant Preiser turned to the shrouded body of the young soldier. The flowers of the tablecloth were cunning. They had shaken off their menace and now resembled something of their intended beauty. The tasteful blend of colours lured the lieutenant back to his hometown of Dinslaken, to the daytrips and picnics beside the Rhine River with Rosa. He heard her say, My darling Andreas. I love you. He heard his voice in reply, Please wait for me, Rosa …

Suddenly, the flowers reverted to the colours of war. He was infuriated by their trickery. They turned and took aim, delivering a crushing blow. He felt powerless to defend himself. He squinted and frowned. The pounding in his head was excruciating. No! Not this soldier. Not this beautiful boy.

The trio spent the next hours in a semi-dazed state, forging on beside their comrades to finally take Hill 165 and make some gains on La Mares Farm, safe under the constant scrutiny of both their lieutenant and sergeant.

Later that night, under a lacklustre sky, the moon hidden behind thick clouds, they stretchered Wolf back to the rivulet on the outskirts of Licy-Clignon and helped dig a grave for him and two other fallen soldiers from the platoon.

The next morning, after the fog lifted, the troops gathered for the burial. Although the dig was large, it was difficult to fit the two sections around its perimeter, but the trio and close comrades of the two other slain soldiers were given prime positions. The remainder of the men fell in behind.

Lieutenant Preiser cleared his throat. 'Men. Soldiers of Reserve Infantry Regiment 273. Words will not be enough today. I know that. Yet our hearts tell us that words are expected. Words are necessary.'

Felix, Bruno and Erich inched closer together. This time, Erich was the first to weep.

'Today we bury three exemplary soldiers, Privates Deppner, Martens and Degenhardt.' Lieutenant Preiser repeated the names, slower and with emphasis. 'Private Wolfgang Deppner from Section A, and Privates Maximilian Martens and Walter Degenhardt from Section B. These fine men died fighting for the protection and honour of their Kaiser and country.'

Erich was shocked. In all the misery of the last hours, he had ignored the other fallen soldiers and now took time to consider them: Max Martens from the coastal city of Kiel who, by rights, should have joined the navy; Max, whose flash of ginger hair bore witness to his mix of Danish and German ancestry; and Walter Degenhardt from a small town near Bochum, who had often entertained his comrades by reeling off the names and birthdates of his eleven siblings from oldest to youngest, and then in reverse. Erich felt strangely comforted. He pictured their faces and was comforted more. Wolf knew them well. Wolf liked them. He is not alone.

'Men! We feel sorrow for these losses, but we can seek comfort in knowing these soldiers are now with God, and that God will protect them. We also express our sorrow to their families and loved ones. We take honour in the fact we have served alongside such heroic men. Sergeants Armbruster and Berg could not have asked for better soldiers. Amen.'

As expected of an officer, Lieutenant Preiser had delivered his eulogy resolutely. He knew it was short and devoid of the usual verbosity that other more senior officers would have entertained, but inwardly, he was in turmoil. The four years of war had caught up with him. *Damn this war! Damn you God! Damn you Kaiser! These boys did not deserve to die in a foreign country, separated for so long from the people who love them. How dare you claim them! This is utter cruelty.* He looked up at the dissipating clouds and tried to gather his thoughts. He noticed the faint outline of a daytime moon hanging low in the sky, waiting patiently for the clouds to float back over her, to let her sleep.

During a lull, Lieutenant Preiser wrote to the families. The letter to Wolf's father was left until last. It was at this time, when he was putting pen to paper for the third time, that the young lieutenant allowed himself to cry.

France

4th June 1918

Dear Mr Deppner,

It is with deep sadness that I inform you that your son, Wolfgang, Private Deppner...

Following Wolf's death, the fighting was intense and his three friends functioned with an uncanny mix of aimlessness and duty. They followed orders, helped their comrades over barbed wire and dutifully carried out their daily routines. They cleaned and fired their weapons, killed the enemy and obediently buried more of their comrades, yet they remained numb. The war had washed them into a vast ocean of indifference. They had become lost and detached.

On the 6th of June 1918, two days after Wolf's burial, Lieutenant Preiser was shot and killed on the outskirts of Bussiares, his death later recorded as a heroic sacrifice to the honour and protection of Germany.

Erich saw the bullet strike with an explosion of crimson and near black. He knew his lieutenant's gallant face would forever haunt him, sprayed with blood, the brave countenance disfigured with pain and anguish.

The lieutenant's death was not instantaneous. His gaze found his men all scattered in chaos. He saw Private Erich Wiese had turned. In those moments before his end, Lieutenant Preiser spoke to Erich, not with words, but with his eyes. You gentle soul. I'm sorry you had to endure such misery.

Realising he had only seconds before he fell to the ground and consumed by a wasteland of corpses and trampled flowers, Lieutenant Andreas Preiser whispered, 'I love you, Rosa…'

Dinslaken

5th June 1918

My darling Andreas, my brave lieutenant,

I have such wonderful news!

Your namesake has come into our world on the 5th of May, a month to the day before I send you this letter. I can imagine your smile as you read this news.

Yes! You are a father my love, and you are going to adore our fine-looking boy.

On advice from our caring neighbour, this announcement was withheld until, at four weeks old, our little Andreas proved he was strong enough to withstand the rigours of a newborn.

The wise Frau Müller advised me that it was undesirable for our fighting men to have extra distractions and concerns for their families. You care so much for your young soldiers, I did not wish to burden you until my pregnancy was over and the news of our little Andreas was as positive as it is now.

My dearest, please forgive me for the delay, but we can now celebrate together!

The streets of Dinslaken are full of smiles for our son. Everyone who knows and respects you, sends their congratulations and wishes you God's protection on the Front.

How I long for this war to end so you can come home and hold your darling son. Every day I see your face reflected in his.

I am so lucky to have you both.

Your devoted,

Rosa

Later, as the entire regiment surrendered to shock, Erich wept and cried out to his two friends, 'I can't endure this misery any longer! Thank God our Wolf didn't see his lieutenant die. What will become of the poor lieutenant's wife?'

Their emotions returned like a crazed, wild boar. Pent-up emotions, some harboured since the beginning of the war, were suddenly released. Felix sat lost in profanities for hours; Bruno thumped his face until his lips split open; Erich cried inconsolably. They were no longer sure of the enemy's identity. Their grief was so intense, so primal, that Sergeant Armbruster almost panicked, but knew he had to bring these men back to the fight. He suppressed any sentiment and took control through force:

'Are you with us, Wittmann?'

'What are you waiting for, Klug? Fire!'

'Wiese, you bastard. I said reload!'

The brutality worked. Not instantly, but within a short period the trio crawled out from the churning ocean; bruised, their bright eyes of youth lost. The voice of their sergeant eventually broke through, enabling them to reload and take aim at the enemy…

Without Wolf, Lieutenant Preiser and the many other killed or wounded comrades from their regiment, Felix, Bruno and Erich fought on into autumn. The wildflowers lost their brightness, just as the warmth of brotherhood and the lustre of their once intense friendship began to fade following the loss of Wolf. All attempts to rekindle their ritual, to form a circle, to touch foreheads, failed. Anything resembling an embrace was carefully avoided, eventually abandoned. The proud and treasured title of quartet, so revered by many in their hometown, would lie forever buried with their beloved Wolf.

With colder weather and likely defeat looming, Felix and Erich watched helplessly as Bruno retreated the furthest into despair. They pleaded with him to stay strong and exchanged concerned looks as he began to talk of never seeing his home and family again.

Chapter 6

2018. February
Tasmania

Conrad, Captain Baz, Martin and Chris, the Focus crew, rendezvoused in the northern suburbs with other members of the Waratah Bushwalking Club and were excited to finally climb Collins Bonnet on the Wellington Ranges. The walking group had gathered to organise a smaller convoy to drive to the start of the walk at a car park on the fringe of the Myrtle Forest.

Robyn, the leader, was pleased everyone had arrived on time and in jovial moods and called for their attention. 'We're expecting good weather today, but as you all know, all that can change in an instant, particularly on the Wellington slopes. Four seasons in one day, and all that.' She described the climb to an altitude of just over twelve hundred metres and cautioned the group to exercise caution as parts of the track were unclearly marked.

'Stick with us, Martin. We wouldn't want to lose you up there!' joked Baz.

The other walkers had warmed to the banter between the four crew members and could not but laugh at Baz's dry wit.

'There's a bit of boulder hopping before we get to the summit,' continued Robyn, 'but, once up there, we should get some superb views. On my calculations, we'll get back around four o'clock, hopefully a little earlier, so that means we'll have time for coffee and cake afterwards.' In a more serious tone of voice, 'Now, with this hot weather lately, there's been increased sightings of snakes, particularly on the Wellington Ranges, so please be vigilant. Any questions before we form our circle for the introductions?' Robyn looked to Martin, anticipating his usual response—'Ah yes, the circle of love!'—but the sound of Captain Baz mumbling something under his breath deterred him.

Due to their similar height and appearance, Martin and Chris had often been mistaken for each other and Robyn had been forewarned that they had recently tried to fool another group by switching their names. She cautioned them, 'Now, I'm on to you two, so don't try your usual tricks.' The group formed the circle. 'We don't have any rookie walkers today, but we might as well stick with tradition and introduce ourselves anyway, just in case we've forgotten each other's names! I'm Robyn, your leader for the day.'

'Bev… Joan… Judy… Liz… Geoff… Vern… Frank… Viv… Rosie… David… Anne… John… Betty… Graeme…'

There was a slight pause as they turned to Martin, anticipating he might be brave enough to repeat his ruse and introduce himself as Chris, but another grunt from Captain Baz discouraged him.

'Martin… Chris… Baz… Conrad.'

In the lead car, with Conrad and Martin as her designated passengers, Robyn guided the convoy over the hills toward Collinsvale. After some initial chit-chat, she got Conrad's attention. 'I've got something interesting for your research on the First World War, Conrad. We're just heading into Collinsvale. Did you know it was formerly named Bismarck?'

'No!'

'Before the war broke out, there was a sizable community of German and Danish immigrants up here.' She explained the Europeans had been enticed by assisted passage back in the 1870s and 80s and became accomplished market gardeners and orchardists, also establishing one of Tasmania's first tourism ventures by opening a coffeehouse. Robyn glanced in her rear-view mirror and was unsurprised to see Conrad's wide eyes staring back at her. 'To think we could have enjoyed delicious German cakes and Danish pastries up here in Bismarck, not Collinsvale, if silly men had not started such a dreadful war that put an end to all that finery!'

Conrad was aware Robyn had experience in editing texts and he always enjoyed her eloquent use of language. Mixed with her charming account of the pre-war Bismarck and growing excitement for the bushwalk, his head whirled with images of the German immigrants tending their fields and enticing tourists into their cosy coffeehouse with the added aroma of baking.

'Oh, and another thing, Conrad. After the war broke out, they interned all the able-bodied men with German backgrounds in camps on Bruny Island, you know, to protect Tasmania from an attack from within. Can you believe it? All those men who were born and raised here, respected members of communities like Bismarck, locked up because their parents or grandparents came from Germany, shunned because of a stupid war on the other side of the world!' Robyn released a disapproving huff.

Conrad gazed out the window and squinted in the mid-summer glare as he looked across to the rolling fields. He noticed the summer heat had transformed the colours of the grasses into hues of silver, beige and gold. He thought about researching Bismarck-come-Collinsvale, and his mind filled with questions about the lives of the pioneering Europeans who had settled there.

'Of course, the name Bismarck was changed because of the rising anti-German sentiment during the war,' said Robyn. 'Some of its residents had anglicised their names and, would you believe, even joined up to fight beside their fellow Tasmanians. What a bizarre world back then.'

Conrad had a few minutes to digest the information before Robyn pulled into the carpark. He and Martin alighted with smiles and predictably gravitated toward Captain Baz and Chris. The four busied themselves with tightening their bootlaces and adjusting each other's packs.

The core group of Thursday walkers, affectionately dubbed the Waratah Ladies, had been thrilled when four new members joined in quick succession. When Conrad arrived, he had recognised Martin from their similar work backgrounds and attempted to alleviate the confusion caused by Martin and Chris' similar appearances: 'It's simple ladies. Martin is slightly taller than Chris, makes terrible puns and wears the flashier outdoor gear. There! That should help.' For the most part it did but, periodically, uncertainty about them could still be heard on the track.

Baz was the last of the four to join and, as with the others, bushwalking was an unfamiliar activity for him. On his first walk, he expressed doubts he would continue long term, but said he was willing to try it out for a couple of weeks. 'Doctor's orders to get some fresh air and exercise, you know.' When he returned for his fourth consecutive walk, the Waratah Ladies smiled at each other, knowing that Baz had also been seduced by the Tasmanian vistas, particularly around the Wellington Ranges adorned with deep-red Waratah blooms in the warmer months.

As Baz got to know Conrad, Martin and Chris on the track and assessed their potential as crew members, he also seized opportunities to catch glimpses of the Derwent River through gaps in the trees when walking along the slopes of Mount Wellington. With the advantage of elevation, he could visualise wind directions and map out potential race courses. 'Hey, Chris. Do you see the line between the casino and Howrah Beach, where Conrad lives? If we had a steady easterly, Focus could easily get there on one tack.'

The Waratah Ladies eventually claimed some credit for bringing the Focus crew together and were always eager to hear about their adventures on the river. They also warmed to Conrad's music interests and, as a reward for their enthusiasm and weekly inquiry, he invited them to his orchestra performances. As he packed his gear for the Collins Bonnet walk, Conrad had made a mental note to invite them to his upcoming string quartet concert.

As the line of walkers ascended through the captivating Myrtle Forest, Conrad noticed the understorey of man ferns, almost double his height, yet still dwarfed by the forest trees that towered above them. He pondered how the European settlers of the former Bismarck would have reacted to the somewhat prehistoric appearance and grandeur of the ferns.

The bushwalkers soon reached a sunny, open slope of sub-alpine scrub and stopped to enjoy their morning break. As usual, the Focus crew formed a close circle and searched their backpacks for snacks. Given that warm temperatures had been forecasted, water was the preferred beverage, but a few walkers were not deterred when they packed their gear and reached for their customary thermos of tea. Others sauntered past in search of a flat rock and made quick, polite comments to give the crew its privacy.

Despite months of racing, Martin still struggled to gain his sea legs and tried to compensate with attempts to impress his skipper. 'That was tricky out on the river yesterday Baz, with the strong sou'wester hitting our starboard, eh?'

'You need to dig out Sailing for Dummies again, Martin. The wind was coming directly from the south.'

'Were you thinking about reefing the mainsail?'

'Um, no. A little difficult to reef under those conditions. Anyway, the wind dropped out for the remainder of the race, so reefing would have been pointless.'

Conrad came to the rescue. 'We've sure had some tough times on the river lately.'

'Some laidback times too, don't forget,' persisted Baz. 'Remember a few weeks back when we had no breeze at all? The river current forced the fleet downstream, for God's sake!' Baz grunted and gazed over to the adjacent mountain range.

Conrad regained his attention. 'I got the same old answer from my neighbour, Wally. He can't sail with us because he's still too busy with work.'

'Huh!'

'He also says five on a boat the size of Focus is too many and someone would need to walk the plank to make room for him. Ha!'

Captain Baz looked at Martin with raised eyebrows. 'Well, I can easily fix that.'

There was a brief pause before Martin realised he had been the target of the taunt. Conrad saw Martin dip his head to disguise an offended expression and tried to make light of it. 'If anyone's going to walk the plank, it would have to be me for failing to convince Wally to get on board, eh?'

From there, the group climbed toward the base of Collins Bonnet with its impressive collar of large dolerite boulders, all the while pairing up with the Focus crew members to catch up on their latest news: winning their races, plans for overnight or multi-day bushwalks, Conrad's upcoming Europe trip and his music interests. 'And, did I tell you I'm shouting my German friends to a live performance of Beethoven's Ninth Symphony!'

The four reached the summit ahead of the others and took in the panorama of the Wellington Ranges, the Derwent Valley and over to Bruny Island. Conrad marvelled at the view of the Wellington Plateau and the western side of Mount Wellington which, from the rear aspect, took on the form of a giant beast raising its front legs as if to pounce. In contrast, many walkers believed the mountain's profile, as seen from the northern suburbs, resembled a sphinx. He noticed the craggy peak of Cathedral Rock. The fine conditions and elevation made its form appear more pronounced, dramatic. He turned to the others. 'Look down there! We need to conquer that peak one day!'

'Wow!' puffed Robyn as she scrambled to the summit. 'You sailors are like mountaineers!' She glanced around at the vastness of the landscape below. 'How lucky we are today! It's not often we get to see all these beautiful views. Usually, we get to the summit and have to make a hasty escape to find shelter from the wind and rain, even in summer!'

The walkers took advantage of the warm weather, found a flat, comfortable rock and settled in for lunch. Conrad was asked about his letter research again and gave a pre-prepared response about commissioning a researcher to investigate information on Wolf's regiment stored at the Military Archives in Freiburg. One walker overheard the conversation. 'What's all this about? What letter? Have I missed something interesting?'

Captain Baz got in first before Conrad's inner voice had a chance to sneer. 'Oh please, no! If you don't know anything about Conrad's German letter—and God only knows how you could have missed hearing about it over the past six months, or more—then please no, don't ask him to tell you about it now. We couldn't bear it. Grab him for a chat on the way down. But I warn you, you'll need at least an hour for the full story!'

Reaching the cars, the walkers felt invigorated by a day of perfect weather, magnificent views and enjoyable chats. Conrad switched on his mobile phone and noticed an email with attachments from his Freiburg contact, but had difficulty reading it on the small screen.

The Waratah Ladies acknowledged his excitement and were not perturbed when he abandoned the post-walk coffee in favour of a hasty retreat home.

In anticipation, Conrad rushed through the door and almost fell onto his computer. It was not long before his elation was dashed. Herr Steinhoff had been meticulous in his research, but his email came as a setback:

> Freiburg
>
> 16th February 2018
>
> Dear Mr. Bentley.
>
> At your request, I have undertaken a search at the Federal Military Archives, Freiburg for the relevant documents pertaining to Reserve Infantry Regiment 273.
>
> I have read all the documents and photographed them—I will send it all in a CD by post.
>
> I've also supplied a link to a book that's available online, written by Lt. Paul Mahlmann (retired) who served with the regiment. No doubt, the book will be of interest to you, but unfortunately I found nothing in it or the other documents referring to a soldier by the name of Wolfgang who was shot and killed on the 3 June 1918.
>
> The problem is, if your Wolfgang had a relatively low military rank, then it is almost certain that nothing would have been recorded about him in either the documents or Mahlmann's book.
>
> As you have already informed me, your previous internet searches were

unsuccessful. Without a specific surname, it would appear you had an impossible task then. Sadly, the same applies now.

Perhaps you can return to your own notes and determine whether there is anything you may have overlooked?

Should you find any new information, I'm happy to make further searches on your behalf.

Yours sincerely,

P. Steinhoff

For a while, Conrad stared at the words on the computer screen. He opened the link to Mahlmann's online book first published in the 1930s, a detailed historical account of Reserve Infantry Regiment 273. Ordinarily, Conrad would not have hesitated to study and translate the relevant pages that described the regiment's movements in early June 1918, but, on this occasion, he was disheartened. He acknowledged that his research might be coming to an end without achieving success.

Gretel arrived home and saw the displeasure on his face. 'What is it?'

'I've hit a dead end with the military archives. It might be time to give up.'

'Ha! I don't believe that for a minute!' As she moved off, Gretel turned and gave Conrad a reassuring smile. She pointed to his folder of documents, a record of his research since June last year. 'Take another look in there, Conrad. I'm sure you'll find another clue. You just need to dig deeper.'

'Ha! That's what the bloke from Freiburg told me to do!'

Conrad reached for the folder and flipped through to the pages which outlined his attempts to write different surnames in the old German scripts in an attempt to solve the puzzle of the German surname in the letter. He looked over his scribbles, arrows and notations. The name Deppner, that he had practised in various sizes, styles and forms, again attracted his attention. Conrad recalled his disappointment in receiving 'no record found' from the Kleve Births, Deaths and Marriages Office, and then supplying alternative, more obscure names, only to become disgruntled when they also returned negative results.

His inner voice made a surprisingly positive call. The name Deppner still looks correct. Try it again, Bentley!

Conrad took a deep breath. Could your name be Deppner after all, Wolf? He opened his web browser and slowly typed the letters…

W—O—L—F—G—A—N—G——D—E—P—P—N—E—R

Chapter 7

1914
Australia Enters The Great War

'What is it, my love?' asked Daisy in her soft voice. Her husband, Frank Swinton, had arrived home from work with a furrowed brow.

'John's been arrested. They're going to ship him off to some internment camp on Bruny Island!'

'Oh, Frank. That's awful.'

Daisy's twin sister, Bessie, was married to John Bloom, the youngest of four children born to German immigrants with the original name of Blume who had arrived in Hobart in the late 1800s and settled in Bismarck, a northern hillside suburb.

'John was born here, for God's sake. This war is making everyone go mad.'

In the summer of 1870, John's maternal uncle, Günter Stummhofer, the newly appointed teacher in the German city of Cleve, had arrived at his sister's house excitedly clasping an Australian Government advertisement. Europeans had been invited to emigrate, enticed with free passage and, in some cases, free land. Scarcely taking a breath, Herr Stummhofer had urged his sister and brother-in-law to seize the opportunity and start a new life on the other side of the world. 'I teach my students about Australia, including Tasmania, its southern island state. I've brought you some pictures of this extraordinary place. The climate is mild and the landscape spectacular. I have no doubt you and your children, and any children to come, will prosper there.'

A few months later, Hans and Marie Blume, their three daughters and other German adventurers, boarded the Victoria in Hamburg and arrived in Hobart in time to enjoy their first spring in the southern hemisphere. The Blumes purchased a pocket of land in Sorell Creek, a small wooded settlement with its own fresh water supply nestled among the northern foothills of the Wellington Ranges.

Alongside British colonists, who were first to settle in the area, the Germans felled eucalypt, sassafras and myrtle trees to build their homes, use as firewood, stoke their ovens, and warm their hands during the surprisingly cold winter months. After a second boatload of mostly Danish immigrants arrived a year later, the settlement was officially recognised as a town and renamed Bismarck. Within a year, the first foundation stone for a Methodist church was ceremoniously laid and most of the Lutheran-raised settlers accepted the minister's invitation to help complete the build and join his congregation. A cohesive community began to thrive, complete with a school, bakery and post office, and, before long, the townsfolk realised that their hillside village would soon need its own cemetery.

The Blumes quickly warmed to the tranquil Tasmanian lifestyle. On many weekends, they sacrificed their work in the fields for trips to Hobart Town to improve their English by conversing with fishmongers, butchers and other shop owners. It was not long before they paid tribute to their new home by anglicising their surname.

Marie Bloom regularly wrote to her brother in Cleve, thanking him for his recommendation that they moved to Tasmania. Herr Stummhofer looked forward to his sister's letters and her charming descriptions of Hobart and its surrounds:

Bismarck

3rd June 1876

My dearest brother, Günter.

Once again, warmest greetings from Tasmania.

Your nieces are growing up fast and we are all enjoying life in our valley. The Bismarck community is very friendly and industrious.

Similarly, our trips to Hobart Town are a constant reminder of just how welcoming the Tasmanians are, marred only by the wretched treatment we sometimes see inflicted on the Aboriginal people.

Günter, I must tell you, the black and white pictures of Tasmania you showed us before we departed Germany failed to show our new home in all its living glory. We marvel at the deep-blue colour of the River Derwent that flows past our capital into the Tasman Sea. We enjoy views of the river from various vantage points around our hillsides. Our nearby forest of myrtle has a rare beauty and an abundance of spectacular plants, including what the locals refer to as man ferns. We can also see Mount Wellington from the valley and its splendour cannot be denied. There are also glimpses of the mountain's adjacent peaks—Collins Cap and Bonnet, named we are told after the first Lieutenant Governor of the former Van Diemen's Land. In late spring and summer, the native Waratah bushes, scattered around the slopes, display bright red blooms that are simply delightful. We sometimes receive heavy snow in winter, but it does not last long as the Tasmanian weather can be erratic. Sometimes it changes many times within the course of the day! Often, there is a light sprinkle of snow on the summit that reminds me of the dusting of icing on a cake.

One of our Danish neighbours has purchased a new camera. I will send you photographs as soon as I can. I know you are forever keen to educate your students about far-off places. The young people of Cleve are lucky to have such a dedicated teacher with a passion for geography!

Yours,

Marie

After many years of tilling the fields, planting orchards, watching their daughters grow into confident women and farewelling them to married-lives in Hobart and beyond, Hans and Marie Bloom were surprised, and in their words blessed, by the arrival of a son. They paraded their newborn through the valley, proudly boasting that they had waived the customary father's Christian name of Hans in favour of John.

John thrived in the clean air of the valley and immediately showed promise when he reached school age.

Bismarck

30th December 1899

My dearest brother, Günter.

Warmest greetings from our island paradise.

We hope you had a joyous Christmas and wish you a healthy and prosperous new century!

Our girls and their families joined us to celebrate the festive season—some making the effort to cross the Bass Strait. It was wonderful to have the whole family back together again. You will be amused to know we are at risk of losing count of how many grandchildren we have!

John is now a joyful seven-year-old and continues to make us feel so young! He is very athletic and loves playing the local sports of cricket and football. His teacher has noticed that he already shows talent on the football field and recommended he joins what is called a 'league' next year. This will mean additional weekend trips to the city, but Hans and I are not perturbed, as it will give us more opportunities to visit our favourite shops and butcheries.

Günter, you would be so proud of your young nephew. I've enclosed a photograph of John dwarfed by his older cousins. You will recognise him from his snow-white hair appearing like a crown above his head, with our delightful Mount Wellington on display in the background!

Are you still planning to visit us one day so you can meet John yourself? I do hope so...

As young teenagers, Frank Swinton and John Bloom met through the Southern Football League and instantly developed a close bond. Frank was surprised, and secretly envious, that his new friend could outdo him on the field. 'It's not fair, John. You're Tasmanian, but with German blood running through your veins, so how is it possible that you are so good at Australian Rules football?'

Both achieved good results at their respective schools and, in the eyes of their parents, sports coaches, peers and neighbours, they effortlessly matured into respectful, kind-hearted young men, admired for their good humour and positive outlook on life.

After finishing school, John worked alongside the orchardists and farmers in Bismarck whilst Frank found a steady position at the South Hobart Tannery. They spent each weekend at football practice in the winter, cricket in the summer, and often raced each other to the summits of various peaks scattered around the Wellington Ranges.

In their late teens, at the invitation of one of Frank's distant relatives who worked at the Mount Bischoff tin mine, the two set off for the small northwest town of Waratah in search of employment and adventure. The relative isolation of the mining community strengthened their friendship and, during rare breaks from the harsh work in the mine, they scrubbed their faces clean and stole away for walks in the nearby bushland. They sat on the banks of rushing creeks or on summits of lofty peaks and mapped out their lives as adults.

As twenty-year-old men, they returned to Hobart with impressive references and practical skills.

'Now we're back in the Big Smoke, John, we need to put our dashing looks and charming ways to good use,' declared Frank. 'We need to meet some fine lasses, mate! Good old Waratah was certainly the place to find steady work and constant rain, but dear me, what a drought when it came to the company of ladies!'

The twins, Daisy and Bessie Webb, had just turned eighteen when they met Frank and John at the Southern League's Annual Ball. Their brother, Tasman Webb, also a star football player, got to know Frank and John both on and off the field and, believing them to be good blokes, took delight in introducing them to his sisters.

'Miss Webb!' cried Frank in his typical, jovial voice. 'To think all this time we've lived in the same suburb and attended the same church, yet how is it possible that we've never met until today? We must make up for lost time!'

Similarly, John pursued Bessie, another sought-after belle of the ball, unable to resist her charming blue eyes and elegant features.

She, in turn, was instantly taken with John's fair appearance and striking blond hair. 'Are you Scandinavian, Mr. Bloom?'

'No, Miss Webb. My parents are German, but I was born here. We live in Bismarck.'

'Oh, how lovely. My family's been on many picnics to the Myrtle Forest.'

Frank and John felt a sense of comfort with this initial exchange and it urged them on to pursue their new love interests in earnest. As with their past adventures of exploring the bushlands around Waratah or dealing with drunken miners who wished to fight, Frank took the lead. 'As you know, John, the art of wooing beauties like our Daisy and Bessie can be a tough sport, and just as tough as the roughest play on the field. Therefore, to achieve our mission and win over these girls, we need to be clever and cover each other's flank. Understood?'

'Loud and clear, Captain Swinton!'

'Good man! Now, watch and learn as I rescue my Daisy from that snotty-nosed school boy and claim her for a second dance.'

Field tactics soon proved unnecessary, as neither Daisy nor Bessie saw the need to waste time with the niceties of courtship or the social norms at dance events. Instead, they politely brushed off advances from other hopeful dance partners—'I'm terribly sorry. I must have a rest'—and willingly yielded to the approaches of their more eager, happy-go-lucky suitors. They sent gracious gestures to Frank and John, signals that their advances would be welcomed without fear of rejection. Similarly, the men disregarded social norms and claimed Daisy and Bessie as their sole prizes for all remaining dances. Frank and John had become utterly besotted by the shared gentleness and beauty of the twins and felt they were embarking on something special. They refused to surrender their delicate hands until the function came to an end.

Within a week, Frank and John audaciously arrived unannounced at the Webb family home and instantly won favour. Within a month, Daisy and Bessie were given parental approval to visit Bismarck, chaperoned by their brother, Tasman. On arrival, Tasman discreetly left the four alone to picnic on the lush green pastures and spoil themselves with Danish pastries and homemade lemonade. Before long, the intense undercurrent of desire had compelled both couples to consider unofficial engagements and Daisy excitedly suggested that the four get married together. 'A double wedding! And soon! We can forego formal engagements and simply get married in the spring. Come Bessie, we have much to discuss.'

John turned to Frank with a concerned expression. 'I don't think our fiancées grasp the significance of my different faith. I must speak with my parents.'

'Your family's well respected by your Methodist minister. He baptised you, didn't he John? I'm sure he won't stand in the way of your love for Bessie and it certainly won't be a problem for you to join our Church of England. Besides mate, it seems our girls have already decided on this plan, so it will take a brave man to fight against it.'

'I like the idea of this double wedding, Frank. I truly do. But I don't want to upset my parents. They gladly changed from Lutheran to the Methodist faith. My father was so proud to help build the church…'

'Don't worry, mate. I'll come with you. Your folks think I'm bonzer and I have the gift of the gab, so leave it to me to do all the talking. Understood?'

'Understood, Captain Swinton!'

To the surprise of both young men, Frank's support was unnecessary. John's parents received them with total understanding and prudence.

'My dear John,' said Hans Bloom with a quiet, reassuring tone. 'We have been delighted in seeing your devotion to Bessie, whom we've grown to love in such a short time. Your mother and I are equally delighted to learn of your plans for a double wedding, with Frank and Daisy. I can see no impediment to this.'

'But Papa. My Bessie is Church of England.'

His parents exchanged knowing smiles. 'You believe your differences in faith to be a predicament, John, but it is not the case. We have already spoken to our minister. It will please you to learn that he knows the Bishop of Hobart very well. We realised long ago, before you were born, John, that everybody soon gets to know everybody else in Hobart. Both clergymen have already discussed this potential union.'

John was dumbstruck and Frank sat with his mouth agape, for once unable to speak.

Tenderly holding his wife's hand, Hans Bloom explained that the Bishop of Hobart was known for his progressive, open-minded views. As a keen conservationist, he had walked through the Myrtle Forest on a number of occasions and once met Bismarck's Methodist minister on the track. Thereafter, the two struck up a cordial, yet professional friendship. 'Your mother and I have anticipated this conversation, therefore we took the liberty of asking our minister to discuss an inter-faith marriage with the bishop. The response was sympathetic, John. The process is uncomplicated and there is no need for you to concern yourself.'

Marie Bloom added, 'Your love for Bessie has not gone unnoticed in the valley, John. Everyone has delighted in seeing you both stroll around the fields, with Frank and Daisy. The four of you have been so absorbed in each other that it seems you were oblivious to all the activity and planning that we have been doing in the background.'

'Mama!'

'A wedding between you and Bessie has been anticipated for some weeks, but I must confess, this idea of a double wedding, with Frank and Daisy, is charming.' With eyebrows raised and a childlike smile, she looked to her husband and suggested, as a testimony to Bismarck's hospitality, that they should hold a reception in the valley.

Frank turned to John. 'That's a bonzer idea, mate!'

John's father agreed and suggested the Church of England in the neighbouring village of Glenlusk would be a suitable venue for a double wedding, making a reception in the valley feasible. 'The Vicar of Glenlusk has visited our fruit markets on many occasions and strikes me as a fine man. I'm convinced the four clergymen would have no objection to our proposals.'

'Oh, Papa!'

'From my understanding, the banns will need to be read in both the Glenlusk and New Town churches. This must be done for three consecutive weeks before the vows are taken. If no objections are made, the four of you will be free to marry and then enjoy a reception in Bismarck.'

'Bonzer!'

'What do we do now, Papa?'

'Leave the planning to us, John. I suggest you and Frank discuss your mother's idea of a Bismarck reception with your fiancées.'

With that, the two young friends raced back to New Town and fell into the arms of Daisy and Bessie, who were equally thrilled at the news.

Frank could not wipe the smile from his face. 'We need to talk to your father. And where's Tasman? We want your brother to be our best man!'

Thereafter, their collective excitement was unmistakable with the pre-wedding church and family meetings their only sources of distraction.

During the reading of the banns, inquisitive Hobart townsfolk sat in the rear pews and peered over the sea of bobbing heads and hats, hoping to get a glimpse of the handsome German from Bismarck and his equally stunning fiancée. They were not disappointed. 'My Lord, what a fine-looking pair. Do you think that's the other sister, the one sitting next to the handsome lad with the permanent grin on his face?'

On an unusually warm spring morning, the dual vows were taken at Glenlusk and, as they entered Bismarck, the bridal parties and procession of guests were greeted by the valley's townsfolk. They strolled under an arch decorated with flowers that spelt the names 'Bessie and John—Daisy and Frank', and ceremoniously shook hands with the Bishop of Hobart, the Bismarck minister and the two vicars. Surrounded by fields of freshly planted vegetables and ready-to-pick flowers grown for the Hobart markets, the Bismarck community hosted the reception in spectacular fashion. The bridal trestles were lavishly decorated with vibrant floral garlands, their fragrance intensified by the warm rays of the sun. The guests, some first-time visitors to Bismarck, were entertained by the festive sounds of a piano accordion and thoroughly spoiled by an abundance of locally produced wine and beer.

Tasman Webb diligently fulfilled his role as best man and ensured all guests were seated before entertaining them with tall tales about the grooms' talents on the football field. His toast to the bridal parties was equally witty, and he took pleasure in the laughs and cheers that echoed around the valley.

Bessie was enchanted by the artistry of the flower arrangements and knew that she would easily warm to her new community with its subtle, yet endearing differences in culture. As her father stood to give his own toast, she struggled to take her gaze from the creative combination of yellow and white flowers, laced together with sprigs of sage and rosemary.

'I thank the citizens of Bismarck for their generosity and friendship that we've all enjoyed throughout this warm afternoon. When it comes to hosting wedding receptions, Europeans certainly know how to put us to shame!' The applause and laughter encouraged Mr Webb further. 'I couldn't be happier to welcome these two fine men into our family. John, who I learned today would have been called Hans back in Germany, has proved himself an ideal match for our lovely Bessie, and we know he will care for her well. What can I say about Frank Swinton, our Daisy's new husband?' He paused and looked around at the anticipation on the faces of his audience. There were charming sounds of farm animals in the distance and insects buzzing around the tables. 'Well, as you will soon learn, I don't have to say much about Frank as, no doubt, he will do all that himself!'

As he basked in the laughter and clapping, Mr Webb glanced at the smiling clergymen. The four had been given pride of place at the festivities and formed an alliance, planning to meet for monthly discussions and possible strolls through the Myrtle Forest.

John's father, Hans Bloom, also observed the four, splendid in their vestments and deep in discussion. He smiled to himself. He looked around at the joy-filled faces of the guests, devoid of any signs of difference in faith or culture, and was deeply grateful to his brother-in-law back in Cleve, dear Günter Stummhofer, the wise teacher, who had long ago encouraged him to bring his family to this far-off place. He returned his focus to Mr Webb, his new in-law, who was still singing the praises of the Bloom family and the Bismarck community.

'John's parents have certainly made us feel at home here, and we thank them dearly.' Someone from the crowd called, 'Hear, hear!'

'I express my gratitude to our four ministers for making this double wedding possible.' The four men nodded in appreciation to another cry of

'Hear, hear!', this time from Frank, who had leaned across the bridal trestle and winked at John. 'I've said enough,' concluded Mr Webb as he invited the guests to toast the brides, his two precious daughters.

During the celebrations, the four newlyweds were overwhelmed by a longing. With carefully planned honeymoons, their yearnings were quickly satisfied. John took Bessie to a guest house in a seaside town of Binalong Bay on the East Coast where, in equal quantities, they made love and bathed in the cool, invigorating waters of the Tasman Sea, all the while admiring the bright orange-coloured lichen that adorned the coastal rocks. At the same time, Frank and Daisy enjoyed their honeymoon in the southern town of Kettering. On the third day, they reluctantly left their hotel and caught the ferry across the D'Entrecasteaux Channel to nearby Bruny Island, where they picnicked in the sun.

Not long after the wedding, the Webbs farewelled their son, Tasman, who left for the Northwest in search of mining work. His mother placed a loving hand on his cheek and implored him to write or visit when he could.

'Rest assured, Mother. I will be back in Hobart for many important events!'

For the next four years, the mateship between Frank and John strengthened further, as did their respective marriages with the arrival of children. Daisy enjoyed motherhood immensely and doted over her two children whilst she and Frank planned more babies. Bessie grew to love Bismarck and warmed to her role as a mother more than she had anticipated. She and John revelled in the affection shown by the townsfolk for their two blond-haired babies. Whilst John busied himself in the Bismarck gardens and orchards and Frank continued to toil at the tannery, the sisters often met to coo over each other's children and whisper secrets about their husbands to each other.

The young couples were content and happy…

Following the declaration of war, both families quickly became alarmed at the rise in anti-German sentiment. Frank learned to hold his tongue in the workplace, but feared for his best friend and their once carefree lifestyle. Before long, suspicion infiltrated the streets and homes of Hobart and the residents of Bismarck, once valued for their charm, were now shunned and subjected to disdain.

Prior to hostilities, Germany had been the main importer of Tasmanian mineral ore but, with supply now blocked and a downturn in production, a disgruntled Tasman Webb returned to Hobart after losing his position at the Mount Bischoff mine.

The irony was not lost on his father who announced, in private, 'England declares war on Germany and Tasmanians are called upon to protect the empire. My son, along with four hundred other miners, loses his job at the tin mine because we must cease trade with the enemy. We are told to brace for economic hardship but, thankfully, all is not lost! The retrenched workers will be spared the dishonour of unemployment if they join the army and fight for king and country. Parents, wives and sisters are told they must feel pride as they kiss and farewell their men because it's their duty to sacrifice them to the war effort. Soon, we are likely to see a call for conscription!'

Although conscription remained unpopular, Tasman Webb, like many of his retrenched co-workers, was eventually seduced by the call to arms. After six weeks of training, he was one of a thousand soldiers who marched past the Hobart Town Hall. Cheered on by unprecedented crowds, including his dazed parents, the young Private Webb boarded a transport ship destined for a war already raging on the other side of the world.

At the same time as normally open-minded Tasmanians joined the boycott of German wares, a bill to prohibit intermarriage was introduced into parliament and petitions were signed to change the names of Bismarck in the South and German Town in the North.

Stunned by the swiftness of events, Mr. Webb senior was heard to say, again in private for fear of recrimination, 'Within a blink of an eye, not only must we farewell our only son, but we also lose our idyllic Tasmania. Our German friends, even their children who were born here, are being demonised and locked up! This war already shows no limits.'

A few weeks later, with those words from his father-in-law still ringing in his ears, Frank's voice could not disguise his own bewilderment and anger at

John's arrest for being a so-called enemy alien. He left work early for fear of striking out and being dismissed, and rushed home, knowing Daisy was the only one who could calm him.

'Calm yourself, my love. We must get up to Bismarck and see Bessie. Their poor children. They won't understand why their father has been taken away.'

Frank looked into Daisy's vibrant blue eyes and his anger immediately melted into affection. He smiled at her reassuringly. 'Please don't worry, my sweet flower. It's all a big mistake. First thing in the morning, your father and I will go to the police station and get John released before they ship him off.'

'Oh, Frank. You are such a good friend to John.'

True to his word, the appeal to the authorities was successful and, within less than a week of pacing a holding cell, John was released on condition he reported regularly to a police station. With the heavy burden of an uncertain future, he held Bessie tightly and whispered assurances to her.

'Thank God I have you back, John. We must see your parents straight away. They are sick with worry.'

Tasman Webb's uncertain future as a soldier in the Australian Imperial Forces was also on everyone's minds.

He wrote home about his sea journey and visiting exotic, far-off places, usually only discussed in geography classes or observed in books. After arriving in Egypt and settling into one of many massive training camps, Tasman sent his family a picture of himself and a handful of comrades standing in the shadows of the pyramids of Giza and the Great Sphinx, the soldiers' broad smiles barely detectable under the brims of their slouch hats.

Tasman's letter and photograph arrived in Hobart in the same week the law was passed to change the name of Bismarck to Collinsvale.

Before long, news of Tasman's death reached his family. They learned he had been killed on the first day of a battle to take a Turkish peninsula and the dreadful news forced them to accept that the invading black clouds of war had reached Tasmania and were likely to hover over it for a long time to come.

'Never have I heard of this place called Gallipoli,' sobbed Tasman's grieving father, this time publicly, undaunted by potential reprimands from those who were likely to perceive his words as unpatriotic. 'A place where young men must kill or die for king and country. But Gallipoli is now a name I shall never forget. My only son dies far from England and even farther from Australia. For God's sake! What kind of god-awful war is this?'

Daisy was inconsolable. She pleaded with Frank, 'Please, my love, promise me you won't get involved in this horrible, horrible war.'

'I promise, my sweet flower.'

Despite his promise, inwardly Frank knew it was only a matter of time before he lost his position at the tannery and would look upon the regular salary of a soldier as a means to keep his family nourished and protected.

The ongoing boycott of German produce had also placed John's work and income in doubt. In secret, the two friends discussed enlisting but knew they faced hurdles, not only a fierce reaction from their wives, but also because of John's German background.

'Why would you want to fight against the Germans, John?'

'I was born here, Frank. This is my home. I love Tasmania and will defend it with my life.'

'But they won't let you in, mate.'

'We will see, Frank. I've heard a couple of other lads from Bismarck, sorry, Collinsvale, have got in. We come from fit and healthy stock, just like you, Frank. We've grown up drinking the healthy mountain water and enjoying the fresh Tassie air. Besides, it's all over the papers—the British Empire needs all the men it can muster for this war! So why wouldn't they take me? We will both make fine soldiers. If we lose our jobs, we won't have much option, Frank!'

'We'll be in a spot of bother if we mention any of this to Daisy and Bessie, mate.'

'I agree. Let's hope the war ends soon. Then we'll be off the hook.'

Chapter 8

2018. August
Tasmania

'Can we try that again?' requested Conrad.

His string quartet was rehearsing the Theme and Variations movement from Haydn's Emperor. The lower instruments are left silent in the first variation, the theme falling to the second violin whilst the first floats around it with delicate counterpoint. The achievement of exactly the right balance between the violins was a tricky problem for even the best quartets, and Conrad wished to rehearse it again.

Fraser, the violist, grumbled, 'Since the cello and viola are not needed, James and I might as well get a cup of tea!'

'Fraser has a point, Conrad,' agreed the leader, Alan. 'Come over to my place for a coffee next week and we'll practise it in our own time. Let's move on to the other variations.'

The rehearsals were in preparation for the long-anticipated charity concert, a program of music from film, some pieces specifically composed for the genre, others borrowed from the masters. Conrad insisted on the Emperor, not only because of its appeal, but because he had invited his German friends and wished to impress them with its nostalgic melody.

Rehearsals were held at Fraser's Sage Avenue home in the northern suburbs. Following fiery debates and Alan's refusal to lead a string quartet if it were named Fab Four or Derwent Delights, they settled on Sage Quartet.

The ensemble had been formed years earlier. One of Conrad's ex-work colleagues approached him to play at a friend's wedding. 'It will be an outdoor affair on the groom's sheep farm in the Midlands, a big homestead with a federation-style veranda. You'll love it, Conrad.'

Panicked at the thought of performing as a soloist, Conrad suggested a string quartet would be more suitable for such an event and immediately set about recruiting players. The choice of leader was in no doubt. He called Alan, a retired music teacher who had extensive experience playing in chamber groups. The two discussed suitable friends for the viola and cello positions and wasted little time in contacting Fraser, a secondary school teacher, who had arrived from the mainland with his young family a few years back, and James, an information technology graduate known for his steady ensemble skills.

After only a limited rehearsal schedule, the quartet arrived at the Midland's wedding feeling somewhat unprepared for the chosen repertoire.

'Just carry on regardless,' encouraged Alan, as they continually shifted their chairs to avoid the sun's rays creeping along the veranda. 'The crowd is more focussed on the bride, anyway!'

It was only after a guest had complimented them on the chosen piece for the bridal procession, the ubiquitous Pachelbel's Canon in D, that the quartet relaxed and enjoyed performing their remaining repertoire.

During the drive home, Conrad knew the quartet had embarked on something special and encouraged the others to continue. Alan was enthused about Conrad's suggestion for weekly rehearsals but initially, the other two were sceptical.

'It's okay for you two retirees,' protested Fraser, 'but James and I still have to work for a living, you know!'

Before long, and inspired by playing reputable quartet repertoire, Fraser and James rearranged their commitments to allow time for as many rehearsals as possible. As word spread, the quartet received further invitations to perform, not only at weddings and a variety of private concerts and soirées but also for a charity concert at a local retirement village. Following its success, the quartet was soon invited back for a second and lost little time in rehearsing new material for it...

After close to an hour of rehearsal, the four were satisfied with the Emperor and called a break.

'I like this Haydn, Conrad,' declared Fraser. 'But don't you think it's a little contentious to play in public? You know, this melody for Deutschland über alles... and all that. Wasn't it about Germany's desire to rule the world?'

'Actually, no. My German friend, who works at the Army Museum, wrote an essay on this very subject, you know, the misinterpretation of the words. They don't translate as a world takeover at all. And anyway, that original first verse, Deutschland über alles... isn't sung anymore. I can explain all this in my concert spiel.'

'Oh, great!' laughed Fraser. 'Conrad plans to give our audience a two-hour history lesson. Pray tell, will we still have time to play the music?' The friendly banter between Fraser and Conrad was often a source of amusement for the other two. 'Knowing Conrad's about to launch into his weekly war letter update, I think I'll bypass the tea and open a bottle of red instead.'

'What have you got to report this week, Conrad?' invited Alan.

'Well, I've got the photo of the Deppner brothers in uniform. I'm interested in your thoughts about their expressions.'

Fraser took a look. 'I assume you mean that one brother is smiling and the other two aren't.'

'Looks more like an odd smirk than a smile,' said Alan.

'Yes! That's what I think.' Conrad was excited someone else had recognised a marked difference between the expressions. 'This photo has bugged me for months.'

'Why's it taken you so long to show it to us?' teased Fraser. 'Ha! It's not like you to hold out on us, Conrad! Who wants a glass of red?'

James looked up from the photo. 'I reckon you're overthinking it, Conrad. Just three different people with three different expressions.'

'Maybe. But I really think something interesting was going on when this photo was taken.'

'Maybe ask your German friends,' suggested James.

'That reminds me,' interrupted Alan, excitedly. 'You took a couple of your German friends to Beethoven's Ninth last week, by the Tasmanian Symphony Orchestra. What did they think of it?'

'Yes, Irene and Paul loved it. I know you don't believe the Ninth is Beethoven's best symphony, Alan, but I have to say, I was in awe. Paul sang along to the Ode to Joy. In German, of course!'

Fraser could not resist. 'I bet the audience appreciated that! Drink up everyone. We need to polish off this red before we get back to playing.'

Alan commented on Conrad's seemingly unending obsession for Beethoven's last symphony. Over the past year, Conrad had stored various recordings of it in his car and seized any opportunity to enjoy a private concert on high volume. He favoured a recording of the West-Eastern Divan Orchestra, a merger of young Israeli and Arab musicians, conducted by Daniel Barenboim. He not only admired the young musicians' energetic performance, but also that they had used Beethoven's music to break down the barriers that divided their faiths, cultures and countries. When it came to his turn to drive fellow Waratah bushwalkers to meeting points, Conrad would invariably issue the warning: 'I'm happy to give anyone a lift, but I don't want any complaints about my favourite Beethoven!'

James suggested Conrad could try to catch a live performance of the Ninth during his upcoming Europe trip.

'Great idea!'

'And you must be getting excited to meet the Deppners in person.'

'Yes! It's going to be good to put faces to names rather than just communicating through email.'

James added, sincerely, 'We all remember how excited you were when you finally solved the riddle of Wolf's surname, Conrad.'

Fraser jumped in. 'Yes! I'm not sure we got much rehearsal done that week!'

Conrad's mind flashed back to February when, after many months of unsuccessful research, he had simply googled the name 'Wolfgang Deppner' and stumbled upon the Deppner family website. A webpage dedicated to Hermann and Martha Deppner, Wolf's parents, reported they had moved from Bremen to Kleve with their four children, which explained why no birth records had been registered with the Kleve municipal offices. He immediately emailed the family representative listed on the website:

Dear Herr Professor Deppner,

My name is Conrad Bentley and I live in Hobart, the capital of Tasmania, an island state of Australia.

As part of my leisure activities in retirement, I study German at university, but I ask you to forgive my poor German in this email.

I regularly meet with a circle of friends, a German discussion group which comprises German-born people and learners, like myself. A member of this group works voluntarily at the Army Museum of Tasmania where he translates German letters and other documents.

Last year, he gave me a copy of a German letter written in the First World War. During my research on this letter, I found your email address on the internet and I'm hoping you may be able to offer me some assistance.

As you will see from the attached copy, the letter was dated Cleve, 17 June 1918. (I understand this town is now spelt with a K). It was written by a father to his son, Otto, telling him that his younger brother, Wolfgang, had been killed near a small village in France.

A Tasmanian soldier wrote on the margin of the letter that he found it on the 8th August 1918, and my research shows a major battle occurred at Amiens on this day. My assumption is that the Tasmanian soldier found the letter on Otto's body and brought it back as a souvenir.

It is very sad to think two brothers died. The letter mentions another brother, Ernst, and a sister named Helga.

Since last June, I've been attempting to decipher the family name which is illegible in the letter. From the outset, I thought the name was Deppner, but subsequent contact with the relevant German authorities did not support this.

By chance, I came across your family's website which may prove Deppner is, in fact, correct.

Some people have questioned why I would go to such lengths to research this letter and have suggested that nobody today would be interested in something that was written a century ago. Perhaps! Nevertheless, the letter grabbed my attention.

It is my belief, the young men mentioned in this letter, and all soldiers who died in the war, have no voice in history. I now wish to give them a chance to speak.

I send you this email in good faith and hope you can solve the puzzle of the name.

Professor Deppner, I respectfully ask you take a look at the letter and let me know if it belongs to your family. I strongly suspect it does!

I look forward to your reply.

Yours sincerely,

Conrad Bentley

Within twenty-four hours, he received an equally enthusiastic reply from retired Professor Willi Deppner, and two days later, a second email from Franz Deppner, who had verified his grandfather's handwriting:

It's inconceivable. It's overwhelming, and it awakens incredible emotions in me. Here I stand holding a letter in my hands that my grandfather wrote one hundred years ago to one of his three sons, all soldiers. A letter that found its way to the other side of the world…

Conrad rushed out to the garden, beaming with excitement as he summoned Wally to the fence: 'I've found them, Wally!'

Fraser poured out the last of the wine. 'So, what plans have you made to visit the Deppners, Conrad?'

'I've emailed Willi Deppner who lives in Duisburg, not far from Kleve, and let him know the dates we're staying with Anke and Pascal in Heimbach.' When they previously lived and worked in Hobart, Anke and Pascal had attended a number of the Sage Quartet performances and knew the other members well. 'Heimbach is close enough to Duisburg for us to catch a train and return in one day.'

'Are Anke and Pascal up to date with your research?'

'Oh, James!' cut in Fraser. 'Of course they would be!'

Alan took control. 'Thanks for the update, Conrad. A live performance of Beethoven's Ninth, somewhere in Europe, would be very special and please say hello to Anke and Pascal next time you send them an email. Now, let's get back to our music. We can look at the Tchaikovsky piece now and revisit the Haydn next week. I take it you have your program notes ready for the concert, Conrad?' Ordinarily, Alan would compere at the concerts but, on this occasion, given Conrad's invitation to his German friends and his insistence on the Emperor, he had willingly handed over the reins.

A few weeks later, Conrad arrived at the venue minutes before the others. He felt a mixture of nervousness and excitement. Initially, his individual practice had proved frustrating, yielding scant improvement. Only in the last few days had he felt confident with many of the more difficult passages, with the help of Alan's advice: 'Treat the music as your friend, not your foe.'

He closed his eyes and took a deep breath. He began to relax...

Moments later, Fraser's voice broke through. 'Wake up, Conrad! Can you give us a hand with these music stands?'

'Ha! Look at you three! I'm now the only one without a beard!'

'Well, you've got half an hour to fix that!' joked James.

'See, everyone! My sense of humour is finally rubbing off on our cellist!'

Fraser coughed. 'I wouldn't say that's a good thing!'

Chas, the social activities organiser for the retirement village, rushed out to greet them. 'Welcome back, gentlemen. What a fine day for a concert. I have everything set up as per your instructions. We've had a good response from the residents and their families, so we're expecting a large audience. What a lovely concept to play music from film. Who thought of that one?'

In unison: 'Conrad!'

'This year, all donations are going to the Blankets for Bangladesh charity, therefore your dulcet tones are going to another good cause. Let me show you to the green room.'

The four knew this meant the kitchen and open pantry area, which gave them ample space to store their instrument cases, tune and warm up unheard by the arriving guests. The others moved off to assemble the stands and left Conrad to pace the foyer...

'G'day Mr Bentley!'

'Wally! What a surprise.'

'A pleasant one, I hope! Your Gretel talked me into it. She's just parking the car and no doubt admiring the gardens out there with my Trish.'

'Geez, you are a dark horse. I hope you like the concert.'

'I'll try not to get too excited, mate. I hear your violin band's not quite ready for Carnegie Hall!'

'Ah, you've been doing some research.'

'Yep. I have a new friend called Mr Google. That's Herr Google in your language!'

Gretel glided in with Patricia. 'The paintings in the entrance hall are lovely, Conrad.'

'I knew you'd like them.'

One resident, an amateur artist, had a flare for depicting the river, mountain and other recognisable Hobart landmarks in vivid colours and simple form. The quartet would be seated beneath one of her best works. Their black attire contrasted with an intense backdrop of colour.

Gretel leaned over and gave Conrad an affectionate kiss. 'Good luck, sweetie.'

A few minutes later, Conrad heard the call, 'Guten Tag!'

His German friends arrived with smiles and high expectations. Paul explained six out of ten members were able to attend, but that Irene was too unwell and sent her apologies. Conrad knew Irene rarely allowed poor health to restrict her social activities, but hid his concern.

Before long, Fraser light-heartedly announced that Conrad's next busload of fans had arrived. Gathered in the hall were half a dozen Waratah Ladies.

'Geez, ladies! I hardly recognised you without your boots and backpacks!'

'And we just saw Baz pull up with Martin and Chris!'

'Wow!' Conrad was becoming overwhelmed.

The quartet made a last-minute tune up before Chas summoned them.

'Steady yourselves and good luck, gentlemen,' came the words of encouragement from their leader.

As they approached the arc of chairs and music stands, as poised and upright as their nerves would allow, they heard whispers and saw movement from the audience. An air of excitement and expectation enveloped the venue. Chas introduced each quartet member and gave a brief overview of their backgrounds before he turned to them, quite theatrically, a prearranged cue for them to begin.

At the conclusion of the first piece, the audience applauded loudly and, as Conrad made his way to the lectern, louder applause rang out.

'Good afternoon, ladies and gentlemen. As Chas mentioned, my name is Conrad Bentley. I will be your compere for this afternoon's concert and will also attempt to play the second fiddle!' He waited for the predicted laughter to subside. 'For your pleasure, we will be performing various styles of music used in film. My role is to guide you through this. We have just played Jesu Joy, of Man's Desiring, from J.S. Bach's cantata Herz und Mund und Tat und Leben.'

Happy with his rehearsed pronunciation, Conrad quickly searched for expressions of approval from his German friends. He also saw Wally smiling back at him warmly.

'Bach's piece has featured in at least twelve movies, including Boogie Nights and futuristic crime thriller Minority Report with Tom Cruise. Oh, and in a couple of TV miniseries.'

Members of the audience nodded and murmured. Conrad felt he had their attention and relaxed.

'Goethe, the famous German writer, described a string quartet as a stimulating conversation between four intelligent people. That describes us to a T. We have lengthy, intelligent discussions about whether to drink tea or red wine at rehearsals, and whether to perform in white or black shirts. We hope you like what we've chosen for today!'

Despite an enthusiastic response from the audience, the other quartet members feared Conrad was embarking on unnecessary discourse. They shifted in their seats. Fraser dipped his head. God forbid! Never again!

'Ladies and gentlemen, as a quartet, we are fortunate to rehearse and perform music by some great composers, and we'll get to these soon! First, we present a collection of pleasant movie themes from Unchained Melody, Titanic, Lord of the Rings and a charming arrangement of Gabriel's Oboe from the film The Mission. We will finish this set with the theme song from Breakfast at Tiffany's, the popular Moon River.'

Conrad momentarily felt a change in the room's atmosphere, something odd. He was unsure what it was, and hesitated before returning to his seat.

Although the mention of Moon River created a burst of excitement from the audience, Alan was concerned they might easily lose interest in what Conrad affectionately called 'dink music'. To his surprise, the audience remained entertained, not only by the pieces themselves, but also by Conrad's detailed research on them. Predictably, they swooned over Pachelbel's Canon in D, and were surprised to hear that it had featured in no less than thirteen films.

'Our next piece is from the 1942 classic, Casablanca, and at least five other films including, would you believe, The Dirty Dozen. It's taken from a famous string quartet by Haydn, known as the Emperor, in German, the Kaiser.'

Conrad steadied himself and explained Haydn had written extensively for the genre and was known as the Father of the String Quartet. Alan began to relax as the concert was about to transition into more traditional quartet music.

'As to the history of the Emperor, it is said that during a visit to England, Haydn was so impressed by the British anthem, God Save the King, that he returned to compose his own in honour of the Austrian Kaiser. This hymn ultimately became the Austrian and German national anthem. It's had a somewhat contentious history, and the words have often been misconstrued, but rest assured, I'm not here to give you a two-hour lecture!'

Conrad was momentarily distracted, not only by Fraser's audible sigh of relief and chuckles from the audience, but also by a return of the odd change in the room's atmosphere. He saw a figure, mostly obscured behind the other audience members, but could make out that the figure was in military uniform. The figure appeared out of place in the crowd. Conrad shook it off and returned to his notes.

'The second movement of the Emperor, which we will perform for you this afternoon, introduces the hymn, with four variations. Each instrument gets its turn to play the melody, supported by the other voices. If you haven't heard this quartet in its original form before, you are in for a treat. Please sit back and enjoy the slow movement from the… Kaiser.'

Some audience members nudged elbows to indicate their recognition of the melody. During the pause, before the two violins played the first variation as a duo, it seemed everyone was breathless. Conrad remembered Alan's advice not to rush his entry—'Let the theme hover over the audience, just for a short while'—but the pause lengthened and unnerved Alan, who had his bow poised in anticipation of Conrad's lead. The expectant audience shifted in their seats as they waited.

Conrad saw the figure in uniform again. The soldier was now standing. He appeared attentive, proud. For a moment, Conrad was taken aback and his breathing became shallow. He felt the blood rush from his face and feared the audience would interpret this as stage fright. The soldier's uniform showed signs of grime and wear, but this time was dry. Conrad knew who it was and felt everything around him slowing down as he looked into the eyes of Wolf Deppner. He was overwhelmed by a rush of conflicting emotions—wonderment, curiosity, unease. Wolf's pleading gaze, mixed with an expression of optimism, was intense. In those few seconds, Conrad sensed Wolf also shared high expectations that the upcoming meeting with the Deppners, Wolf's living relatives, would bring the story of his life cut short to the forefront. The task, initially exciting for Conrad, now felt onerous. Conrad fought hard to keep his composure, not only for the performance but also to reassure Wolf. Yet self-doubt crept in, including doubt that Wolf's presence could be anything but logical. He expected his negative inner voice was about to snarl at him, but instead, to his surprise, Conrad heard a softer, younger voice. A voice he had heard once before on the day he received the letter.

'I applaud you giving a personal voice to this beautiful music, Mr Bentley. You are amongst friends. Please continue…'

During the intermission, Alan jostled beside his players. 'I believe we've just heard our quartet at its best.'

'The Emperor took my breath away, Alan,' said Conrad.

'I had a similar experience during your lengthy pause! I thought we'd lost you there for a moment.'

Conrad saw a flash of Wolf's face again. Internally, he was still questioning the logic that such visions were possible.

'Conrad? Are you still with us?'

'Yes, yes Alan. You know, so many people have come up to me and said they loved the Emperor. My friend, Paul, was nearly in tears.'

'For the right reasons, I hope!' joked Fraser.

'How are we going to match this in the second half, Alan?' Conrad appeared somewhat rattled.

'I think the Tchaikovsky will do the trick.'

Fraser seized his moment. 'By the way, after this concert, I will need to take a break from the quartet to concentrate on my studies.'

'Really? With Conrad's trip to Europe in six weeks, I'm not sure a break before he leaves would be a good idea.'

'I'm really sorry, Alan, but I'll get a promotion out of it. We can restart rehearsals when Conrad gets back.'

As Fraser and James moved off, Alan turned to Conrad. 'The rot is going to set in. After such a long break, it'll be difficult to get the quartet back together again. Mark my words, Conrad.'

'It's only for a couple of months. We've worked so hard, Alan. A break will do us all good.'

Alan attempted to make light of it. 'Well, there goes any plans for a debut concert at Carnegie Hall!' Yet deep down, he had grave concerns that the quartet would fold. Conrad's words of encouragement failed to reassure him.

'Welcome back ladies and gentlemen, and it's good to see nobody has made a run for it during the break!' Conrad searched for the spot where he had seen Wolf but accepted his mind had more than likely played tricks on him again. He took a deep breath. 'Our next piece has been used in thirteen films between 1988 and 2015, perhaps most notably in Paradise Road from 1997. It is the slow movement from Tchaikovsky's first string quartet. I hope you enjoy our performance as much as we've enjoyed rehearsing it over the past few weeks.'

Alan was aware Conrad had prepared copious notes about the history of this quartet and how it was performed for Leo Tolstoy, who had been brought to tears by its beauty. He was puzzled why Conrad withheld the information and appeared distracted.

Despite this, their performance was heartfelt and again left the audience breathless. Alan feared the remaining music, of a lighter nature, would disappoint them, but their rousing applause proved otherwise. Shouts from the audience for an encore echoed around the room.

After the concert, Chas congratulated them. 'Please don't pack away your lovely instruments just yet. I'd like to get a photo for our newsletter. By all means farewell your guests, then please meet me at the staircase.'

As Chas rushed off, Alan turned to his quartet. 'We did well today, gentlemen. The hard work we put into the Tchaikovsky really paid off. Now, I assume you've reached a consensus on this long break.'

'Yes,' from the violist.

'I'm happy with that,' said James.

Conrad smiled. 'I'll be fresh as a daisy after my Europe trip and raring to get back to the Emperor!'

Chas arranged the four musicians on the staircase. Alan struggled to hide his concern while Conrad watched his guests leave in procession. He saw waves from the Waratah Ladies and his German friends filed past with appreciative smiles. Paul raised his arms in a bravo-type gesture. The three Focus crew members followed.

'Well done,' congratulated Martin. 'Loved the Tchaikovsky!'

'Same here,' said Chris with a smile.

From Captain Baz: 'See you next week for the race.'

Gretel strolled out with Patricia, again admiring the artwork.

Wally gave a thumbs up. 'Moon River was a real hit, fellas!'

Chas declared the afternoon was a resounding success and that he intended to talk to the social committee about a date for a third concert next year. 'What will be your next theme?' Alan mumbled something under his breath. Conrad also sensed a slight loosening of the tight thread that had held his quartet together. 'Okay. Just one more shot. The player without the beard, sorry I forget your name, please switch with the cellist so we can get a picture of the two violin players standing side by side. That's it. Now, I need a smile from the leader!'

Conrad observed the last guests shuffling to the exit and was disappointed that he caught no further sight of Wolf Deppner.

You fool, Bentley! You've said it yourself, this is all illogical. Get a grip.

88 | A Soldier's Quartet

Chapter 9

1916
Tasmania Deploys More Troops

A year after their brother-in-law, Tasman Webb, was killed at Gallipoli, Frank was retrenched and John's work in the fields of Collinsvale completely dried up. A new Tasmanian battalion, the 40th Battalion, was formed as part of the 10th Brigade, 3rd Division, a necessary expansion of the Australian Imperial Forces. The two friends could not ignore the aggressive and convincing recruitment drive sweeping across the island and, as they entered a makeshift recruitment depot in the city, its portico festooned with imposing Your Empire Needs You and For King and Country billboards, they shared mixed feelings of apprehension and purpose.

After scrutinizing Frank and John's applications with ancillary information rushed in by a concerned-looking aide, a burly sergeant looked up from his desk with a frown. 'Applicant Bloom, it says here that you spent a short period under arrest, in preparation for a transfer to an internment camp. What pray would be the reason for that?'

'That was nothing, Sir,' cut in Frank. 'It was just a simple misunderstanding. My mate, John, well, he's as Tassie as they come. Like me, he's very keen to defend the empire, Sir.'

The sergeant was from northern Tasmania and unfamiliar with some of the southern place names. He looked at John with a curious expression. 'Applicant Bloom, I also see here that you reside in Collinsvale, which previously had a German name.' The sergeant was too quick. He turned to Frank. 'Now, listen to me, Applicant Swinton. Before you are tempted to interrupt me again, it's 'Sergeant' to you, not 'Sir', and this time, if you don't mind, I would prefer it if your mate, Applicant Bloom, speaks for himself. Understood?'

'Ah, but—'

'I said, do you understand, Applicant Swinton!'

'Yes, Sergeant!'

'Now, Applicant Bloom, what have you to say about all this?'

'Yes, it's correct, Sergeant. I live in Collinsvale with my wife and children and I've worked for orchardists and farmers up there before all the pastoral work dried up. Now I'm here with my good friend, Applicant Swinton, to join up and fight the Germans.'

'And the internment camp issue?'

'Just as Frank… I mean Applicant Swinton said, Sergeant. That was all an unfortunate misunderstanding. It all got sorted in no time.'

The sergeant was less than convinced that the eager Applicant Bloom would ordinarily pass army protocols, but he was under immense pressure from up the ranks to enlist all able-bodied men. An overwhelming number of potential soldiers rejected due to poor oral health had hampered recruitment in Tasmania. After a slow morning intake, he was swayed by the presentation of these two healthy, strong men.

'Okay, you two, listen to me carefully. If you pass the medical and have good teeth, can string two sentences together, write your own names and impress the officer sitting back there, whom you must address as 'Sir', then I have little doubt the 40th Battalion will take you.' Frank and John turned to each other and smiled. 'Now, give me your full names and dates of birth.'

'Francis Stanley Swinton, born 26th of April 1894.'

'John Henry Bloom, Sergeant. I was born in Tasmania on the 22nd of September 1893.'

'Good. Now, sit over there and wait to be called in for the medical. And for God's sake, Applicant Swinton, let your mate speak for himself. The medical staff will not be as forgiving as I am. Understood?'

Frank and John observed the ebb and flow of uniforms darting in and out of various processing rooms. The proud smiles of the successful applicants added to their excitement.

'Do my teeth look clean, John?'

When they arrived home as recruits of the 40th Battalion, scratching their irritated skin under stiff, new uniforms, they were astonished to see their wives attempt smiles. Although inside, both Daisy and Bessie were burning with fury by the betrayal, they knew their places in a man's world gripped by war.

A few days later, as Frank and John boarded a military bus to transport them to basic training, Daisy whispered in Frank's ear, 'I think we are having another baby, my love.'

After what seemed days rather than weeks, Daisy and Bessie were unprepared and overwhelmed by the reality of farewelling their husbands. On the brutally cold first day of July 1916, they stood sobbing on the pier with their children and the other families, waving at the troop transport ship Berrima as it pulled away. At first, it was an effort to recognise their husbands in the sea of khaki until they made out their familiar smiles and saw them returning enthusiastic waves from the stern. The sisters clutched each other in an attempt to muster a reciprocal gesture.

Their father drove them to Sandy Bay to see the last glimpse of the Berrima before it disappeared down river. They hugged their children tightly, knowing their lives would be forever changed, and prayed for the war to end before their husbands reached Europe.

On board, the two friends noticed the colour of the Derwent River appeared a deeper blue under the winter sun. John pointed over to his beloved Bismarck with its chimney smoke wafting over the hills. From a southern aspect, Frank marvelled at how Mount Wellington resembled a sleeping lion, a sentinel. They noticed a crowd of people running along Sandy Bay Beach and returned waves in the hope that some of the distant figures were their wives and children. Already, they imagined a return trip up the river and wondered how a post-war Hobart would greet them. With a combination of heavy hearts and excitement, they sailed past unfamiliar places and landmarks.

Frank turned to a soldier beside him. 'Do you know the name of that craggy peak to the left of Mount Wellington, mate?'

'It's Cathedral Rock. I'm from down the Huon Valley, so I get to see it a fair bit. The mountain hides it from you city folk.'

Frank grabbed John's arm. 'Mate! I can remember seeing this Cathedral Rock when Daisy and I were down the channel on our honeymoon. The mountain hides it from us as if it were secret treasure.'

'It looks pretty impressive, Frank.'

'Let's make a deal that we climb it when we get back from this war, eh?'

'It's a deal, Frank!'

As the ship entered the Tasman Sea and headed north toward the Bass Strait, the two friends felt the spray of salt water on their cheeks and pondered the thrill of visiting exotic ports.

'I'm glad I've got you beside me, John.'

'Same here, Frank.'

'Let's shake hands on another deal. Let's promise to look after each other and both come back, safe and sound.'

'Forget the handshake, Frank!' John wrapped both his arms around his brother-in-law, his best friend. 'Of course we'll look after each other!'

Chatper 10

1914
Germany Enters The Great War

'Where did Wolf rush off to, Martha?'

Hermann Deppner had noticed his youngest son's absence and called to his wife from the landing. The Deppners were readying themselves for church, but Wolf's disappearance had made Hermann feel anxious. An event to farewell Cleve's finest, including his three sons, was set to take place after the service.

Cleve, a small town in the Lower Rhine region, close to the Dutch border, had not escaped the vigorous recruitment drive and Hermann was sensible enough to know his sons were model recruits for the country's hasty mobilization.

His neighbour, Detlef Graf, Cleve's resolute and well-respected foundry manager, had not concealed his enthusiasm. 'For goodness' sake! What kept the Army from reaching us for so long? We have the finest men to offer!'

Despite enjoying their life in Bremen, the Deppners' numerous visits to Martha's cousin, who had married a Dutchman from across the border in Aalten, had created a desire to move. They were attracted by the intimacy of a smaller town and, as their trips to Aalten passed through Cleve, they eventually chose this as their new home.

They arrived in 1909 in a convoy of trucks and vans. The commotion had created a welcome spectacle for the inquisitive townsfolk. Their new neighbour, Herr Graf, who employed the majority of the town's able-bodied men and hopeful applicants from afar, could not ignore the noise as the three Deppners leapt from the vehicles, surveyed their new neighbourhood and playfully threw their younger sister between them like a toy. Herr Graf instantly assessed the young Deppners' employability potential and, at the earliest opportunity, announced to their father that he had work for the taking for all three at his foundry.

Wolf Deppner would later decline Herr Graf's offer, as he had known from a young age that his future lay in teaching. He was nearing sixteen on his first day at Cleve Grammar School. At lunchtime, after the morning lessons, he weaved his way through the dining hall and randomly selected a table of three. Somewhat surprised by Wolf's confident introduction, but quickly charmed by his friendly smile, the three responded:

'Welcome. I'm Erich Wiese.'

'My name is Bruno Klug. Pleased to meet you.'

'Hello. I'm Felix Wittmann. I'm the one who keeps these other two in line!'

The three were close friends, but Wolf's arrival triggered the formation of a new, cohesive group, and their teachers quickly observed the development of a unique clique. The grades of Bruno and Erich improved remarkably and the positive change in behaviour of the frequently recalcitrant Felix validated the group. Their bond appeared unbreakable and the four soon became known as 'the quartet', the source of such title lost with the passage of time. They paraded through the streets of Cleve with a certain prestige as their title slowly became part of the town's vernacular and was carried over into their adult years.

Felix Wittmann was the best-looking member of the group who had not been without an admirer since the age of thirteen. His friends were envious. They accepted that they lacked Felix's charisma: a mixture of bravado and natural charm. He was the first of the four to shave and could easily sport a robust moustache. His wit had masked what he lacked in academic ability and his flair lay more in swaggering around the streets of Cleve, lifting his head higher whenever he felt the eyes of the girls were following his gait. 'Sorry, ladies. My heart now belongs to the lovely Lina Hartmann!'

For the past year, Felix had been employed at Herr Graf's foundry, having proved himself worthy within the first week—'That Wittmann boy is a good worker. He can teach the other members of his so-called quartet a thing or two!'

Bruno Klug had mousy-coloured hair and light brown eyes, but was unremarkable in most physical aspects. Moderate in manner, he offered a certain warmth to the quartet. Well-raised and educated, his steady work ethic was instantly recognised when he began an apprenticeship at the Klugshof Brewery under the supervision of his uncle.

His friends immediately exploited his position at the brewery and nominated Felix as their spokesman. 'Bruno, my dear man. Please get us some free beer! An apprentice has a duty to sample his wares, and it is the duty of his friends to assist.'

Initially, Bruno had regretted the pilfering, but soon reconciled his guilt with the prestige he gained from the others. Wolf and Erich had pleaded with Bruno to join them at Teacher Training College. At first, he had been tempted, but his sense of family loyalty steered him toward the apprenticeship. Whenever the quartet stole away into the fields to talk, embrace, and drink their plunder, there was a mutual sigh of relief that Bruno had chosen the brewery over teaching.

Erich Wiese was a thinker and daydreamer. He lacked Wolf's ability to take learning in his stride at the Teacher Training College and easily became anxious about his schooling, relying on the other members of the quartet for support and reassurance.

Herr Graf's daughter, Frieda, was attracted to Erich's somewhat serious manner. She and Lina Hartmann had been best friends since a young age and often mused over their four prized friends. Both girls shared similar height and build. Lina had light hair and a delicate complexion, whilst Frieda's face displayed stronger features. Both were popular with their peers and teachers and, more recently, held in high regard at the Cleve Finishing School for Girls.

The love-stricken Erich admired Frieda for her intelligence and shrewdness, but initially favoured her beauty. His interest in art allowed him to detect the subtle changes in her dark eyes when exposed to different light. Erich seized every opportunity to benefit from his friendship with Wolf, who acted as agent in facilitating contact between the two lovers. Erich peered over the gate that separated the Deppner and Graf courtyards, trying to catch sight of his beloved Frieda's raven-hair. He waited in hope for Frieda's invitations to visit whenever her disapproving father was absent. Frieda had found Erich differed from the other men of Cleve. Like her, he envisioned life beyond the small town and, as a result, their mutual attraction intensified.

Erich was blond, his hair bleached lighted by the summer sun. Frieda confessed to Lina that her admirer's Scandinavian appearance had been part of his appeal. Erich was usually self-conscious about his slim build, but the flattering cut of his recently issued uniform gave him a newfound air of confidence.

Felix, Bruno and Erich soon came to realise that it was Wolf who added strength and a unique quality to the quartet. He was kind and steadfast, but also had a humorous side to his personality. From a young age, Wolf's parents had delighted in his energy and ability to entertain the family with his yarns and well-rehearsed tricks. He would race after his older brothers and pester them to include him in their pursuits. His younger sister, Helga, soon followed suit, and the bond between the two youngest siblings grew strong. She would affectionately stroke his face and play with his thick hair, proudly declaring that her favourite brother would one day make the finest husband to the luckiest girl in the whole of Germany.

As a teenager on the threshold of manhood, the Cleve townsfolk warmed to Wolf's carefree nature, but it did not negate his ability to be circumspect, particularly about his career choices. After he met his three best friends, Wolf felt secure, somewhat indispensable, admired and important. He felt as though he needed little else to help him navigate the path to adulthood.

Wolf's parents worried about his hasty enlistment, as did most parents of Cleve, but they equally accepted that it would have been futile to argue against it. They acknowledged Wolf was an integral member of his quartet, a group that appeared to think and act as one. They hoped the quartet would turn out to be the most definable factor in protecting Wolf in combat.

The Grafs, Wolf's neighbours, had moved to Cleve in the late 1800s. Germany had begun negotiations with the neighbouring Dutch Railway Authority to improve trans-border lines, and Herr Graf saw an opportunity to gain work and establish a good reputation before opening his own foundry.

As an uncomplicated, self-made man, Herr Graf was strongly influenced by the social norms of his era. He had no time for reflection or unnecessary emotions, and detested the teachings of Sigmund Freud, believing them to be dangerous hogwash. His father had taught him from a young age that the mind must be a straight road, with no detours, curves or intersections: 'Don't let your mind wander, Detlef. This is foolishness. Never let your head fill with voices of doubt or pointless self-talk. Decent, hardworking people, who keep looking ahead and never doubt themselves, are the ones who succeed in this world!'

His wife, Gertrud Graf, was tall with lean features who took pride in the special dark hue of her hair, drawn back to fit with the fashion. She tolerated many of her husband's disparaging comments and sermons—'Teacher Training College is filling young Wolfgang Deppner's head with rubbish! Where is the good for any man to learn about philosophy and art?'—Lately, most of Herr Graf's discourse had been about the war and how he could profit from it.

On a sun-filled autumn day in 1914, Herr Graf flaunted his high standing in Cleve by hosting the post-church festivities for the families of the first recruits and selected dignitaries. He planned a ceremonious farewell for his own son, Johannes, the three affable Deppners, Wolf's three friends and a handful of other recruits. He intended to parade the soldiers before his hand-picked guests, make a comment on their immaculate uniforms and toast them with imported champagne: 'I'm happy to have Klugshof beer in reserve, but these brave recruits deserve a much more dignified farewell!' Uninvited townsfolk speculated on how the extravagance of French champagne could be possible in such austere times.

Wolf had disappeared after breakfast and was yet to return. His mother, Martha, sensed her husband's rising unease as he called to her from the landing. 'Wolfi's gone to meet his friends, Hermann.'

'I hope they won't be late for the service!'

Martha Deppner doubted the quartet would attend church. She still thought of them as boys. Martha's disposition was cheerful. She had a warm, full face, crowned by thick auburn hair. Wolf, her youngest son, shared her temperament and appearance, whilst Otto and Ernst resembled their father. The youngest child, the precocious and lovable Helga, was a mix of both parents and was doted upon by the entire family. Secretly, Martha felt relieved that she had only one daughter to guide through a world ruled by men, a world now disrupted by war. She was aware her neighbours' daughter, Frieda Graf, felt the pressure of living in such a world and often overheard Herr Graf promote the benefits of sending Frieda to finishing school to educate her on how to care for a husband and raise children. Martha flinched at such sentiment and was thankful she had married her dear Hermann for love, rather than to meet societal expectations. Still, she too had questioned the logic of bringing children into an increasingly turbulent and uncertain world. She knew the current views of the men of Cleve were more pragmatic than her own and was aware that her husband and Herr Graf discussed such matters when they met at the fence for their weekly talks.

The original owners of the Graf and Deppner homes had erected a gate between the two properties, the purpose of such a feature a constant source of irritation for Herr Graf who vowed to keep it closed. The interconnecting gate stood slightly lower than the paling fence and allowed the neighbours to see each other's faces.

At first, their conversations had been polite, neighbourly exchanges, strictly governed by Herr Graf's proviso to discuss only matters of gravity. Despite their different backgrounds, initially a source of discomfort but eventually replaced by a mutual respect, the two men began to look forward to their meetings. Through billowing pipe smoke, they discussed subjects as far-reaching as politics and religion.

Conversation rarely referenced Herr Graf's son, Johannes. There was tacit acknowledgement that Johannes Graf could not compete with the determined and popular Deppner offspring, or Wolf's quartet, for that matter. Johannes did not share his father's passion for the metal manufacturing industry and, despite his father's efforts to persuade him otherwise, he was unwilling to surrender to the vocation that was expected of him. He became increasingly unsure of his place in the world and, like his sister and her unofficial suitor, Erich Wiese, wished to see what opportunities lay outside his hometown. Herr Graf failed to see his son's hasty enlistment as subterfuge for an escape from Cleve.

Lately, most discussions between Herr Graf and Hermann Deppner at the gate had focussed on Cleve's support for the war effort, worthy suitors for Herr Graf's daughter and, of course, his profitable foundry.

Hermann Deppner lit his pipe and approached his neighbour, who was already standing vigil at the gate.

Earlier that morning, Herr Graf had also observed Wolf hastily leave the house. Armed with this knowledge, he saw an opportunity to launch an attack. 'I trust Wolfgang and his friends will attend the church service, Deppner? This is such an auspicious occasion. It would be disrespectful if any of our recruits were absent when Father Schilling dedicates his sermon to them, wouldn't you agree?'

'Yes, Herr Graf. This is certainly a great day for Cleve. And we thank you for hosting today's farewell.'

'We are very proud that our Johannes was the first of Cleve's finest to enlist. This certainly encouraged others to follow his example, don't you think? Gertrud and I will celebrate the great contribution our son will make in defending the Fatherland.' Hermann Deppner was unable to respond. 'If Johannes had ten brothers, I would offer them all to the Kaiser!'

Such a declaration now left Hermann completely dumbfounded. There was a brief awkward silence and he avoided eye contact.

Herr Graf took a puff of his pipe. A plume of sweet-smelling, expensive tobacco wafted over the gate. He had a fleeting urge to inform Hermann that he had been recently approached by government and military officials touting potential contracts. He was gratified, not only at being sought for his expertise to manufacture modified railway tracks that would transport men and equipment into enemy territories, but also because he had been requested to keep all negotiations confidential. It appealed to his ego to think of the request as top secret.

'When does your Johannes leave for active duty, Herr Graf?' Hermann waited for Herr Graf's carefully crafted reply. He was aware Herr Graf had sought an audience with the recruitment officers and persuaded them to re-assign Johannes to a different unit, reportedly because he was not prepared to allow the immature group, the so-called quartet, expose his Johannes to peril on the battlefield.

'He leaves next week. You know, Deppner, once we shore up the Eastern Front and rightfully reclaim our border regions, we will defeat the British and French and our soldiers will be home within the year.'

'I do hope so.'

Herr Graf was not finished. He cleared his throat. 'When the war is over, I'm happy for Johannes to stay on as part of any occupational force to garrison either France or Belgium, but even further afield, if need be.' With that, Herr Graf checked his pocket watch. 'It's time, Deppner. Please don't forget your new camera for the post-church festivities. You have given a promise to take photographs, have you not? Let's put that Kodak contraption to good use!'

The men turned and marched off. As usual, Herr Graf's head was lifted higher.

Following the usual commotion of gathering coats and hats, the Grafs formed a column on the footpath and waited for the Deppners to join them. Within a few steps, the street filled with other churchgoers, respectfully nodding and lifting their hats to their revered foundry manager. The procession marched along the street to the same rhythm. There was a collective sense of pride that the war would bring prosperity to the Fatherland, and to Cleve.

Frau Graf was less convinced, but wisely kept any dissent to herself. She had British relatives and shared fond childhood memories of visits to England. A regular exchange of letters continued until the overtures to the war had sounded. She felt the loss of such an important part of her life and now harboured dreadful thoughts of her son, Johannes, fighting against his British cousins.

Herr Graf, who secretly detested his wife's British lineage, had tried to quell her disquiet. 'My dear Gertrud. Germany's ties through the Victorian bloodline have weakened. The British treat our Kaiser with disrespect. They should not meddle in our affairs and did not hesitate to declare war against us. In my opinion, Britain has felt the poor cousin for a long time, always in the shadow of her more sophisticated German family. It's a convenient opportunity for Britain to break free from us. And we will not complain!'

Such posturing left Frau Graf speechless. Past images of walking beside her kind and affectionate aunts in the lush English countryside flashed before her. The hope of one day introducing her children to their English cousins was all but dashed as she listened to similar anti-British sentiments expressed amongst the congregation and in Father Schilling's sermon. Frau Graf realised the war cry that had rapidly spread across Germany, was now well entrenched in her hometown.

At the same time, Wolf and his friends were in the field beside Herr Winkler's house, drinking beer, laughing and playfully punching at each other's arms.

Erich Wiese noticed some of the flowers were already losing their vibrant colours, surrendering to the approach of autumn, but he was not disappointed with their brown stems and faded blooms. He saw beauty in the autumn tones. He looked around at the perennials and herbs that had escaped Herr Winkler's garden and sprung to life in the field, never to be tamed by fences or walls, and marvelled at the clumps of sage that had survived such a hot summer.

'Ah, look at this colour fading from purple to almost blue,' he mused.

'Ha! Erich! You make me laugh,' snorted Felix, but there was no malice in this. Like the other two, Felix respected Erich's aesthetic gift.

'What's the time?' asked Bruno. 'Aren't we going to be late for church?'

'We're not going to church!' declared Wolf. Mouths fell open around him. 'We're going to stay here, drink Bruno's beer and listen to Erich harp on about flowers or far-off places. We're going to admire our new uniforms and have fun. Anyway, the sermon's already started. We've missed it already.'

Astounded, but equally delighted by Wolf's boldness, Felix cried, 'Wolf! That uniform has given you such courage!'

Encouraged by the alcohol, the four felt like mavericks ready to take on the world, but also knew that their elation would be replaced with melancholy once the beer ran out.

Felix verbalised what the others were thinking. 'We need to make a pact. Here. Today. We need to promise to look after each other in this war and come back as the quartet.'

The last bottle was passed around and emptied. They moved closer to each other, into a circle, their arms draped over each other's shoulders. The four men moved their heads forward, slowly, until their temples almost touched. Each looked into the other's eyes and saw the same expression—a mixture of determination and apprehension. They closed their eyes and regulated their breathing until the four independent sounds merged. The formation lasted for a few minutes, as they swayed gently and felt the warmth of the sun on their backs. Usually, they would have broken their brotherhood embrace sooner, but today they held on to their ritual, fearing it could be lost to the war.

'Now,' said Wolf, as they unlocked their arms and sat on the grass. 'It's time for one of Erich's stories. What have you been daydreaming about lately, Private Wiese?'

Erich took a deep breath and retold a favourite story about their past geography lessons with Herr Stummhofer and the pictures of Canada and Australia on his classroom walls. 'And Tasmania! Remember? Herr Stummhofer had relatives there, in a town called Bismarck on the other side of the world. I want to go there. To Tasmania!'

Felix taunted, 'Why leave Germany, Erich? Isn't your uncle's house down south, in Heimbach, far enough from Cleve for you?'

No, thought Erich. Heimbach is not far enough for me, not by a mile. When this war is over, I want to go to the ends of the earth!

The last time Erich had visited Heimbach, his uncle announced that he intended to bequeath his home and belongings to his only nephew. 'Erich, my dear boy, you have been eternally good to me, helping me repair the fences and paint the house. You have eased my loneliness since your dear aunt passed away. As gratitude, this house will be yours one day.'

The faithful nephew felt a special affinity with his uncle's adventurous spirit, a quality Erich's father had been forced to bury under the burden of work. The uncle and nephew often hiked through the lush green of the Eifel Forest with its high canopies of swaying branches. A few times, they bivouacked under the stars...

'No, Felix. I love Heimbach but it's time we saw the world.'

'Oh! I see, Private Erich Wiese. So now you're saying that it will be all of us who go off travelling to god-knows-where!'

'Yes, Private Felix Wittmann.'

'The quartet goes to Canada and Australia. Is that what you're suggesting, Private Wiese!'

'Yes, Private Wittmann.'

'Well, this is all very interesting... Private Wiese.' Felix raised his eyebrows and looked to Wolf and Bruno for support, but they were alarmed by his uncharacteristic terseness and dipped their heads. The sun's rays were intense. The effects of the alcohol, the uncomfortable, stiff uniform and rising fear of losing everything that's familiar to him, had made Felix cantankerous. 'And what about my Lina? What will she say when her soon-to-be fiancé comes back a war hero, only to wave her goodbye because he's off with his friends to explore the world? Answer me that... Private Erich Wiese!' His voice now sounded hostile. He fired the final shot. 'And what about your beloved... Frieda?'

A shadow had been cast over the quartet, and the mood soured. Erich's cheeks reddened. Felix was close to tears. The four avoided eye contact and looked to the ground.

After a long silence, Wolf came to the rescue. 'I applaud your fascination with travel and far-off places, Private Wiese, as we all do. But I have a question.' He waited for the others to look up. They saw him grinning. 'Tell me, please. How does one actually get to Canada or Tasmania?'

Felix jumped in with a veiled apology. 'By camel, hot air balloon and boat, you fools! For God's sake, don't you soldiers know anything about the world?'

Felix grabbed hold of Erich and hugged him. With that, the shadow lifted, and the quartet rolled around in laughter, laughing longer than necessary, knowing that this could be their last such opportunity for a long time to come.

They unravelled themselves, stood, and adjusted their uniforms before marching off to the celebrations at Herr Graf's house. With every step, the effect of the beer lessened, and they approached the festivities with trepidation, knowing they were about to face displeased parents and certain disapproval from others. Wolf's earlier bravado was left behind with the empty beer bottles in the field of flowers…

After all the guests had gathered at the Graf residence, Wolf and his friends, splendid in their brushed-down uniforms, tiptoed inside.

'Wolfi! Thank goodness you're here!' Martha Deppner tenderly placed a hand on Wolf's cheek. 'You will need to apologise to your father and Father Schilling.'

'Yes, Mama. And to Herr Graf, no doubt!' He kissed his mother lovingly, and imagined his friends receiving similar receptions.

The unmistakable odour of beer followed the four around the house as they politely greeted guests and hugged their families and friends, sometimes in group formation, other times in pairs or individually.

Some guests were indifferent to the quartet's earlier indiscretions, but Herr Graf was predictably riled. In his mind, by deliberately avoiding the sermon, they had disrespected the entire town. He knew he would find it difficult to pardon them. He started to pace and puff.

Frau Graf quickly manoeuvred beside him. 'My dearest, Detlef. How special it is to gather everyone in our home to farewell Cleve's finest. This is such an important occasion.' She summoned him briefly with her eyes, then looked back and forth to the nearest guests, inviting them into her ploy. 'We do look forward to your speech!'

'My dear Gertrud. Yes, you are right. This is certainly a special day for Cleve.'

The quartet assembled in the drawing room and was followed by a group of admiring younger guests.

Frieda Graf positioned herself between Wolf and Erich and strategically grabbed their hands. 'You look so handsome in your uniforms!'

She threw Erich a bashful smile, quite juvenile for her age, and he realised he had been the sole target of her compliment. Frieda felt emboldened by the joyous occasion and ignored the likelihood that her father would be hovering to scrutinise her moves. Herr Graf had expressly forbidden any exchanges between Frieda and Erich that would encourage notions of a courtship—'One must plan the process of engagement and marriage with care. The most worthy suitor for our daughter's hand must be stringently vetted.' To Herr Graf, Erich Wiese was an unsuitable contender and should be discouraged, no matter how harshly.

Frieda was aware Erich, like most other men in Cleve, was intimidated by her father, but impressed that he was yet to fully retreat in fear. She had grown to love Erich and waited for him to pull her aside and declare his love for her, all the while accepting her father was likely to finish the victor.

As Herr Graf confidently strutted from room to room, ensuring his guests were enjoying the event with equal quantities of champagne and merriment, Erich seized his moment. He grabbed Frieda's hand and led her off to an empty room.

His words spilled out. 'I love the blue colour of your dress! I love you Frieda!'

Instantly, Frieda realised his clumsy declaration of love was born out of a sense of urgency. She responded kindly. 'I love you too, my dear Erich. But, my Papa... he...'

Erich knew it was unusual for Frieda to be tongue-tied. It confused him. He had an urge to insist that they run away together, to hide at his uncle's house in Heimbach, but instead chose: 'I know. I know. Your father does not approve of me!' He paused. His plan to hold her, kiss her and shower her with compliments was fast disappearing. 'I don't know why your father dislikes me so much.'

Such an insipid response displeased Frieda. *Has he learned nothing about courtship from Felix?* Yet the splendour and fresh smell of his uniform quickly softened her mood. 'We can't talk here, Erich. Not today.'

'But Frieda. I'm off soon. I might not see you again.'

His hasty choice of words irritated her once more. She knew not only her father, but also time, was her enemy. 'That's right, Erich! You... the quartet has decided to leave us. You enlisted, willingly, without talking to me. You didn't even fight it. You just blindly signed up!' Erich heard the exasperation in her voice as she kept up the salvo. 'Do you know how that makes me feel, Erich? To be left here with all the miserable women and old men, waiting for you to return?'

He was shaken. 'I will write to you, Frieda.'

She panicked. Her father had said nothing, but she knew he would not grant them permission to exchange letters. 'Erich. Please. We cannot write to each other.'

There was silence. She believed she could hear Erich's heart beating and longed to reach over and touch his tunic.

'I know, Frieda. I know. We cannot defy your father.'

With that, the blood sport of courtship made an uninvited entrance and jostled in between the two lovers. Frieda succumbed to intense emotions and fell prey to the game. 'Oh, Erich! Why have you given up so easily? Have you learned nothing from Felix about how to treat girls? The art of courtship? You just said you love me and now you're ready to discard me! You don't love me at all!'

Erich was startled. 'I do love you. Of course I do, Frieda.'

'How do I know that is true?'

He took her hand. He summoned her full attention. His expression was gentle, loving. 'I love you, Frieda, with all I have in my heart. I cannot express it in any other way.'

There was a pause as they looked into each other's eyes. He had redeemed himself, and Frieda dismissed the awful game of courtship as quickly as it had arrived.

'I will write to you in secret, Erich.'

'I don't understand.'

'I have a plan. I will arrange it with Lina. When she writes her love letters to Felix, you will also hear my words of love for you.'

Erich pondered the ploy and knew Frieda was clever enough to accomplish it.

They heard guests yelling and laughing outside the door. He must act quickly. He reached into his uniform pocket and brought out his gift. A sprig of sun-bleached sage plucked from Herr Winkler's field only hours before. Without words, he thrust it into Frieda's hand. She was genuinely touched and wondered how Erich knew she preferred simple, heartfelt gifts. She was impressed that he had remembered her favourite colour. As the inebriated guests tumbled into the room, she placed the gift in her apron pocket.

The celebrations continued. The house staff served sufficient canapés and beverages to ensure all invited dignitaries were impressed with Herr Graf's generosity. The dining room became the hub for the younger guests. There was a constant coming and going and the sounds of chatter with chinking of glasses.

Felix approached Herr Hartmann, Lina's father, to ask for her hand in marriage, but the extra champagne he had drunk for courage failed him. He stuttered during his prepared speech, practised on Wolf over many days.

Herr Hartmann was forgiving. He took hold of Felix's hand. 'Felix, my dear boy. Come home safely from this war and you shall have my daughter's hand!'

The Hartmanns and Wittmanns hugged each other whilst Felix rushed off to find his fiancée. He bounced into the adjacent room with a beaming smile, grabbed Lina, and kissed her. Some of the younger guests, school friends and acquaintances, grasped the significance of the kiss and cheered.

Excitedly, Frieda and Lina escaped to talk about the unfolding events. At the door, they intercepted Bruno and Erich, who recognised Lina's joyous expression as a clear sign that Felix was successful in his quest. As Frieda passed Erich, she kissed him, deliberately resting her lips on his cheek longer than a courteous gesture. It left Erich speechless and filled with love.

Felix waltzed around in delight and the growing excitement attracted more of Cleve's younger generation, grateful that the older guests had finally set them free from serious conversations about the war. 'Come on, lads! Let's get some more of old Graf's free champagne!'

Before long, Lina and Frieda reappeared hand in hand, almost skipping. They grinned and giggled like a pair of naughty schoolgirls.

Felix was intrigued. 'What are you two scheming?'

'My dear Felix. My precious fiancé. The quartet is not the only group to hold secret meetings in Cleve, you know. Frieda and I regularly hold our own. We talk about how handsome you are while we plan our own very important things!'

'Stop teasing. Tell us!'

'When your train leaves to send you off to fight, Frieda and I have decided to steal away from the finishing school and come to the station. We are going to give you a private farewell of a thousand hugs and kisses!'

Wolf and Bruno smiled at the thought of such a clever plan. Erich's face expressed sheer delight at the thought of receiving more kisses from Frieda, while Felix tilted his head and winked. 'Ah, you two little devils!'

A protective dome had formed over the Graf household, cocooning everyone under a temporary blanket of pleasure and celebration. Only flashes of uniforms, darting in and out of rooms or huddling together in celebratory packs, gave any hint to the outside world.

'Everyone come! Please follow me out to the courtyard! My neighbour, Herr Deppner, has a new camera and wishes to take photographs of us all!'

The guests were shepherded outside, curious about the promise of a photography session. The midday sun had warmed the courtyard, an expansive area that could comfortably accommodate a large crowd.

Herr Graf confidently entered centre stage with his hands stylishly placed in his waistcoat pockets. Behind him towered a dark paling fence, an imposing backdrop that accentuated his profile. 'Come on, Deppner! Out you come with that Kodak contraption of yours!'

As if he were a station master, ushering passengers to their assigned carriages, Herr Graf instructed his subjects on different poses. Some were compliant, others needed coercion. He basked in the role and looked forward to reading about the event in tomorrow's newspaper. For that purpose, he had invited a local reporter, but only on the proviso he left his camera behind—'Thank you, but I've commissioned my own photographer.'

Herr Graf offered Hermann Deppner advice on what angles were suitable for single, pair and group shots. He arranged the soldiers and their families, with and then without Father Schilling, the mayor and other dignitaries. He consented to the teacher, Herr Stummhofer, posing with some of his former pupils. The younger children obeyed orders as to whose hand to hold, where to stand, and how to give their best smiles. With the sound of Herr Graf's commands echoing around the courtyard and heat from the intense sun, most of the guests began to feel overwhelmed by the unrelenting spectacle. Photographs of the soldiers, without the clutter of civilians, were left to last. A guest bravely called out that the quartet should pose for a shot. Herr Graf dismissed the suggestion with a snort. It was left to Wolf's mother to mention that the very last would be of her three sons.

'Yes, of course, Frau Deppner. Of course, my dear Martha, you are correct. A photograph of your brave boys is certainly in order.' Herr Graf took hold of Martha's hands and surprised her with a moment of genuine tenderness, then, 'Come on, Deppners. You heard your mother. On the double!'

Frau Graf was beginning to believe her husband was either intoxicated or revelling too much in his director's role. Her heart warmed at knowing so many of Cleve's citizens, including her dear neighbours, would later treasure these photographs. She tried to ignore thoughts of war, but the sight of the last three handsome Deppners, all lined up in their spotless uniforms, filled her heart with dread.

'That's right, you three, stand in front of the fence. Wolfgang, you change places with Otto so Ernst is in the centre. That's a much better composition, wouldn't you say Deppner?'

The shift in angle gave Wolf a clearer view of Erich and Frieda. They had taken advantage of the distractions and were holding hands, low and out of sight. Wolf's heart raced when he noticed Frieda had pinned a sage flower to her apron. He recognised it as the one he had seen Erich pick earlier. Erich's desperate gift of love.

Wolf grinned. His cheeks puffed up as his grin spread wider into a smile. He saw the defiant act of holding hands as bold, perhaps risky, but he was proud of them. He looked back and forth from the lovers to his father, who was fumbling with the camera under a constant barrage of instructions from Herr Graf. Wolf's smile lingered and began to intrigue some of the guests. He received a disapproving look from his father, but the champagne had weakened his ability to compose himself, to hide his smile, to mask his true feelings. He could not look at the camera as seriously as his brothers. He glanced back at the two lovers and involuntarily laughed, then coughed in an attempt to disguise it. He felt immature, like a schoolboy, and could sense the stiffening postures of his brothers beside him.

Otto made a desperate attempt to thwart a calamity. 'Steady yourself, Wolf. You're upsetting Papa and Graf.'

It came too late. The blast hit them.

'For God's sake, Wolfgang. Stop smiling!' The force of Herr Graf's roar shocked everyone. There were gasps from some guests as he fired a second round. 'What on earth do you think is so amusing? Be serious, you fool! You're off to war, for God's sake! How can you defend our country with a childish attitude like that!' Herr Graf coughed and sputtered then, in a louder roar, he unleashed: 'Stop laughing, you fool! You are a disgrace. You should be ashamed of yourself. The whole of Germany will be ashamed of you!'

The guests were stunned. The volley of insults appeared excessive, unwarranted. They sensed the foundry manager had uncharacteristically lost his composure under duress.

Erich and Frieda released their hands in fright. Wolf's sister, Helga, wept. Wolf's mother put a hand to her mouth to prevent the sound of her distress from escaping, while Frau Graf readied herself to intervene.

'For God's sake, Deppner! Just take the damned shot. Now!'

Shaken by the shouting, Otto and Ernst nervously shifted position and fired wide-eyed expressions at the camera. Wolf desperately tried to compose himself, and almost succeeded. His father jumped at the bellowing beside him and, just a second too soon, took the photograph. Wolf's inwardly private, caring smile was forever ensnared by the indifferent camera.

Herr Graf turned and pushed his way through the guests, muttering expletives under his breath and avoiding any eye contact. He grabbed the arm of a reporter who was busily making notes. 'Print any of that and I will personally see to it that you are fired!'

For a few moments, the guests were unsure what to do before shuffling inside with murmurs and coughs, eager to escape the heat. Frieda Graf moved off and looked back at Erich as if to say, Please don't follow me. Johannes Graf watched his father storm off. He fidgeted, unsure if he should stay outside or follow the others. Otto grunted as he and Ernst left their younger brother staring at the ground. Martha Deppner moved beside her husband who, still clutching his camera, was looking through the gaps in the gate to the safety of his own courtyard. Lovingly, she took hold of his hand and led him inside.

Wolf's three friends approached him and waited for him to raise his head.

Felix gave him a slap on the back. 'Come on, lads! Let's give that god-awful champagne a miss and have some Klugshof beer instead!'

Frau Graf chased after her husband. She took his arm and whispered, 'My dear Detlef. I know you are upset. Wolfgang is young. He didn't mean any harm. Please calm yourself for the sake of the guests. You still have your speech to give.'

He knew she was right. He had an important task to perform. His speech would relieve his embarrassment and redress his unfortunate outburst. He looked lovingly at his wife and, in that moment, recognised how much of their son was reflected in her face. His mind raced back in time. He saw his little Johannes bouncing on his knee, giggling and demanding, More, Papa! More! He remembered the three Deppner boys arriving in Cleve, so very young and energetic. His mind returned to the present, to the boys as men, dressed in uniforms and ready to fight. Herr Graf clasped his chest. It was nothing pathological. He was overcome with emotion, an unfamiliar rush of feelings. His straight road had reached an intersection of uncertainly and his mind flooded with voices. He heard Hermann Deppner pleading with his Wolf, Please steady yourself for this war, my son. I pray your friends will protect you. He heard himself plead with his own son. My dear boy. My dear Johannes. You must protect yourself in this war.

Initially, Frau Graf was alarmed by her husband's penetrating glare. She saw intense emotion on his face and tears welling up in his eyes. She knew it was not the effects of champagne, or solely due to the unfortunate event in the courtyard. She sensed his unfamiliar inner pain and, in that moment, she adored him. 'I love you, Detlef,' she said, and hugged him before any guests sought them out.

Bruno's parents took hold of their younger children and hugged them firmly. His uncle was close by and assured them Bruno's position at the Klugshof Brewery would be held over until he returned. Erich's parents embraced in silence. They had lost two infants before he was born and knew the torment of grief. They refused to contemplate a world without their son. The Hartmanns and Wittmanns grouped together, shaken but supportive, desperately trying to ignore Herr Graf's outburst and focus more on Lina and Felix's engagement. The best friends, Lina and Frieda, held each other's hands tightly and whispered assurances to each other. Hermann and Martha Deppner gathered Otto and Ernst in their arms and attempted smiles of encouragement. Helga rushed over and screamed, 'I don't want my brothers to go!' The other guests embraced. Some of them wept.

Like an ominous forecast of the horrors to come, the protective dome over the Graf household had fractured. The Great War had begun.

The children of Cleve soon developed furrowed brows from listening to adult discussions on the latest news about the Eastern Front or the Schlieffen Plan.

Helga Deppner, the once vivacious schoolgirl, no longer skipped around the streets or visited friends. Within weeks of losing the company of her brothers, and Wolf's quartet, who so often entertained and spoiled her, she had become morose and preferred to spend time alone in her room.

Her parents summoned her to a meeting with the Grafs as they sorted through the newly developed farewell photographs. Once, excited by the lively presence of men parading in uniform, Helga was now deeply pained to see those same dear men displayed in a procession of static black and white prints. To her, trivial chatter in times of war seemed incongruous and offensive. Discussions about her embroidered summer tunic, Herr Stummhofer's plans to move to Cologne, of Lina busily planning her post-war wedding and the loveliness of Frieda's favourite blue dress all but lost in the matt-grey of a photograph, disappeared into the background until Herr Graf's disparaging comment about one particular photograph attracted her attention.

'Unfortunately, this one has been spoiled by Wolfgang's display of impertinence with his childish smirk. It is a pity to deny you a photograph of your three boys, Frau Deppner, the one you wished for, but I suggest you discard this one. Throw it in the fire!'

When the opportunity arose, Helga seized the contentious photograph and rescued it from further criticism and possible destruction. Later, she looked at it closely and focused on Wolf's mischievous grin. She thought back to happier times when her favourite brother was forever smiling and carefree. Where are you now, Wolf? Are you safe? Abruptly, her mind flooded with images of the quartet covered in blood and dirt. No! I cannot bear it!

With tears falling, she carefully placed the photograph in an ornately carved box which contained a cache of her treasured keepsakes, letters, drawings and her personal diaries. She locked the box and fell sobbing on her bed.

'Wolf! My darling Wolf…'

Chapter 11

2018. September
Europe

On their first morning in Heimbach, Conrad and Gretel woke to the sounds of Anke and Pascal preparing breakfast. After travelling around Europe for three weeks, in and out of hotels, a good night's rest had offered some relief to their fatigue.

As he clutched pre-paid return train tickets from Cologne to Duisburg, which Pascal had kindly arranged, Conrad could not conceal his excitement at finally getting to meet the Deppners. Yet he harboured some doubts that everything would go as planned. After landing in London, he had difficulty operating the international roaming function on his mobile phone and relied solely on emails with Willi Deppner to confirm their arrival time in Duisburg. A last-minute check, before Anke drove them to Cologne on her way to work, still revealed no replies, and Conrad was worried Willi might have misunderstood his poorly written German in the emails and would not be at the station to greet them…

'Do you think you will recognise them, Conrad?' asked Gretel as they alighted in Duisburg.

'I'm not sure.' Conrad and Gretel waited for other passengers to disperse from the arrival platform. 'It doesn't look like they're here. Let's go.'

As they caught up with the throng of commuters shuffling toward the main entrance, Gretel cried, 'I think that's them!'

Conrad peered over the heads in front of him and, in the distance, saw two figures excitedly waving flags. He recognised the German tricolour, Dutch and Australian flags, but it was the Tasmanian flag, with its red lion as the state's emblem, that caught his eye.

'Welcome to Germany.'

'Welcome to Duisburg.'

Willi Deppner and Piet Janssen, a dutchman with a connection to the Deppner family, introduced themselves. Willi stood slightly shorter than Conrad and was measured in his movements and communication, whilst Piet towered over them all.

In collaboration with Piet, Franz Deppner and a handful of other relatives and acquaintances, Willi had founded the Deppner family website, uploading historical records, family stories and anecdotes dating back to the 1500s. They called their most recent webpage, Letter of Fate from the First World War 1918: Hermann Deppner writes about the death of his son, Wolfgang. His letter found a century later in Tasmania. Willi, Franz and Piet, addressed in Conrad's emails as 'the trio', had honoured Conrad by listing him as a co-author to the story. Shortly before the Bentleys departed for Europe, Willi had informed the group that the website had inexplicably crashed.

'Piet and I must take you to our favourite coffeehouse so you can recover from your train journey.' Willi saw Gretel frown and slipped into English. 'They serve an assortment of delicious German, Dutch and Belgian cakes, and Piet will recommend his favourite.'

Gretel turned to Conrad with raised eyebrows. 'Huh! All those wasted hours on the flight over with your German lessons, and look, they speak perfect English!'

Willi came to Conrad's rescue. 'We'll endeavour to be kind to you both, as I suspect Conrad would also like to practise his German while he's here.' Conrad gave a thankful nod. 'After the coffeehouse, we'll have a short tour around the Duisburg city centre, then take you to my house where my wife, Sigrid, will serve afternoon refreshments.'

'I hope she's not going to too much trouble.'

'I'm certain she is, Gretel! Coffee with cake is a tradition in Germany. You will not be able to avoid it.'

Conrad was curious. 'Will we get to meet Franz?'

'Who is Franz again, sweetie?'

'He's the ninety-year-old grandson of Wolf's father, the man who wrote the letter back in 1918.'

'Just turned ninety-one!' corrected Willi. 'Yes, you'll get to meet him later.'

'Where do you fit into the story, Piet?' asked Gretel.

'My great uncle married Martha Deppner's cousin. Martha was Wolf's mother, so that makes her Franz's grandmother.' Piet saw Gretel struggle to keep up. 'Sorry Gretel, I know the family connections can be a little confusing and certainly harder to explain in English! We plan to draw up a family tree to make it all easier to understand.' He described inheriting the Janssen dairy farm in Aalten where, in 2013, he found a suitcase filled with documents, diaries, letters and other collectables, property that belonged to the Deppners and their neighbours, the Grafs.

Gretel smiled. 'Ah yes. I remember Conrad showing me a newspaper clipping about this suitcase and how you tracked down Deppners to hand it back.'

'We'll show you all these items later,' said Willi. 'The story about the suitcase of treasures, and the other posts on our website, helped your husband find us.'

'Ah, yes. Sending emails to anyone and everyone in Germany for eight months before realising all he needed to do was google Wolf's name!' She gave Conrad a hug. 'But I'm proud of my hubby. Some people call him tenacious because he won't give up until he finds what he's looking for.'

In the early afternoon, with full stomachs and the international flags in hand, the four arrived at Willi's house to a warm welcome from his wife, Sigrid. 'I will not take no for an answer, Gretel' she insisted, as she served cake with lashings of whipped cream.

'Thank you, Sigrid. And you speak English too! I love the watercolours. Did you paint them yourself?'

As Gretel and Sigrid moved off to inspect the artwork, Conrad turned to Willi. 'What's the latest on the website?'

'All the posts seem to have disappeared, but we're on the hunt for someone to help us fix it.'

'I'm sure you'll get the posts back. I spoke to my friend, Pascal, last night. He's a computer expert and reckons the posts are likely 'archived'. I'm not exactly sure what that means, but it sounded promising.'

'They're here!' Sigrid rushed for the front door. 'Come in Franz. The charming Tasmanians are excited to meet you.'

From his photos, Conrad instantly recognised Franz Deppner's cheerful, round face, but was surprised by the ease of his stride and youthful smile.

Franz immediately reached for Conrad's hands. 'I personally thank you, dear Conrad. I believe you were destined to find my grandfather's letter and bring it back to us. That's why we've called it the letter of fate.'

'I wish I could have brought the original with me but it remains the property of the Army Museum of Tasmania.'

'Ah, that's of no concern. At least we finally get to meet you in person instead of those emails. Now, please introduce us to your Gretel.'

Franz had arrived with his wife, her brother and sister-in-law. Conrad admitted he was unlikely to remember everyone's names and joked that name tags might have been helpful. He noticed places were set at the table, with one extra.

Sigrid offered more cake. This time, Gretel declined and stood her ground, but Conrad yielded. The conversation segued from one topic to another, and the Tasmanian guests were bombarded with questions. Conrad saw Franz Deppner continually nod in approval and observed that a smile and contented expression were rarely absent from his face.

'He's here!' Sigrid rushed to the door for a second time.

Conrad was curious about the identity or purpose of another guest but, as he entered, his resemblance to Franz was unmistakable. Conrad noted his confident stride, solid build, friendly smile, and thick, somewhat unruly hair streaked with grey. He surmised that the ninety-one-year-old Franz would have sported the same thick hair in his youth.

'Hello, you must be Conrad.'

Willi introduced the additional guest. 'This is Stefan Busch. Otto Deppner's grandson.'

'Pleased to meet you, Stefan. This is my wife, Gretel.'

As they returned to the table, Conrad noticed the others were exchanging knowing looks. Gretel realised Conrad had failed to grasp the significance of Stefan's introduction and gently placed her hand on his leg. It alerted him to what he had overlooked. 'Oh my God!' He was a little embarrassed by his high-pitched shriek. 'Otto Deppner's grandson? But I thought, I mean, didn't Otto, on the Western Front, didn't he...?'

Franz Deppner slapped the table, and the others leaned back and clapped.

Sigrid was the first to speak. 'My dear Conrad. We have overwhelmed you with this surprise. I do hope it's a pleasant one.'

As if on cue, Willi added, 'Yes, Conrad. We must apologise. When we first heard from you, Stefan was dealing with a family bereavement, therefore we didn't wish to disturb him at such a difficult time. With all the excitement of our subsequent email exchanges, a tsunami of emails as you so aptly describe them, we neglected to tell you that your assumption, that Stefan's grandfather died in battle, was incorrect.'

It was Stefan's turn. He smiled at Conrad reassuringly. 'My grandfather was taken prisoner on the 8th of August 1918, within the first hours of the Battle of Amiens. After that, we believe he spent quite some time in England as a prisoner of war before returning to Kleve, but we are yet to confirm all the details. I'm on board now to lead this part of the research. My hope is that we find some more clues about how my grandfather's letter found its way to Tasmania.'

Stefan passed the baton to Franz, who explained that frisking captured soldiers and taking their processions was a common practice, as had happened to him when he was captured by the Russians in the Second World War. 'The main purpose is to gather intelligence, but another is to take souvenirs. We assume your Tasmanian soldier might have obtained the letter for this purpose, as a souvenir of the war.'

They paused. Gretel leaned against Conrad's shoulder and took his arm; a supportive, loving gesture. The guests observed he appeared distracted. His mind was racing and he began to feel foolish about his hasty conjecture that Otto Deppner had been killed.

Once again, Sigrid came to his rescue. 'Poor Conrad. We've bombarded him with too many details. Let's take a break from this discussion. More cake, Gretel?'

'No thank you, Sigrid. And I believe my husband has also had enough.'

'Nonsense!' called Franz in German, with a boyish grin on his face. 'I can tell by your husband's eager expression that he's ready for more!'

'Sorry, what did Franz say, sweetie?'

Conrad supressed his own grin. 'He said Sigrid would be insulted if I didn't have another slice.'

From there, the conversations weaved around some contentious issues, including German politics on asylum seekers and a rise in neo-Nazism and right-wing extremism across the globe, the awkwardness of such topics saved only by Gretel's suggestion to discuss matters of a more light-hearted nature.

Conrad described his delight in visiting Europe for the second time, admiring the Palace of Versailles and staying with his pen friend in Waldshut-Tiengen on the Swiss border. 'We had a great time giving a lecture on Tasmania at his daughter's high school and my friend sings in a community choir. We were invited to a rehearsal and sang our hearts out in German, English and Italian!'

Conrad expressed their excitement in finishing the holiday in Malta and nodded to Gretel to report on her family in Stuttgart and the visit to her mother's original family home in the former German-speaking Sudetenland, in Czechoslovakia, before the family was expelled to Germany at the end of the Second World War.

Franz Deppner added, 'There are still German-speaking enclaves across our borders in Belgium and France. These places have changed hands many times over the centuries. The Alsace region in France is one of my favourite places to visit, especially the beautiful city of Colmar. Both French and German is spoken there. You know, it's hard to imagine any scenario that would cause real borders to go up again. When it's the language, culture and friendship that bind us, borders and walls become irrelevant.'

The words resonated with Conrad for a few moments. 'Yes, what's surprised me the most about Europe is that it's so easy to travel between all the countries. One blink of an eye and you wouldn't even know you've crossed a border!'

Despite the jovial atmosphere, Conrad was becoming impatient with the small talk and felt relieved when Willi produced the suitcase of memories. He was keen to see the items close up and hear their stories.

Willi ceremoniously arranged some of the items on the table and Gretel could not hide her delight. 'Look at this summer tunic. I love the hand-embroidered flowers. And there are lovely butterflies hiding amongst them!'

'How do you say 'butterfly' in German?' asked Conrad. He received a joyful chorus of 'der Schmetterling' in reply.

'And look! There's a matching embroidered handkerchief. These are such lovely treasures.'

'Yes. My Aunt Helga was known for her embroidery,' said Franz.

Gretel picked up another item, a pressed flower mounted behind glass with ornate brass brackets. 'This looks like salvia. It's faded a bit, but the original colour must have been lovely.'

'We're not altogether certain of its significance. We know from a brief entry in Aunt Helga's diary that it belonged to Frieda Graf. The Grafs were the neighbours of my grandparents. Take a look at the inscription on the back, Gretel.'

From my devoted Erich, 1914. Frieda G.

'Who was Erich?'

'One of Wolf's friends. He had three close friends—Felix Wittmann, Bruno Klug and Erich Wiese. They all fought in the war together and helped bury Wolf, as described in my grandfather's letter. Young Erich Wiese had a love interest in Frieda Graf.'

'Ooh! Now I know there's romance in this story, I'll start paying more attention to my husband!'

'The four soldiers were called 'the quartet', but we can't find any reference that connects them to a musical group.' He knew this would grab Conrad's attention, who looked up, wide-eyed. 'I can remember my family talking about a quartet when I was a boy, but I never really understood what it meant. Who knows Conrad? Maybe Wolf and his friends were members of a string quartet, like yourself!'

'A quartet of friends who go off to fight in a war together…'

Conrad's words floated above the table. It allowed everyone time to reflect on the other stories from the suitcase that might remain untold. Conrad imagined Wolf and his friends in uniform, smiling, proud. Did you play in a string quartet, Wolf? Who was the leader? Who played the cello, the viola? How did you protect your precious instruments from the shelling, from the mud and grime? He recalled Alan, his own quartet leader, had once mentioned that such incongruous things, such as quartets in uniform, did occur during the Great War, but he snapped from his musings before his inner voice had a chance to make its first appearance in Europe and denounce his thoughts as absurd.

'My Aunt Helga also wrote about the quartet in her diaries. It appears they were well known by this title in their hometown.' Franz paused to ensure he had everyone's attention. 'It's very sad to know only two members of the quartet survived the war.'

'What!' gasped Gretel. 'Did another one die?'

'Sadly, the young Bruno Klug was reported as missing in action.'

'What an awful waste of young lives.' Gretel let out a disapproving huff.

Franz opened a decorative wooden box. Inside were photographs, items of jewellery and what appeared to be folded letters and sketches. 'Aunt Helga kept most of her keepsakes in this box. Here's the photograph of Wolf, Otto and my father, Ernst. The one we sent you, Conrad. There's an inscription you haven't seen...' Franz turned over the photo and held it up. *My three brothers I rescued from the fire.* 'We know it's Aunt Helga's handwriting, but the meaning eludes us.'

'I've been interested in this photo for a long time, but now it's even more intriguing.'

Willi laughed. 'Yes, Conrad. We were all entertained by your speculations about Wolf's expression. I believe the English word is... overthinking!' He allowed the laughter to subside. 'We now know that this photo was taken in the courtyard of the Graf's home. The same empty garden beds and tall paling fence are in other photos taken on that day. We think the pictures were taken during an event, possibly a farewell for the soldiers. The house no longer stands following the Allied bombing in the Second World War.'

'Can I see the other photos?' Conrad knew their visit was coming to an end and felt the need to get as much information as possible.

'All in good time, Conrad. We're having Helga's diaries typed up. When that's done, we'll send you everything.'

'Is there a photo of Wolf's quartet in the courtyard?'

'Not that we could find.'

'Why were the young girls sent across the border?' asked Gretel.

The group turned to Franz for a response. 'From my understanding, when the war ended and Germany was garrisoned, an occupational soldier on horseback struck Frieda's mother with a whip, in anger. Because of this, my grandparents and the Grafs probably feared for the safety of their young daughters and sent them off to Aalten to live with Piet's distant relatives, you know, for their protection. Frieda eventually moved to England to live with her British cousins. Willi tried to get more information about all this, but the trail went cold. It's likely Frieda Graf changed her name to get a passport, but again we're not certain.'

Gretel sighed, 'Ah, I do hope Frieda got a chance to say goodbye to her admirer, this young Erich Wiese, before she left. He must have been heartbroken.'

There was a natural pause in the conversation as the cups were refilled. Franz explained Helga eventually returned to Kleve, but left her keepsakes behind in Holland. 'Why? We're not exactly sure.'

'Do you remember her well?'

'Yes Conrad. Aunt Helga and my father were quite close. She stayed with us for many years after the war. I was her favourite nephew.' Franz dipped his head to conceal his smile. 'She told me I reminded her of Wolf.'

'Yes! I can see the resemblance in the photo! You both have the same cheeky grin!'

'In time, she moved back to the family home to care for her ailing parents, my grandparents, Hermann and Martha Deppner.'

'Ah!' said Gretel. 'I'm starting to understand the family tree.'

'After my grandparents died, Otto, Stefan's grandfather, took her in. She died in her seventies.'

Conrad looked at Stefan. 'Your grandfather? Otto Deppner? Now I know he survived, what happened to him after the war? I take it he had a daughter, your mother, and that she married someone named Busch?'

Stefan nodded. 'There's more to research about my grandfather. All in good time, Conrad, but Helga did keep a letter from him…'

Western Front

2nd August 1918

Dear Papa, Mama and Helga,

I sit here holding the letter about Wolf's death. I am in shock and cannot envisage a life without him. His death is the worst blow of this unrelenting war. Other comrades share similar grief and we all hope for an end to the hostilities so we can return home and comfort our loved ones.

To my dear Mama, to offer a son to fight for the Kaiser is honourable. To lose a son is insufferable. I long to kiss you.

I have faith in the Red Cross to bring us news about Ernst. The Eastern campaign was particularly hard, but I feel in my heart that he has survived, and is alive. We should not give up hope!

To my dear, sweet Helga. You have sunk into a deep hole. Please, for all our sakes, cheer yourself so you can help Mama and Papa with this awful grief. This is the mission I give you. I know you are strong inside and can do this.

The battalion has moved closer to Le Hamel, east of Amiens, where we expect more heavy combat. I shall write again as soon as I am able.

I love and cherish you all.

Papa, I will keep your letter in my breast pocket until the war ends. That way, I will know Wolf is close to my heart.

Your loving,

Otto

Conrad felt there was too much to absorb in too short a time. He regretted organising only one visit.

Franz sensed the urgency. 'Aunt Helga also kept a letter from the widow of Wolf's platoon commander, Lieutenant Preiser. It would appear my grandfather paid her a visit…'

Dinslaken

29th June 1918

Dear Herr Deppner,

Thank you for your visit. To make the long journey to Dinslaken would have been a great strain on you.

I think of my husband every day. Our son, his namesake, reminds me of him so much.

I feel such pain that my dearest Andreas died without knowing he was a father. I wrote to him, but the letter was returned unopened.

What grief we share from the war, Herr Deppner. However, your words of encouragement have comforted me greatly. Please write to me when you hear news of your surviving sons. I long for such cheer.

The gifts from your wife and daughter arrived today. Please pass on my gratitude. The gloves will warm the hands of my little Andreas in the coming winter and I will treasure your daughter's embroidered napkins. They are simply exquisite. She has such a talent. You must look forward to the day when she can return from Holland.

Yours sincerely,

Frau Andreas Preiser

'Oh, Conrad!' cried Gretel. 'Was the lieutenant killed as well? This is all very sad.'

Many questions and thoughts whirled around in Conrad's head. He wondered whether Wolf also made his presence known to his relatives. He was tempted to ask them, but his inner voice cautioned him. Don't be a fool, Bentley! They'll think you're a madman.

'Are you still with us, Conrad?'

'Yes, Franz. I'm sorry. I'm sorry. There's so much to take in. I wish I had time to read Helga's diaries and look at the other photos. I have so many questions.' He felt nauseous. 'May I please have a glass of water?'

As Sigrid dashed into the kitchen, Willi advised, 'You will not get all your answers today, Conrad, and some pieces of the puzzle will always remain lost. I fear the time has disappeared from under our feet and you will miss your train if I don't drive you to the station soon. You mentioned in your last email that your Heimbach friend will be waiting to collect you in Cologne.'

'But… what are we going to do with all this information?'

'Our first task is to restore the family website.'

Conrad looked to Stefan Busch. 'I don't know anything about you, Stefan. Do you live in Kleve? What do you do for a job?'

'It's okay, Conrad. I'll send you a tsunami of emails outlining my life story.'

Franz suggested Conrad needed to add Stefan to his email list. 'Instead of Dear Trio, you'll now have to address us as Dear Quartet.'

As Willi fetched his car keys, Stefan reported that he and his French wife were visiting her family soon, and that they also planned to make a detour through the villages and landmarks mentioned in the letter—the Clignon area and Amiens. 'I've been in contact with the Mayors of Licy-Clignon and Bussiares. They have recommended we meet with a local historian, a military enthusiast who's apparently an honorary member of the American Marine Corps. He gives lectures in America and leads tours around the battlegrounds of France for people researching their family members who fought in the war. We're hoping he can help us identify the sites connected to Wolf's fate.'

Franz Deppner reached for Conrad's hands again. His grip was surprisingly firm and his expression earnest. 'Before you go, Conrad, we wish to give you an important mission.' Franz's expression intensified as he summoned Conrad's full attention. 'We have the face of the letter's author, my grandfather, Hermann Deppner. We have the face of my father, Ernst Deppner. We have the faces of my two uncles, Otto and the fallen Wolf. Sadly, we are yet to see the face of the Tasmanian soldier who took the letter of fate back with him to the other side of the world. What are you going to do about that, my friend?'

Conrad inhaled. Good grief, he thought, it's going to be like finding a needle in a haystack! 'I'm not sure, Franz. I suppose I could research which Tasmanian regiments fought in the battle of Amiens, but I think it's going to be hard to find him without more clues. I don't even have a name.'

Willi smiled. 'The absence of a name has not been an impediment to you before, Conrad! We already know you are… sorry, what's the English word again, Gretel?'

'Tenacious.'

'We are confident our… te-na-cious comrade from Tasmania will solve this piece of the puzzle. Now, one last thing before you go.'—Conrad braced himself for another difficult mission—'We are giving a presentation about the letter of fate to my community group in November, all four of us now that Stefan is on board. Of course Conrad, we would like you to join us as our guest of honour.'

Conrad contemplated his answer. 'That's a lovely invitation Willi, but I don't think we can do two trips to Europe in one year. I'll be there in spirit.'

'Please everybody, say your farewells.'

'I'll wrap you two slices of cake for the journey.'

'No thank you, Sigrid,' answered Gretel before Conrad had a chance to accept. 'We have strict instructions from our Heimbach friends to leave room for more coffee and cake tomorrow. We're visiting Anke's parents.'

As Willi Deppner drove around the corner and headed for the station, Conrad was overwhelmed by what he would later call his 'blitz visit to Duisburg'.

Behind his sunglasses, tears of elation, frustration and expectation welled up in his eyes.

'Sweetie! Look!'

Conrad raised his head and saw a line of figures on the footpath, jubilantly waving the international flags. A salute to his visit and friendship.

He was moved to tears.

Chapter 12

The Great War
The Tasmanian Soldier's Story

In August 1916, Frank and John shivered on the deck of the troop ship Berrima as it lumbered toward the Southampton wharf. They stood shoulder to shoulder with the other men of the 40th Battalion. Exhilarated from their voyage through warmer climates, the soldiers swapped a Tasmanian winter for a chilly start to the northern autumn and, without delay, commenced gruelling training in the English countryside to prepare them for trench warfare.

In late November, the battalion was deemed 'sufficiently battle-ready' and ferried across to France as part of the Australian 3rd Division, the shock of an icy crossing making their thoughts of home more intense.

At the beginning of the following year, the battalion took part in minor skirmishes but was predominantly held in reserve. During recreation, Frank and John displayed their football prowess and visited numerous small villages.

In late March, Frank received highly anticipated news of the arrival of his third child. 'Listen to this, John,' as he excitedly fumbled with the letter:

New Town

2nd March 1917

My love, my dearest husband.

You are a daddy again.

A darling girl arrived only days ago, and she is healthy and lovely...

'I'm so pleased for you and Daisy, Frank.'

'What news from Bessie, mate?'

'Much the same.' John chose not to spoil Frank's elation and kept Bessie's words to himself:

Bismarck

4th March 1917

Dear John.

I miss you deeply.

I have thought long and hard about protecting you from this news, but to witness the horrible treatment of our German families and friends, without you by my side, is simply awful. I feel so shaken. I cannot bear this alone.

Our once wondrous life in the valley, in this place they now call Collinsvale, is disappearing before my eyes. The apricots sit wasting on the trees, the ripening apples are neglected and plagued with pests and the coffeehouses have closed, along with the school and church—hopefully only temporarily. It will also sadden you to hear that our lovely German butcher in Hobart was assaulted and his shop vandalised. Words fail me!

Your parents are so lovely to me, but they cannot hide their sadness. I am sorry to upset you with all this, but I need you more than ever.

Rest assured, there is also good news. Frank would have told you about the arrival of another daughter. To hold another baby allows me to forget the troubles here. She has stirred such feelings of joy in me. We must have another child, John! Another reason for your swift return.

The children miss you terribly. When they smile, I see your face. They take after you in every way. In Hobart, people stop me in the street to admire their blond hair. How cruel it is that I cannot boast about their German grandparents. When will this madness stop?

Please come home to us safely, my darling...

Not until the first week in June 1917 did the men of the 40th first experience major combat at Messines in Flanders. A year in advance of the attack, British, Canadian, Australian and New Zealand miners and engineers had painstakingly burrowed under the German lines to lay thousands of pounds of explosives.

Frank and John felt the violent tremors caused by the quick succession of blasts and were overwhelmed by the surreal spectacle of black earth, chalk, steel, fire and bodies of the unsuspecting Germans that mushroomed into the pre-dawn sky. They gave each other a brotherly nod before they were sent into the fray, stumbling around the huge craters left by the blasts. Alongside their comrades, they pushed hard to take the Messines village and were, at times, close enough to see their own fear reflected in the eyes of their enemy.

For many weeks, the two friends sat together on many piles of rubble that were once beautiful cities and villages dotted around the Western Front, now all but destroyed by senseless bombing. They often caught glimpses of shattered cathedral steeples, ghostly towers that appeared now and again through the smoke and dust. Like other comrades, they felt shaken by their first taste of heavy losses, yet relieved that they had avoided the main drift of the enemy's ruthless, experimental use of chlorine gas. As they observed lines of shocked and nearly blind, gas-stricken victims being shepherded past them, they felt immense pity.

Trying to ignore the distant hammering of bombardment, Frank and John sought refuge in their most recent letters from home.

'Listen to this from Daisy, mate.'

New Town

3rd June 1917

Dear Frank,

You are going to love our little girl. She has grown so quickly and her brother and sister dote over her so much...

Frank wiped away tears, a mixture of emotion and the residual effects of the gas. 'I can't wait to see my newborn. After all this time away, my other children won't recognise me, and maybe I won't recognise them either.'

'Yes, you will Frank. Look! Bessie has sent me a picture of them all. You can't mistake your children. Thank God they take after their mother!'

As they stole a moment to laugh and glance around at the other men, all similarly chatting and proudly sharing photos, their Platoon Commander Lieutenant Brown approached them. 'Ah, Swinton and Bloom. Good news from home, I take it.'

The lieutenant's smile and kind heart soothed Frank in an instant. 'Yes, Sir. My new baby is growing stronger by the day and my other children are just bonzer.'

'Splendid! You know men, it's times like these, when we can forget about the fight for a brief moment, that I'd give my right arm for a beer!'

'I agree, Sir,' said John, with a blissful smile.

In a slightly more serious tone of voice, 'That was a tough battle and we all deserve some rest. When we lose so many fine soldiers from our battalion, it's a crying shame we can't give them a proper send off and raise a glass in their honour.' The lieutenant took a seat and lit a cigarette. For a while, Frank and John observed him deep in thought.

Like most men of the 40th who found it hard to find work after war broke out, Alfred Percival Brown had joined up as a corporal in his mid-twenties and accompanied his assigned platoon from Hobart to England, resolutely supporting them through the extra training and ensuring they were sufficiently prepared for the life in the trenches. Toward the end of 1916, he was promoted to lieutenant, and an increased respect from his men came with it. They believed he expertly carried out his officer duties whilst not altogether losing his ordinary-bloke ways to rank.

Inwardly, the lieutenant had begun to struggle with the harshness of the war and the shock of losing good men under his command. He accepted it was his duty to demonstrate a stiff upper lip and ensured he only let down his guard when alone. During lulls, he found himself staring at flowers, glimpses of colour that had sprung to life in the shelled fields, or blooms left unattended in abandoned gardens. Many times, he saw wheat fields with splashes of red, clusters of poppies that boasted their vibrant colour under a bright sun. The colours of Flanders and France made him reflect on the futility of war. The beauty of these countries that he once only knew from geography books or magazines, but now seen up close, was disappearing under heavy bombing. For the sake of morale, he suppressed such thoughts when mingling amongst his men.

'Remind me, you two. Which part of Hobart are you from?'

'I'm from New Town, Sir,' said Frank.

'Ah, not far from me, Swinton. I come from Glenorchy. We were practically neighbours. It's a wonder we never met before the war. Hobart's such a small place.'

'Too right, Sir.'

'And what about you, Bloom?'

'From Collinsvale, Sir.'

'Ah yes, the former Bismarck. I've walked through the Myrtle Forest a few times in my younger days. It must be difficult for your folks right now. People with German backgrounds are copping it a fair bit, I hear.'

John dipped his head.

'It's madness, Sir,' chipped in Frank. 'I've known John since we were lads. We met on the footy field and worked together in the mines on the West Coast before we got married and settled down. John's parents are decent, hardworking people. It's not fair the war has reached Tassie and made a mess of things there too.'

'I agree, Swinton. I agree. But I don't reckon it will get much better back home until this damned war is done and dusted.' He looked at John. 'In the meantime, you need to keep your head high, Bloom. You are doing Tassie and the British Empire a great service and your folks will be proud of you.'

'Thank you, Sir.'

'You know, you're not the first German descendant who's fighting with us over here. Back at the training camp in England, I met an officer who came from German Town in Tassie's North, but I think the powers that be have changed the name of that town too.'

'It's madness,' repeated Frank.

'This war has taken some strange turns, and now involves almost the entire world. Our job is to focus on our assigned missions and follow orders. Simple as that, men. And that's all we can do, for now.' The lieutenant took a puff of his cigarette and looked closer at the two friends from Hobart. 'It's a wonder they didn't use you as a German interpreter, Bloom. I take it you speak the mother tongue?'

John was somewhat surprised by the question and hesitated to respond. 'My parents decided to learn English when they arrived in Hobart, Sir. They speak a bit of German with some of the neighbours,'—John thought to himself that it was unlikely any German would be spoken now—'but I was raised to speak English. Whatever German I know, I'd rather keep to myself, Sir.'

For a moment, an awkward pause jostled in and lingered between them. Frank shifted his position slightly closer to John. He was protective of him and concerned others might overhear and misconstrue the conversation. The three reflected on the situation back home, where Australians with German backgrounds were now classed as enemies of the state, people not to be trusted.

'Well, you speak perfect English, Bloom! Or should I say, Tasmanian! And that's good enough for me. Besides, I wouldn't want to lose you from the platoon. You're a good soldier and one hell of a gifted footballer! If it weren't for you and Swinton, we wouldn't have any chance of beating those other hopefuls on the footy field, now would we?'

'Too right, Sir!' answered Frank. 'With all this talk of footy, it reminds me of the after-match beers. I'd give my right arm for one!'

'Me too!' came a cry just metres away. A similar cry was heard coming from farther down the line, and one more, until the entire squad was heard clapping and cheering.

From the outset, Frank and John had held their lieutenant in good regard. As they watched him weave his way through the other men, slapping them on their backs and chatting, their respect for him strengthened. They glanced at each other and smiled.

'He's a good bloke. I like our lieutenant.'

'Same here, Frank.'

'He doesn't have any airs and graces. He's like one of us, John, but with pips. After the war, when I meet up with him in Hobart, I'll be sure to shout him a beer or two.'

'I'll join you, Frank!'

After the brutality and shock of the Messines' battle, the men of the 40th joined the continual rotation of troops in and out of the trenches. For relief from combat, they spent an equal amount of days in the secondary lines, played football or enjoyed the occasional, but oh-too-short, recreational leave.

At times, a handful of officers attempted to boost morale by putting on comedy skits. The troops were repeatedly entertained by the confident larks of Lieutenant Brown in costume.

'He's certainly a natural on stage, John!' laughed Frank.

To some, such frivolity, with a backdrop of smoke from distant shelling, would have appeared incongruous but, in many cases, it prevented soldiers from breaking down.

Frank and John continued to lead their squad to victory, not only in friendly skirmishes on the football field but also on the battlefields. They regularly received praise from their superiors. Nevertheless, all the men of the 40th Battalion knew the sport and whimsical stage shows were only temporary reprieves from the ever-present war that raged just beyond the slopes…

By the end of March 1918, the Australian troops were recalled from Flanders to the Somme to bolster the Allied forces that had amassed to halt the Spring Offensive, known to the Germans as Kaiserschlacht—the Kaiser's Battle.

As the 40th Battalion marched toward Amiens, the men passed many bouquets of dried flowers—wreaths that had been fashioned by grieving soldiers and placed on the ground in honour of their fallen mates. Frank noticed a posy of blue cornflowers and yellow daisies, fresh enough to display their original colours, and immediately thought of his sweet flower waiting for him at home.

Exhausted and dirty, with little or no sleep for two nights, they finally arrived on the northern banks of the River Somme and set up camp near the village of Morlancourt. As dawn broke, they watched hundreds of British soldiers in retreat for a well-earned rest and realised that they were there to replace them.

Frank and John felt a sense of foreboding and tried desperately to ready themselves for the upcoming battles. The fighting resumed almost immediately and their advances placed them less than two hundred metres from enemy lines, where John feared he would finally look into the eyes of his German cousins.

From then on, the combat intensified and the Australian ideal of mateship was severely tested under bombing raids, rain, mud and dreadful waves of chlorine gas.

Under such intense pressure, Frank and John struggled to support each other, both physically and emotionally, and their once impenetrable fortress of friendship cracked and became vulnerable. Frank suffered from severe headaches that he could not shake, and his vision and mind started to blur. He began to see John less as the spirited German from Bismarck and more comparable with the dirty-faced, ugly Germans, living or dead, he now saw daily on the battlefield.

John sympathised with his ailing friend and sensed a weakening of their bond. He feared the war had taken its toll. I'm worried about you, Frank, he thought. It's not like you to look so angry.

Frank became suspicious of John's increasingly concerned looks and frowns. He misconstrued them as malicious and calculating. One night, he woke from a nightmare—John had been standing over him with his rifle, bayonet attached, sporting a malevolent grin, his fine face replaced by the soiled appearance of the enemy. Frank tried to curb his odd, hostile thoughts, but he heard voices in his head that were louder and more convincing than his weakening logic.

'What's happening to us, Frank?' pleaded John during a lull.

'Nothing. Just leave me alone. My head is pounding and your questions are making it worse. For God's sake, John! Go and wash your face!'

On the night of the 28th of March, Lieutenant Brown led a raiding party on a small thicket west of Morlancourt. The attack had limited success and resulted in heavy losses on both sides, however the lieutenant received adulation from his fellow officers and was cited for his bravery. Yet, as he sat down to write letters to the families of the fallen, he saw little reason to be rewarded for so-called gallantry and feared the fighting was increasing with a vengeance.

In the Morlancourt assault, John suffered a shrapnel wound to the shoulder and was transported to an aid station well to the rear.

In his absence, Frank had time to reflect. He reproached himself for thinking ill of his brother-in-law. He wrote in his diary, *I've finally found hell on earth and stooped to a low in my mind and thoughts that will shock my loved ones…* but within a few days, his headaches and distrustful thoughts about John resurfaced. Following another push over the top, he returned to trench and sat in the usual pool of muck and misery, feeling anger toward John for leaving him to suffer alone.

Recovering in a field hospital tent, John asked a nurse to write a diary entry for him, *This war has no boundaries. It turns country against country, man against man, and now I fear, friend against friend…*

Weeks later, the battalion learned the Germans had retaken Messines, a brutal blow given that so many of their comrades had been slain in the first battle to liberate the town a year before.

Infuriated and bewildered, Frank felt the war had almost crushed him, and desperately yearned to fall into the arms of his wife. That night, as he tried to fall into a much-needed slumber, he whispered up to the dark sky, 'Oh, how I miss you, my sweet flower.'

Recovered sufficiently from his injury, John returned to the battalion and immediately took his tired and broken brother-in-law into his arms. 'I'm here now, Frank. Don't forget I'm your best mate.'

Glimpses of their friendship rekindled for a couple of weeks but, cruelly, their fragile truce was short-lived. During one of the many battles on the Somme, Frank had noticed John hesitate to fire. 'What are you waiting for, John? Reload!'

John buried his face in the dirt and wept. 'What the hell are we doing here, Frank? This is all wrong.'

Frank heard a voice yelling in his head, Private Bloom doesn't want to kill Germans any more. Leave him! As Frank pushed toward the enemy lines, his anger, that his brother-in-law had frozen in combat and left him dangerously exposed, turned to fury. Take this, you dirty Huns!

It was not until the battle ended that Frank learned John had been wounded, this time severely. Frank watched as John was stretchered away, eventually transported to England for surgery. Frank was numb. He felt no compassion. There was no love for John now. Instead of a decent farewell gesture, Frank thought, I hope the nurses wash the filth from your face, John Bloom—or do you now call yourself by your German name of Blume?

Lieutenant Brown was there to see John off. 'You'll be in safe hands, Bloom. Good luck, soldier.'

He turned and noticed Frank appeared to be in a trance. Frank's vacant and peculiar expression alarmed him. I'm losing this one…

Days later, during a night patrol, Frank heard the Germans singing their national anthem. The sound floated above the foxholes, the fine voices blended in skilful harmony. Frank and some of his comrades recognised the melody and found themselves enjoying its charm.

Suddenly, Frank imagined he heard John's voice in the choir. He gasped, believing the anthem was now a weapon of intimidation. His paranoia returned, this time like the attack of a crazed beast. From that point on, he developed a hand tremor and suffered terrible nightmares about his brother-in-law, his best friend, crawling over the border to Germany, proudly dressed in a German uniform and turning with a sneer as he took aim at his former comrades. Frank convinced himself that John was and had always been, the enemy. His lieutenant often threw him concerned looks, but Frank hid his suspicion and waited for an appropriate time to expose John's treachery. Now and again, a faint voice of reason questioned his illogical thoughts, but the grip of war was stronger. Cunningly, and within a frighteningly short time, the paranoia completely overwhelmed him, and he was powerless to fight against it.

At the same time, in an English military hospital, recuperating from numerous shrapnel wounds and surgery on his left leg, John craved the company of his only true friend. He sensed the war had finally turned Frank against him and desperately wished to talk to him, take hold of him, to reassure him.

When their letters reached home, their wives detected subtle changes in language and careful choice of words, or more brutally, the absence of words. As their children chased each other around the garden, oblivious to the torment of their fathers, Daisy and Bessie cried in each other's arms.

'They don't speak of their friendship anymore, Bessie!'

'When they return to us, we must be prepared to mend their bruised minds and hearts.'

'My Frank is going to find it impossible without John, yet he writes nothing about him. Oh, Bessie. I can't bear to think of my Frank as an angry man. I want him back. I want him to be the same old Frank. I hate this war!'

'We've already lost a brother. Our husbands' shattered friendship is another casualty. My sweet Daisy, when this war is finally over, it will fall upon us to nurse them, to make things right again, and pray we never see another war.'

Toward the approach of the northern autumn, Frank's last strand of fortitude to fight was all but lost, buried with many of his comrades under the churned and bloodied soils on the Western Front. Not even the arrival of fresh American troops could cheer him. His fear of returning to Daisy, a disgruntled and broken man, and the thought of not recognising his children, panicked him. His paranoia worsened. He stole away to read his letters and look at his family pictures, but the smiling faces of his children only added to his pain. He felt himself falling into a vast sea of indifference and madness.

One night, he heard a voice telling him to end it all, to leave his rifle, walk off into the darkness and simply let an enemy bullet claim him. It was only Daisy's faint whisper for him to stay strong that held him back…

As the battalion reached Amiens, the frantic exchange of orders, buzzing of reconnaissance planes, arrival of more Canadian dominion forces, further distribution of American troops into the Australian units and the corralling of massive tanks alerted the men to a major battle.

On the evening of the 7th of August, Lieutenant Brown revealed the plan to put an end to the stagnant trench warfare with a massive coordinated attack. 'This is it, men! Tomorrow we're in for the big stunt. The 40th will be held in reserve until the lads in the initial push have done their job, then we'll join them over the top. So, clean your rifles well and thoroughly check your gear.'

Frank woke shortly after 4.00am to a thick, menacing fog. The battle erupted with a barrage of mortar fire before the first wave of soldiers pushed blindly through the mist and smoke, with only the sound of enemy gunfire to guide them toward their target. The men beside Frank tried to talk to him but were drowned out by the roar of shelling. They watched in awe as huge British Mark V tanks, resembling black monsters, lumbered past their reserve post. They saw them as beasts on a mission to intimidate and frighten the enemy into submission and retreat.

It was not long before a line of captured Germans appeared, some too young to shave, all disoriented by the choking smoke and the thunderous sounds of the ensuing battle. Frank saw expressions of uncertainty and humiliation on their faces and, in some cases, relief.

Under the surface, Lieutenant Brown was becoming rattled by the unfolding chaos. Outwardly, he kept his composure. He approached Frank's squad. 'We've received orders to frisk these Germans. The command post needs urgent intelligence. Privates Swinton, Birch and Peters, report to Sergeant Hill from C Squad and start searching them.' He realised his words had been lost behind a wall of noise and confusion. In a louder, more staccato voice, he repeated: 'Swinton, Birch and Peters! Report to Sergeant Hill. We don't have much time. Take everything the Huns have.' Another troop of tanks crashed past. The lieutenant was hardly visible through the mist and smoke. He bellowed, 'The rest of you men stay here and wait for me to return.'

Frank and his two comrades positioned themselves beside a makeshift trestle table and waited for the disarmed Germans to be pushed into place. Without instructions, the prisoners appeared to know what was required of them and immediately emptied their pockets of letters, photographs, handdrawn maps, sketches, watches, service books, lockets and other mementos from home.

From behind, an officer yelled, 'Come on, you dirty Huns! Hand it all over. Schnell! Schnell!'

The prisoners saw another line of tanks bob up and down as they lurched toward the fray. They panicked at the grinding sound coming from the black beasts and fumbled with their belongings. Some dropped to the ground.

'Pick it up, you dirty Huns!'

Frank heard muffled orders coming from every direction as the officers and sergeants paced up and down, cursed and yelled. He sensed they were under immense pressure and that some were failing to cope. He looked up at the face of his first prisoner but only recognised the defiant expression of a brute caught in a trap. Frank flinched. The face was plastered with weeks of grime. The only distinctive feature was the prisoner's bloodshot eyes that stared back at him. At that moment, Frank had an urge to lean over and punch the face, a symbolic act to punish the German Army for the misery and hurt it had caused, but the frantic hollering from behind him brought him back to his task. He gathered his first booty and, as Sergeant Hill passed by, dropped it into the collection box before dismissing the first German with a flick of the wrist.

The next prisoner was shoved forward. This time, Frank was taken aback when he saw a relatively cleaner face with full rosy cheeks and a submissive expression.

Obediently, the prisoner started to empty his pockets. He looked up and surprised Frank with, 'Mein Name ist Otto.'

Frank looked into the prisoner's tear-filled eyes. He did not see fear or hate in them, just sadness. Images of John and the German immigrants tending their fields in Bismarck flashed before him.

'Sind Sie Australier?'

Frank thought the question was audacious and that the prisoner was trying to disarm him with words. *I know how to fool you, mate!* 'No, mate. I'm Tasmanian.'

The ploy failed. Instead of silencing the prisoner, it encouraged him. Frank was astounded when he heard, 'Ach, Tasmanien. Ja. Ja. Ich kenne—I know Tasmanien.' The prisoner had pushed out the words. They were said in panic, or perhaps relief. Frank saw the prisoner start to tremble. 'I know

Bismarck in Tasmanien. Mein Bruder—my brother, Wolf. Er sprach von dem Ort Bismarck!'

With his rudimentary German, Frank grasped the meaning of the words, and it completely baffled him. He felt everything around him slow down. The horrible sounds of the fighting disappeared into the background. 'You know Bismarck? In Tasmania?'

Privates Birch and Peters flashed each other a worried look.

'Ja! Bismarck. In Tasmanien.'

'You know my mate, John?' Immediately, Frank felt foolish. He realised his question was illogical. But the mention of John's hometown had confused him.

Otto frowned. He had not understood. The prisoner to his right became uneasy and whispered something cautionary.

The words of warning came too late. A roar exploded from behind. An enraged Sergeant Hill barked: 'What the hell are you doing, soldier! You're not here to fall in love with a Hun, you bloody idiot. Now, finish the job!'

It was Otto who reacted first. He dipped his head. He realised the yelling resulted from his interchange with the nervous, yet seemingly compassionate Tasmanian.

'Come on, mate. Hand it all over,' whispered Frank.

Otto complied, then reached into his tunic breast pocket. He touched the letter from the father and quickly withdrew his hand for fear of surrendering his last precious memento from home. In his mind, he saw an image of his younger brother, Wolf, lying dead beside a small French village. His tears fell.

'Come on, mate. Give it to me.'

Wiping away his tears, Otto produced the letter. Both men took hold of it and briefly exchanged knowing looks. Otto's hand trembled. 'Von meinem Vater.'

'From your father?'

'Yes, von meinem—from my father.'

Otto released his hold. The letter was exchanged. For a moment, it seemed everything around them had now come to a standstill. Frank heard nothing. He thought of his own treasured letters and looked up at this so-called barbarian Hun who seemed to know something about Tasmania and John's Bismarck.

Otto took a gamble. 'Mein Bruder ist tot.' Desperately trying to hold back more tears, he tried again, in English. 'My brother Wolf... he is dead.'

Frank was moved.

The officer witnessed the further exchange and ordered Sergeant Hill to take immediate action. Frank felt the rush of swearing and waving of arms approach him even before the furious sergeant reached the trestle table and nearly upended it. 'Enough, you bloody fool! Drop everything into the box. Now!'

The sound of an almighty blast, far closer than anyone could have expected, roared through the dissipating fog and made everyone and everything shake. Frank was startled by the force of the sound, and the letter fell to the dirt.

As he was led away, Otto turned and gave Frank a nod. The gesture left Frank with an unwanted image of the enemy, the demon, transformed into a vulnerable human being.

'Fall in!'

Frank swivelled and noticed the letter at his feet. He scrambled to retrieve it from the dirt and ash. He was unsure of protocol and searched for Sergeant Hill, in vain. He heard a second order to fall in. Without further thought, he placed the letter into his breast pocket.

Over the next few days, Frank witnessed the processing of over a thousand German prisoners, most looking exhausted and miserable. The prisoners were corralled for a photograph, presumably to be sent around the world as propaganda for the current Allied victories. Frank suspected the prisoner who had given him the letter would be amongst them. His face recorded for history. The prisoner's name eluded him. He took out the letter and looked at its contents for the first time. He saw the name Otto. Yes! That was it!

Frank choked and gasped. At the top of the letter he recognised the place name Cleve. A voice in his head shrieked, John Bloom's parents come from Cleve! Bloom's parents are Huns!

Confused and shaken, Frank tried to reach deep into his mind for logic, but a sharp pain ripped through his head and his entire body felt heavy. He read the letter again, desperate to find a surname. Was this Otto also called Bloom? No! It would be Blume.

Frank's mind raced and thumped. He started to feel infuriated by the prisoner's apparent trickery. How dare he try to trap me with his English! He deciphered some other names, but the German script infuriated him further. He heard a voice break through. All Huns are your enemy, Private Swinton. Don't you forget that!

He shook his head and shoved the letter back into his pocket.

Within a week, dirty and tired from the constant fighting and dodging German aerial bombing, the men of the 40th reached Warfusée, just east of Villers-Bretonneux, where they bivouacked amongst the numerous abandoned enemy foxholes scattered about the village.

During a lull in the shelling, Frank finally had an opportunity to approach his platoon commander.

'Sit down, Swinton,' invited Lieutenant Brown with his customary reassuring smile. 'What's so important for you to leave your mates and seek out a stuffy old officer like me?'

'I don't know what to do about this letter, Sir. It's followed me into battle since the morning of the big stunt. It's German, so I want to be rid of it.'

'I'm not sure I understand.'

'It should have gone to the command post with all the other items we frisked from the Germans. I made a mistake and this letter got left behind and… and… then, with all the fighting, I… I… well, I didn't have time to worry about it… until now, Sir.'

'Again, I'm not sure why you think there's a problem, Swinton.'

'I should not have kept it, Sir. The letter was part of the intelligence gathering and…'

The lieutenant smiled and tried to settle Frank's unease with a tongue-in-cheek response. 'Well, Private Swinton, let's think about this for a moment. After our gains at Amiens, and now that we're eyeing off a final crack at the Hindenburg Line, I don't think your German letter is going to interest the powers that be, or win us the war.'

'I suppose not, Sir.'

'Just keep it as a souvenir.'

'No! I don't want it. I don't want the filthy letter.' Frank lowered his head, but his voice was still fierce. 'I hate the Germans. I've had enough of the lot of them!'

Lieutenant Brown was unprepared for such an outburst. Recalling Frank's close friendship with John Bloom, he felt such a hostile remark, even in the arena of war, was out of character. He became concerned and tried to make light of it. 'Calm yourself, man. Now, listen to me, I'm sure I can get someone to translate this damned letter of yours. If there's nothing of use in it, then I will stand by you when you're court-martialled for withholding information. But, if we find the letter contains vital information that can single-handedly end this war, once and for all, then I'll stand beside you in London when the king pins a medal to your chest. How does that sound?'

Frank recognised the carefree Tasmanian humour. He missed it, but was unable to smile.

'Now, Swinton. You say you got it on the morning of the stunt, the 8th of August, yes?'

'Correct, Sir.' He attempted, unconvincingly, to describe how this prisoner seemed to have some connection to Tasmania, with John and Bismarck, but backed off when he saw Lieutenant Brown's incredulous expression. 'With all the noise coming from the stunt, I dropped it, Sir. And then... and then... it was too late to...'

'Calm yourself, Swinton.'

'Sorry, Sir. It's been a tough few days. I don't want this rotten letter in my pocket anymore. It's given me headaches.'

'Have you seen the medics?'

'No. There's no need if I can get rid of it.'

'Well, let's hope you're right.' Lieutenant Brown considered his next move. 'Hand it over. Let's see what's causing you so much grief.' The lieutenant took a cursory glance at the handwriting, then looked up. He still detected resentment and scorn on Frank's face, a complete contrast to the once likeable joker of the platoon. He was alarmed by Frank's agitation over a seemingly innocuous German letter and his veiled attacks on John Bloom's character. He took a risk. 'Have you heard from Private Bloom lately?'

Silence, a cough, and then a gruff, 'No!'

The lieutenant pressed no further. 'Okay, Swinton. I think it's time you get back to your mates and enjoy the rest period while you still can. Forget this letter and tell a few of your jokes. That's an order!'

Later that night, Lieutenant Brown looked over the letter and, due to his limited German, found it mostly an indiscernible scribble. The town of Cleve, and its connection to the infamous King Henry VIII caught his attention. He made out four names—Helga, Otto, Ernst and Wolf. He speculated they were siblings and wondered if the letter was full of hope and bright news until he picked out a passage citing the name Lieutenant Preiser, a rank that could indicate unhappier content. He detected nothing that might relate to John, or his name Bloom, and chose to disregard Frank's ramblings. After a while, he dismissed the letter as having little value other than a memento from the war. On the margin of the letter, he wrote an inscription based on what Frank had told him.

Lieutenant Brown sighed as he folded the letter and placed it between the pages of his field diary. I have my own letters to write, he thought. Sad letters to loved ones back home about their fallen sons, brothers and husbands.

He raised his head, looked beyond the encampment and pondered whether his German counterpart, Lieutenant Preiser, was undertaking the same dreaded task, somewhere else out on the Somme…

By September, the Germans had retreated back to the Hindenburg Line and it was not long before the Allies cut a swathe through their defences. News of the Bulgarian and Turkish surrenders, combined with further victories on the sports fields and the issue of winter clothing, lifted the battalion's morale.

Frank briefly allowed himself to feel some semblance of relief that he could soon be home, but Germany's capitulation failed to ignite the same level of jubilation he saw on the faces of his comrades. He was horrified by a rumour that his battalion could be deployed to garrison Germany once victory was declared. He simply wished to return to his family. The uncertainty caused his moods to fluctuate, as if he were a capsized boat at the mercy of the wind and swell.

A few weeks later, whilst he gazed at his trembling hand, Frank heard his lieutenant call: 'Cheer up, Swinton. We're not off to garrison Germany after all. We're off to the city of love instead. Paris!'

Chapter 13

1919
The German Soldiers Return Home

'Papa! Wheel me back a few paces so Herr Deppner can see me.'

The neighbours had gathered for the first time since Johannes Graf's discharge from the military hospital. As Hermann Deppner craned his neck to see the wounded Johannes over the top of the gate, his wife Martha approached the pitiful scene. Through the gaps in the gate, she caught a glimpse of Johannes in a wheelchair, the fresh white bandages a stark reminder of his recent leg amputation.

Johannes had been advised to convalesce in fresh air and sunshine for both his physical and psychological recovery. Most of the returning soldiers were expected to suffer greatly from the effects of trench warfare. New experimental treatments had started to filter out from the major clinics, but as yet, there had been no discussion about the meaning of psychological trauma in the Graf household.

Ordinarily, Martha Deppner would have allowed the men their privacy, but the war had created subtle changes to social norms. She became impatient. 'I'm tired of you stubborn men and your senseless ways. For goodness' sake! Just open the gate!'

'Frau Deppner!'

'Martha!'

Both men were taken aback by Martha's intense glare, but her repeated demand left them little choice but to obey.

'Give the damned thing a good pull from your side, Deppner!'

'Push, Herr Graf!'

Johannes sat patiently, somewhat embarrassed that he was amused by the scene. Martha moved in and seized the top of the gate with both hands. It shifted, and something snapped. Balls of rust and shards of decayed wood fell to the ground. For a moment, the four faced each other from either side of the open space and waited for someone to break the silence. The gate swung back and emitted a squeal.

Johannes waved away the dust. 'Good morning, Frau Deppner.'

'Oh, my dear boy!' The men were unsure of what to do next. Martha took control. 'Hermann! Wheel Johannes inside. Herr Graf—Detlef! Fetch your wife. We are going to sit and talk in the parlour like civilised people, not over fences or through gates! I'm afraid I can only serve tea. The war has taken away many precious things, including our coffee rations.'

'I have freshly ground coffee beans!' declared Herr Graf.

The Deppners exchanged an incredulous look but resisted inquiring how such luxuries could be acquired under occupation.

'Thank you, Detlef. That will be lovely. Now, off you go and fetch Gertrud. I haven't seen her for days.'

Within minutes, Frau Graf arrived with a broad smile and a freshly baked cake. Again, the Deppners exchanged a furtive look but could not disguise their delight at the unexpected treat.

They manoeuvred the wheelchair to the table. At first, Johannes felt the subdued laughter with coffee and cake was absurd in such turbulent times, but he was soon surprised by how quickly the social discomfort of his amputation disappeared behind the veil of conversation. At one time, he had become fearful that his prolonged exposure to men in pain, men who had screamed out from their hospital beds after realising they were missing their wits and limbs, would also blight him irreparably. Yet, in the Deppner's parlour he momentarily forgot his wound as he listened to his parents and neighbours engage in small talk and waited for them to turn their attention on him. Johannes was determined to question anyone who trivialised the impact of the war. His ghastly experiences on the Western Front and his leg amputation were personal reminders of what happens when men from different countries cross borders and oceans to fight each other, and it had made him assertive.

'I'm being sent to Düsseldorf to get fitted with an artificial leg,' he told them. 'The doctors warned us that the sight of returned soldiers who are blind, mad or have missing limbs will become commonplace. I'm among the fortunate. I only lost one leg!'

The other four sat speechless.

It was Johannes' father, Herr Graf, who was first to respond. 'I believe there's been great advances in prosthetics since the… since the…'

'Since the war? Since our defeat, Papa? Yes. Correct.'

'It is such a relief to see you back safely, Johannes.'

'Thank you, Herr Deppner. Please, is there any news of Otto and Ernst?'

'The Red Cross informed us only yesterday that Ernst has been found safe in the East and will return home soon. For an interminable length of time we heard nothing, so this news is such a relief.'

'And our Otto was permitted to write to us from the English internment camp,' added Martha Deppner, gleefully.

'I can't wait to see them both again.' Johannes knew it was going to be difficult to acquaint himself with the notion of two, rather than three, Deppner brothers. 'Mama tells me your Helga is enjoying her time in Aalten.'

He deliberately omitted the name of his sister, Frieda, who had accompanied Helga across the Dutch border. Frieda had recently written to say she had found work in a local newspaper office and wished to remain in Holland. She also spoke of plans to visit England and Johannes was aware his father was troubled by this news.

Martha Deppner was less circumspect. 'Helga writes that she and Frieda love their walks together through the dairy pastures.'

Herr Graf mumbled something under his breath.

Hermann Deppner broke the awkward silence. 'Helga will return home as soon as we feel it is safe for her to do so.'

Johannes understood Germany would need to bear the brunt of retribution for a while, and not only financially. The report that his mother had been viciously whipped by a garrison soldier had filled him with anger for weeks, but he suppressed his lingering resentment in the presence of the Deppners. 'The current hardships will pass. We will learn from our mistakes and rebuild our lives.'

His words surprised and impressed the others.

'You have grown so wise,' said Martha.

His response was equally surprising. 'The wise teacher, Herr Stummhofer, came to visit me in the hospital!'

'This is the first we've heard of this,' whispered his mother.

'Were you in his geography class with… with…?'

'With Wolf and his quartet? Yes, Frau Deppner.'

'What a kind gesture for him to visit you.'

'I told Herr Stummhofer how I had many plans to leave Cleve before the war, to see what the outside world could offer me.' The others dipped their heads, knowing such plans were now unlikely. 'There's something he said to me. It heartened me.' Johannes coughed. His mother feared he was about to weep and placed a gentle hand on his cheek. 'Herr Stummhofer said the way to see the world is not by travel, but by the honour and adventure of teaching others about it.'

The four looked at each other and took a moment to consider Herr Stummhofer's insightful words. They recalled their own sense of adventure when younger. The Deppners reminisced about their bold move to Cleve and how their children revelled in their new surroundings. Frau Graf reflected on her visits to England and the help she received from her aunts and cousins to improve her English; and Herr Graf contemplated the impact of his father's strict discipline that smothered any chance of boyish adventure.

'I will enrol at the Teacher Training College as soon as I have the strength.'

'Oh, my dear Johannes!'

'What wonderful news!'

'My hat goes off to Herr Stummhofer!'

'Papa?'

Herr Graf checked himself. Ordinarily, he would have bellowed 'Nonsense!' to such trivial ambitions, but, on this occasion, he felt strangely comforted by Johannes' declaration. 'I am glad to hear you are looking to the future, my dear boy.'

Later in private, he would confess, 'My dear Johannes, what this awful war has taught me is that one's life and fortunes are sometimes at the whim of fate, something that I have never contemplated, or indeed, experienced until now. I want you to know your plan to become a teacher is well received. Of course, I had expected you to work for me, ever since you were a boy, but this new development cannot make me happier at a time when our country and our lives are in turmoil. I am very proud of you, my son.'

'Herr Stummhofer also told me he paid visits to all the wounded of Cleve, and to the parents of the fallen or missing. He said the visit to Bruno's parents was particularly distressing.'

It was reported, Herr Stummhofer had flinched at Frau Klug's screams of anguish: 'What on earth do the words 'missing in action' mean to a mother? No! No! No! Unless someone shows me the body of my beloved Bruno, I refuse to believe he is gone or entertain the notion of a sham funeral.'

Johannes turned to face the Deppners. 'My dear Herr and Frau Deppner, I expect the visit Herr Stummhofer paid you would have been as equally difficult.'

Wolf's parents both let out a whimper.

'I cannot imagine the grief you feel for the loss of your precious Wolf,' continued Johannes. 'If I am to be honest, I admit that I never had much time for his quartet. I was jealous of their close friendship. But now, to know that it no longer exists, with the loss of Wolf and Bruno, is incredibly difficult to accept.'

Johannes reported that Herr Stummhofer had recently encountered Felix Wittmann on the street:

Standing alone, looking dazed and disoriented, Felix had escaped a meeting with Lina's family to finalise the wedding plans. He needed a quiet place, but froze in his tracks, unsure of his whereabouts. 'I lost them, Herr Stummhofer. I left Bruno and Wolf behind in France. I couldn't save them.'

Herr Stummhofer had been alarmed at the sight of Felix in such distress. 'Wittmann! You must shake such guilt.' The teacher disregarded convention and immediately took hold of the tormented soldier. Onlookers passed by without curiosity. The citizens of Cleve had become accustomed to seeing young men with vacant stares, sobbing or learning how to walk with a crutch. 'The war has claimed too many victims, Wittmann. I'm devastated the quartet did not survive the war, but I cannot ignore the joy of seeing you back, safe and well.'

At first, Felix had struggled to find comfort in Herr Stummhofer's words. The bleakness of the war flooded his mind. He could still feel Wolf's agonised face turn cold in his hands as if it were yesterday. He recalled the sorrow and sobbing over Lieutenant Preiser's death. And Erich's screams still reverberated in his head: Where's Bruno?! I can't find Bruno!

Felix and Erich had woken in the middle of the night to find Bruno had inexplicably vanished. The sight of his rifle left behind, leaning against the sodden wall of the trench, was an ominous sign that Bruno's grief had smothered him far more than anyone had realised. They raced against time to find him, frantically searching bomb craters and turning over corpses grotesquely draped over barbed wire, before they heard the dreadful, ill-timed command: 'We cannot search for Private Klug any longer. Fall in!'

Felix sensed Herr Stummhofer was trying to rescue him from the turmoil in his head. He detected the faint sound of Herr Stummhofer's words, but Erich's awful screams grew louder: No, Felix! Damn it! We are not leaving until we find Bruno! With tears streaming down their faces, the two were manhandled back into line, their shattered world growing more intolerable with the loss of another friend and the looming German defeat.

Herr Stummhofer heard Felix moan more than once, 'Oh, Bruno. Oh, Wolf', and understood that for many years to come, demons would haunt the soldiers who had survived the war.

'My dear boy,' he said, 'you must keep looking to the future and your family for solace.'

Felix wept. 'I've lost Erich too. He's taken off to the Eifel, to his uncle's house in Heimbach. Lina and I want him to come to our wedding but he won't answer my letters.'

Herr Stummhofer considered his response carefully. 'My dear Felix, I also grieve for Bruno and Wolf, but you must not carry this extra burden of Erich's departure.'

Never before had the teacher used the Christian names of the quartet, but on this occasion he had felt the need to rescue Felix with familiarity and gentleness. Felix always believed his teacher had favoured the others, yet the mention of their names reassured and comforted him.

'It will take time, Felix. Your dear Erich Wiese is damaged. You are a painful reminder of happier times.' He gripped Felix by the shoulders and summoned his full attention. 'You will need to forgive this war for robbing you of your friends. I know you have the strength to do this, Felix. Now, go to your Lina and make your plans for the future.'

He farewelled Felix with a reassuring handshake and a request for a wedding invitation…

As beams of sunlight inched their way into the Deppners' parlour, Wolf's father recalled his own meeting with the troubled Felix Wittmann:

'I'm so sorry, Herr Deppner. I vowed to keep your Wolf safe, but I failed. We buried him near a small French village, beside a brook.' Felix sobbed uncontrollably. 'Then… Lieutenant Preiser got killed and… and… Bruno went missing. Herr Deppner, it's just too much to bear…'

Hermann's mind wandered further back to the moment he had arrived in Dinslaken with a heavy heart to offer his condolences to Lieutenant Preiser's grieving widow:

'Frau Preiser?'

'Yes…'

'Wife of Lieutenant Preiser from Reserve Infantry Regiment 273?'

Rosa steadied herself against the doorframe. 'Yes, I'm Frau Preiser, but I'm sorry to say my husband is…'

'Please forgive my intrusion. My name is Hermann Deppner, from Cleve. My son, Wolfgang, also served with RIR 273. Your husband wrote to me about my son's death, only a few days before he also, sadly… I'm here to offer my sincere condolences for your loss.'

Hermann paused, twisting his hat in his hands. He tried to hold back his tears, realising his pent-up emotions over Wolf's death were eager to escape and likely to hinder his prepared speech. The sight of the distressed widow had unnerved him.

'Oh, Frau Preiser, this war…'

'How terribly impolite of me, Herr Deppner. Please, do come in.' A small child crawled between them. 'Andreas, my darling, this is Herr Deppner.' She feigned a smile and toyed with her hair. 'He's not walking or talking yet.' As tears rolled down her cheeks, she explained how the lieutenant had died without knowing he had a son.

Rosa produced her unopened letter, returned by the war ministry, but it was too much for Hermann to bear. He apologised for his abrupt departure and left the distraught widow in search of a safe place to sit and weep in private, to remember his Wolf…

The Deppner's parlour was now filled with sunlight.

Johannes spoke of his regret in not seeing Erich Wiese before he had departed for Heimbach. 'I hope Erich also has the inner strength to fight against the horrors of the war.'

Frau Graf was also reflective. She let her mind return to 1914, to the image of her daughter, Frieda, covertly holding Erich Wiese's hand during the soldiers' farewell in the courtyard. She felt such pity for the Wiese boy and was uncomfortable whenever she passed his parents in the street. But her daughter was not yet ready to see her own destiny as a dutiful wife and mother.

Herr Graf spoke about releasing Felix Wittmann from his foundry. Bruno's uncle had offered Felix a secure position at Klugshof Brewery, to start when he regained his strength and wits. 'Wittmann was one of my best workers before the war, but I don't begrudge him replacing Bruno Klug. The town brewer has weathered the storm well and fortunately remained untouched by this damned foreign takeover!'

Herr Graf's humiliation was well known. His foundry had been acquisitioned under the rules of post-war occupation and he had been effectively relegated to a position of office boy, often forced to deliver any profits to designated banks for war reparations. With foresight, Herr Graf had destroyed any ledgers or documents pertaining to his war-time contracts before they could be confiscated and scrutinised. Reports of the arrests and interrogations of less astute business men from neighbouring cities had filtered through. Herr Graf had resigned himself to being patient. He believed the dishonour in losing governance of his foundry was temporary and that he would reclaim it, and his wealth, once Germany was freed from its shackles of guilt.

'Cleve waits for the day when you can regain your rightful position, Papa.'

Herr Graf grunted and coughed. 'Huh! Those imbeciles who have taken over my company know nothing about the metal industry, let alone bookkeeping. In their wisdom, they have sacked my accountant and are running the place at a loss. I suggested they focus their efforts on potential post-war contracts, but they refused to listen!'

'What a frustrating situation for you, Detlef,' said Martha Deppner, unconcerned she had broken with convention and engaged in matters of politics. She knew all businesses were struggling under the burden of occupation and reparation. 'I'm sure our new Weimar government will eventually put an end to the chaos.'

The five sat quietly and contemplated their futures in a new Germany with its shifting politics, relinquished territories and redefined borders.

Johannes checked himself. He still felt phantom sensations of his missing limb and was impatient to adjust to its absence...

'Enough of this solemn mood!' demanded Frau Graf, her frame silhouetted by an intense beam of light streaming in from the window behind her. 'The war has covered our streets in misery for far too long.'

She was determined to steer the conversation to brighter paths. She looked over to Martha Deppner, who nodded in agreement. Frau Graf had feared it would take much longer to see happiness on the face of her broken son, but was encouraged when Johannes returned her smile.

'I want to talk about happier things and happier times. I want to hear more about Frieda and Helga's life on the dairy farm. Detlef! We must visit our Frieda. I've never been across the border and I miss her dearly.'

It was Martha Deppner who replied. 'Oh, what a wonderful idea, Gertrud. We shall all go. Even you, Johannes! You will adore my cousin. She writes and tells me how much she treasures the company of Helga and Frieda.'

Frau Graf sighed. The thought of travel was delightful, but she was not finished with her plea for happiness. 'I'm going to plant roses in the courtyard again. I miss them.' She turned to face her neighbours. Tears welled up in her eyes. 'I'm going to plant a rose in honour of your Wolf.' She was encouraged by the eager faces looking back at her, urging her to continue. 'I want to visit Bruno's parents and offer my condolences. Martha and I will meet and plan gifts for Felix and Lina's wedding. I want my darling Johannes to tell us more about how the doctors are going to mend his broken body and how he is going to rebuild his life as a teacher.' She paused and took a breath. She waited until all eyes were upon her.

'I want happiness to return to Cleve!'

Chapter 14

2018. October
Tasmania

'How do the Germans say 'idiot', Conrad?'

'Like that, but with the sound of 'yacht' at the end—like 'idi-yacht'. They also say 'Dummkopf'. Why do you ask, Baz?'

The other crew members, Martin and Chris, grinned at each other in anticipation of their Captain's response.

'Because you're a… Dummkopf! To think for months on end we had to suffer all your ramblings about trying to find the Deppner family when, instead, all you had to do was google Wolf's name. When you finally met up with the Deppners, I bet they said you were a Dummkopf!'

After returning from Europe, Conrad had been eager to get back onboard Focus and give his crew a full report of his travels. Rehearsals for his string quartet were stalling as Fraser, the viola player, was still busy with his study and yet to confirm a return date—'See, I told you the rot would set in,' was his quartet leader's response.

Coupled with that, Conrad was yet to register for a Waratah bushwalk. He had hoped the fresh air on the river would ease his frustration.

'Yep, I agree. I'm a Dummkopf. Don't worry, I've copped it from everyone.'

'We know. According to your wife, it was all such a waste of your time when you could have been doing jobs around the house instead!' taunted Baz.

So far the race had been uneventful and, as Focus reached upriver to the first marker, the sounds of frivolity and laughter coming from its deck aroused curiosity from nearby crews.

As they settled into a north-westerly breeze and maintained a reasonable distance behind the forward fleet, Conrad took photos of the white sails ahead of them, spectacularly swaying on the river.

Baz predicted the wind would freshen once they made the turn and knew Focus would respond well with the extra speed. 'We'll try and keep up with Tin Shed, just ahead of us, then I'll pass it at the marker. So Conrad, we'll be on this reach for a while. Here's your chance to talk about your trip.'

'Where do I start?'

'Well, we got all the emails about France and Belgium; the big sob story about missing out on a Beethoven concert; staying with your pen pal and his family who live not far from the Swiss and French borders, the one who sings in a choir and took you along to a rehearsal; and seeing Gretel's relatives in Stuttgart. Oh, and the trip to your mother-in-law's old house in Czechoslovakia.'

'Glad to hear you read all my emails,' smiled Conrad.

Chris piped in, 'And we got the thousands of photos from Malta!'

'Just tell us about your friends in Heimbach and the visit with the Deppners. That should see us through this leg!'

'Heimbach was great. We visited Anke's parents and gave them a garden concert on the violin and viola. Here, take a look, Baz. I've got some videos of it...'

'Ah, maybe next time, Conrad. I don't want to take my eye off Tin Shed.'

'We did some delightful walks along the banks of Heimbach's river and, on the last day, Anke and Pascal took us to a place called Ordensburg Vogelsang.'

'Geez, that's a mouthful!'

'It's an old Nazi training school in the foothills of the Eifel National Park. The place is now a museum.'

'Well, I bet that was riveting.'

'I found it interesting, Baz, but war museums and stuff aren't Gretel's cup of tea, and Anke got a bit overwhelmed by it all. But I can see why the Nazis built the thing up there. The views are amazing. It makes you feel like you're on top of the world. Invincible.'

The sun's rays warmed the cockpit as Conrad recounted his meeting with the Deppners—'What? They greeted you at the train station waving the Tassie flag!'—He held their attention with descriptions of nausea from overindulgence on cake, excitement at looking over the artefacts from the suitcase of treasures. He mentioned Wolf and his friends had been known as the quartet.

Martin was intrigued. 'What, like your string group?'

'Who knows? It's not the first time I've heard of soldiers forming a string quartet in the First World War! But it could have been just a pet name. Bit of a mystery, really. There's nothing in diaries about Wolf and his mates playing music together, and no photos to back it up.' Conrad explained how Stefan Busch planned to do more research on the fate of his grandfather, Otto Deppner. 'This Stefan bloke seems more tenacious than me!'

'I doubt that!' mocked Baz.

'Stefan's meeting some war expert in Licy-Clignon and Bussiares.'

'Been practising your French, Conrad!'

'Yes, Baz! Anyway, they are going to look at the place where Wolf got killed, then they're heading off to Amiens. And while Stefan's off visiting France, good old Franz Deppner asked me to search for the Tassie soldier who brought the letter back with him.'

'Really?' This time Baz was intrigued. 'How're you going to do that?'

'To be frank, I haven't put my mind to it yet.'

'I doubt that!'

'Too busy trying to organise my own quartet. We've had another invitation from the retirement village, but our violist is too busy at the moment, so that's on hold.'

Baz put on his official skipper's voice. 'Looks like your time's up, Conrad. The lead boats have rounded the marker. They've got a good tailwind for goosewinging. Might pay us to get our pole set up before the turn. You okay with that, Martin?'

'Aye, aye, Captain.'

'By the way, Conrad. Did you find out if the Germans use the term goosewing?'

'They say 'Schmetterling' instead. It means butterfly.'

'Well, that makes sense. With the boom out one side and the headsail spread out on the other, then yes, I suppose that would look more like a butterfly.'

Martin added, 'The Germans have a beautiful butterfly and we have an ugly goose!'

'I think that's the most intelligent thing you've said for quite some time. Now, head up to the bow, my little… butterfly and get our… goosewing ready. Chris, give him a hand.'

After a few moments, Baz turned to Conrad. 'All jokes aside, Conrad. I think you've done a great job with all this war letter stuff. We're all proud of you.'

'Thanks, Captain.'

'It must have been good to finally meet the Deppners.'

'Yep.'

The reason Baz wanted a private word was revealed. 'By the way, how's your neighbour, Wally, coping after all that shit in Melbourne?'

'Oh, you saw his son on TV too.'

Days earlier, Conrad and Gretel had sat watching a news report in disbelief. A right-wing rally, reinforced with an unmistakable band of neo-Nazis, had taken place on the streets of Melbourne. While Conrad questioned the legitimacy of such rallies in Australia, Gretel put her hand to her mouth in shock at the sight of Wally's son, Andrew Archer, looking dishevelled, crazed-eyed and inexplicably giving a Nazi salute. Stunned by the footage, they sat in a daze for a few minutes before racing next door to offer Wally and Patricia support.

'Crazy stuff, Conrad. Is Wally okay now?'

'Not sure, Baz. He and Patricia took off to Melbourne on the ferry. We're still waiting to hear from them.'

'I know Wally would have raised his boy to be respectful. All this neo-Nazi shit just doesn't make any sense.'

'I can't work it out either. Wally knew something was up, but you just don't expect that Nazi shit to happen here in Australia.'

Conrad immediately thought his statement was naïve, given the worldwide rise in right-wing ideology. He reflected for a few moments and his mind returned to visiting the former elite training school on the edge of the Eifel Forest, with its remaining buildings exhibiting the short-lived attempt at Nazi glorification and superiority. He recalled posing for a photo as foreground to a colossal statue of a Teutonic torch bearer. When he had looked at the photo afterwards, Conrad saw himself dwarfed by the statue's height and symbolism. The strange reaction he felt from seeing the ostentation of the former training facility, juxtaposed with the beauty of the landscape, had stayed with him for days…

'Okay, you two butterflies! Leave the… Schmetterling pole where it is for now and come back until we round the marker.'

With metres to go before they made the turn, the crew took a few more moments to relax.

Baz reported, 'By the way, Conrad, while you were in Europe, Martin and Chris took me to on my first overnight walk, to Lake Rhona.'

'Ah, nice. Did you get to pitch your tents beside the lake on the quartz sand?'

'Yep. But I'm telling you, Martin's idea of only one tent between the three of us wasn't one of his brightest. Hey! Are you two… butterflies still walking the Overland Track next year?'

'Yes! We should all do it!' suggested Martin, unable to contain his excitement.

The others took a moment to consider the proposal, then nodded in agreement. Baz complimented Martin on his second intelligent comment of the race, but clarified that he would only consider the five-day trek across the world-renown Overland if they took an appropriate number of tents. Baz had accepted that joining the Waratah Bushwalking Club had opened up trekking opportunities that he never knew existed, extra experiences that he could enjoy with his crew.

Focus edged closer to Tin Shed with another boat, White Fang, a larger yacht with a sleek hull, just in its wake. The three boats glided around the marker almost neck and neck, with Focus flanked by the other two. They straighten up.

'May the best boat win!' called Captain Baz, grinning and bracing himself against the wheel, leaning forward as if he were readying himself for a sprint. His crew was somewhat surprised to see a rare boyish side to their skipper and smiled at each other. 'Back up to the bow, Martin,' he ordered. 'It's time for you to do your real butterfly act.'

After the turn, Conrad took a photo of Mount Wellington and noticed feathery white clouds were dancing over its summit. He recalled his delight when the Aboriginal language name, kunanyi, had been added to its title under the dual naming policy. The angle of the mountain from the river allowed Conrad to trace some of his favourite tracks along its slopes and up to the summit. He marvelled at how the profile of kunanyi/Mount Wellington could change depending on the multitude of vantage points around Hobart. As Focus made ground on the lead boats, the breeze on his face was calming…

'Shit! Baz! Look out!'

'Shit!'

Tin Shed had made a sharp turn to port, which caused its rigging to bounce and thump violently. The whip-cracks of its flapping sails were louder than anyone could have expected. Pressure on the rudder had snapped the steering cable and its skipper lost control. Desperate screams came from its crew as they attempted to drop the sails before a split-second decision was made to cut the lines. The sails were released and flailed wildly, like the tentacles of an enraged sea creature emitting an intimidating growl.

Baz realised there was no time to take evasive action. 'Grab hold of something!'

The horrendous sound of splintering fiberglass seemed more powerful than the collision. Tin Shed rammed the mid-starboard hull and forced Focus to lift out of the water. Conrad tried to break his fall as he flew to portside. Chris could not catch him. Baz gripped the wheel and desperately searched for Martin who had disappeared behind Tin Shed's collapsing sails.

Over the radio: 'White Fang to box… White Fang to box… Emergency call… Collision mid-river… Rescue boat needed… Over.'

Baz regained his balance and snapped into action. 'Get up there, Chris! Find Martin and drop the mainsail.' He saw Conrad cradling his left arm. 'Is it broken?'

'Maybe. I don't feel too good.'

'Just sit there and don't move.' Baz frantically tried to keep control at the helm but Focus was now at the mercy of the offending boat, the wind and the swell. 'Chris! Get Martin back here and start the engine!'

The sound of yelling and swearing from Tin Shed's crew reverberated across the water's surface. There was a second emergency call from another boat as Focus and Tin Shed were forced side by side and alternately bobbed up and down with the swell. The sound of their hulls screeching and jarring against each other added to the distress.

'Shit, Baz. I'm so sorry,' yelled Tin Shed's skipper. 'I lost steering. Are you taking on water?'

'Not sure.'

Martin rocked back and forth in the cockpit. He looked in shock.

Chris yelled from below. 'Baz! The engine won't start!'

'Leave it!'

'Baz! There's water down here.'

'Shit!'

Martin vomited over the side. 'I'm sorry, Baz.'

'It's okay, mate. We'll get you off soon.'

White Fang had dropped its sails and was now under motor, circling in anticipation of further assistance. Its skipper called, 'Rescue boat's on its way. Anyone hurt?'

'We're all okay on Tin Shed.'

'Not good here. And we're taking on water.' Baz quit the helm, joined the others in the cockpit, lowered his head and uttered a succession of expletives to himself.

Chris moved closer beside Martin and whispered assurances to him.

Conrad cradled his arm a little tighter and moaned in pain.

The four sat motionless and waited. The sounds of the scraping hulls, concerned radio transmissions and nearby crews scampering around their decks, their only distractions…

※

After Conrad and Martin were transferred to the safely of the rescue boat, Captain Baz and Chris clambered aboard Tin Shed.

Baz noticed White Fang was still circling, not ready to give up offering support until everyone was safe. He felt strangely comforted by a flash of White Fang's hull raised slightly out of the water on a turn, the angle of sun's rays giving it a spotless, sparkling appearance. He gave Conrad and Martin a reassuring nod before the rescue boat motored off.

On the way to the marina, a large swell caused Conrad to suffer a severe wave of pain. He closed his eyes and contemplated the impact of a broken arm. He knew his inner voice was eager to make comment and invited it to do so. Come on, then! Say it!

That's the end of your Sage String Quartet, Bentley!

Chapter 15

1918
A Tasmanian Soldier Longs for Home

'Private Swinton!'

Frank turned and saw his lieutenant hastily bidding farewell to fellow officers and summoning his attention as he crossed the bustling street.

Lieutenant Brown had noticed Frank staring into the River Seine and speculated he was also feeling similar disappointment that the river running through the French capital lacked the colour and breadth of their Derwent River back home.

Frank had accompanied his comrades through the streets of Paris, but the friendly revellers and spectacle of the King of Belgium's visit failed to lift his mood. He was now alone on the river bank, morose and lamenting his former self.

'Good to see you, Swinton! Did you get a glimpse of the king?'

'Yes Sir.'

'The Parisians put on a splendid parade for him, didn't they Swinton?'

'Yes Sir.'

The officer looked at him closer. 'What's all this, Swinton? I saw you staring into the river, looking all glum. Why aren't you off with your mates, drinking the wine and dancing with the pretty French girls?'

'I only dance with my Daisy back home, Sir.'

'Of course, of course. I understand. But cheer up, man. The war is over and you'll be home soon enough.' Lieutenant Brown was concerned that Frank's depressive mood had not improved with the signing of the armistice. 'My God, it's so cold out here. Come on, Swinton. Let me shout you a coffee. Or even better, a beer!' He ushered Frank into a nearby café...

As he looked up from reading the menu, the lieutenant noticed Frank's mind was elsewhere and tried desperately to bring him back. The short supply of coal throughout Europe made heating difficult and, even amongst the horde of happy patrons, laughing and chinking their glasses, the interior of the café remained chilled. He shivered and noticed Frank was lightly dressed and appeared oblivious to the temperature. 'Aren't you cold, Swinton?'

'No Sir.'

'Well, I suppose Tasmanians are raised to be tough, eh?'

'Yes Sir.'

'What are you planning to do in Paris, Swinton?'

'Not much, Sir.'

Impatience forced the officer to harsher measures. 'Have you heard from your good mate, Private Bloom?'

There was a brief silence. 'No!'

'Why not, Swinton?'

'We don't write to each other, Sir.'

'That makes no sense to me.'

Frank looked up. His eyes were bloodshot, and his mouth was quivering. His words spilled out. 'He's German, Sir.'

'What? What the hell are you talking about, Swinton? Bloom's not a German, you silly fool. He was born in Hobart!' The lieutenant attempted a laugh and tried to make light of the remark, but inwardly he was shaken. Like most of his men, he knew Frank suffered bad nerves, but it alarmed him to see that Frank's fragile grip on reality appeared all but lost. He panicked at what he could do. He felt his mind was racing against time. In a softer voice, the lieutenant used Christian names in the hope it would soothe and rescue. 'Frank, please listen to me. John was born and raised in Hobart. You know that.'

It failed. 'That may be so, Sir, but Bloom is not the man he once seemed.' Frank shook and stuttered. 'I've watched John very… I watched Bloom closely since we got over here. He changed…' Frank could feel himself falling into a bottomless chasm. Something was squirming inside him. It urged him to continue. 'Bloom is devious. He cannot be trusted.'

'What?'

'Did you read the German letter I gave you, Sir?'

'Yes, well as far as my German can get me.' The lieutenant was bewildered.

Frank dipped his head and mumbled, 'It was written in Cleve. Bloom told me years ago that his parents came from the same place… from Cleve… in Germany… Mrs Bloom's brother is still a teacher there… in Cleve.' Frank rocked in his chair and let out a groan, something that sounded not quite human. 'Bloom's mother writes to her brother all the time, Sir.'

'I'm still not following you, Swinton.'

Through gritted teeth: 'The Hun who gave it to me… the letter… he, he seemed to know them… the Blooms… I think he talked about them… I'm not sure. Yes, he certainly talked about Tasmania and Bismarck… I think he talked about them too. They all come from the same place, Sir. They must know each other.'

The lieutenant became impatient with Frank's illogical rant. 'For goodness' sake, man. What are you—'

'I was there when Bloom enlisted, Sir! I asked him back then, you know, why anyone with German blood would want to join up to fight their own people… I was shocked that Bloom was so keen to join up. It didn't make sense to me.' Frank paused and considered his next words. 'But it makes sense to me now. Bloom didn't enlist for the right reasons… Do you… do you follow my meaning, Sir?'

'No. But I fear you're about to tell me.'

Frank's eyes widened, and he audibly inhaled. The lieutenant held his breath. 'Bloom is a German spy!'

With that, Lieutenant Brown lost his composure. 'That's bloody nonsense, Swinton!' He felt the release of pent up anger hidden deep in the pit of his stomach, likely since the beginning of the war. He thumped the table with both fists. The table lifted and the sound of glasses smashing was as loud as his outburst.

Patrons in earshot ceased conversation and glanced over at the disturbance. The Parisians had become accustomed to the sounds of distant bombing but felt that this new sound of anger was out of place in their now liberated country.

A bold waiter approached them. In broken English: 'Please, my friends. The war is over. No more fighting.' He paused and waited for the two Australian soldiers to look up at him. He smiled. 'Wait one moment. I bring you champagne.'

The lieutenant was tempted to lean over the table and grab hold of Frank, to shake him, but instead whispered, 'Listen, Frank. I don't know what's going on. You've either gone completely mad or you're a bloody fool. Either way, I'm not standing for it.' He inhaled, then let out a loud sigh. 'This war has claimed too many lives, too many good men have died. And for what? For us to turn against each other? For us to go mad and forget our best mates?' The lieutenant's hands shook. He pushed them hard against the tabletop to steady them. He could feel tears building. 'No! I will not allow this! Do you hear me?' He paused. He willed Frank to raise his eyes but realised he needed to try harder. He disregarded the risk of upsetting the other patrons again. 'You listen to me, Frank! You know John Bloom was born in Hobart. You know he's Tassie, through and through. He's loyal, and he is your mate. You know all this. This rubbish about him being a spy is bloody ridiculous and I won't stand for it.' The lieutenant was almost breathless. 'I'm not going to sit back and let you be swallowed up by a war that is now over. No! You must lay down your weapon and be done with it.'

The waiter returned. In a calm voice: 'Please enjoy the champagne and allow it to warm your hearts. We thank you for rescuing our country.'

They drank a whole glass and refilled.

As the champagne flowed through Frank's body, he felt an unfamiliar sensation of warmth. He shivered and realised he had dressed unwisely. He took a deep breath and started to weep. He was unsure of his conflicting thoughts and emotions, but he knew they were raging against each other in his belly. He heard Daisy's voice sing in his head. Come back to me, Frank. I love you.

Lieutenant Brown leaned back in his chair and thought, If I win this last battle and bring Swinton back, such a deed would be far more rewarding than any medal from a king.

'Frank, I want you to listen to me…'

The smiling waiter returned and topped up their glasses. 'Enjoy, my friends.'

'… listen to me carefully. You will write to John, and soon. I am aware he and the other wounded soldiers will be shipped home in the next week or so. You are to forget this rubbish about who is the enemy. You hear? The war has ended and you need to make peace.'

Frank looked up. Tears were now streaming down his cheeks, but neither men were concerned with the inquisitive looks from the other patrons. Frank shook his head in disbelief. Why have I allowed myself to fall so deeply into this pit of anger and misery?

The lieutenant waited. He saw Frank start to return.

Frank sensed a quietening of his thoughts. 'Oh, Sir. I will. Yes, I will. I will write to John.'

'Splendid, Swinton. That's music to my ears.'

Frank's shivering increased. The lieutenant reached over the table and grabbed Frank's hands to steady them.

'Sir, I feel like I've gone mad. I need John beside me. I don't want to go home a madman.'

The lieutenant clutched Frank's hands tighter. 'Calm yourself, Swinton. Everything is going to be fine.'

They sat for a while; heads lowered. The lieutenant allowed himself to relax. He heard Frank mutter John's name to himself more than once. The lieutenant waited…

'Now, Swinton. I understand you don't want to join your mates and go out dancing, even though I reckon it would do you a world of good.'

'But Sir, I—'

'Yes, yes, I know. You only dance with your darling back home. I understand.' The laughter and merriment of the other patrons broke through and reached them. The lieutenant was relieved to see Frank's cold, expressionless face had regained some colour. 'At least take yourself off to the Palace of Versailles. You will see beauty there. It has huge gardens and open spaces. We've been stuck in cramped trenches for too long. It will allow you to feel free.'

'Yes Sir.'

'Those are my orders—write to Bloom and visit the beautiful gardens at Versailles. Understood?'

For the first time in what seemed a lifetime, Frank attempted a smile. 'Understood, Sir.'

'Splendid! Now let's finish this champagne and see if that waiter can find us some decent beer instead. We need to talk about Hobart, Swinton!'

A few days later, with images of the Palace of Versailles fresh in his mind, Frank wrote:

Paris

2nd December 1918

Dear John,

I'm still stuck in France and hope this letter reaches you before you board your ship and head home.

It has been too long since we talked to each other. I miss you, John. I regret finishing this god-awful war without my best mate beside me.

I want to tell you so much, but first I need to confess that I've been such a fool...

Feeling as though he had crawled out from an ocean of despair, Frank celebrated Christmas with a sports afternoon and realised he had not lost his on-field skills to war or a trembling hand. As he kicked the winning goal, he spotted his lieutenant smiling back at him and was warmed by celebratory hugs from his teammates. Happiness returned, marred slightly by the disappointment of receiving no reply from John.

'I reckon you've missed the boat there, Swinton,' was the lieutenant's witty, but helpful reply. 'I think Bloom went home earlier than expected, but it's only one letter. Write to him again and he'll get a splendid surprise when he arrives back in Tassie.'

Frank's mind was suddenly awash with images of Hobart and the smiles from his loved ones. 'Oh, Sir. I can't wait to get home.'

Chapter 16

2018. November
Tasmania

'What's happened?' Gretel had collected Conrad from his German conversation session and was surprised to see his furrowed brow.

'Irene's been diagnosed with pancreatic cancer.' He paused before adding that in true Irene-style, she was putting on a brave face. Conrad recalled his father's battle with cancer and how he had similarly masked the pain and fear with reassuring smiles in the years and moments before his death.

Gretel put her hand to her mouth but failed to smother her gasp. 'That's horrible. Beautiful Irene. How cruel!'

'She's going to have surgery. I think it's called the Whipple Procedure. Anyway, the whole group is devastated. I want to help her as much as I can, but I can't do much with my arm in this bloody sling.'

'Don't be so hard on yourself.' Gretel took hold of him. 'I've got my art class soon, but I can give it a miss if you want me to stay home with you.'

'I'll be fine.'

'Oh, sweetie. This is just awful. I'll get inspired and paint something as a gift for Irene.'

'That's a lovely idea.'

'Are you sure you're okay?'

'Yes, I'm sure. Now drop me home, then go and enjoy yourself. That's an order!'

Ordinarily, before the river accident, Conrad would have lessened the shock of Irene's news with the diversion of violin practice. As a poor substitute, he checked his emails and was pleased to find one had arrived overnight from Willi Deppner. It lightened his mood:

Dear Conrad,

We hope your broken arm is recovering well. We were so entertained by the photos of your grandchildren, all dressed as doctors and nurses and caring for their injured grandfather!

The quartet, as you affectionately call us, gave its presentation on the letter of fate—I've attached our PowerPoint slides.

The presentation lasted close to an hour and was a great success. Many people in the audience are now inspired to check their own family histories from the First World War—to bring the past back to life!

I started off by introducing the empty chair on stage and explained it was such a shame that our Tasmanian friend was unable to join us.

I showed the photo of us during your Duisburg visit and pointed out you, holding the Tasmanian flag, then described your island paradise. The audience was captivated by your latest beach photo.

Piet read out your original email that you sent to me in February 2018. Conrad, I urge you to read it again. You will see how far we have come since you found us!

Franz read out the letter his grandfather wrote over one hundred years ago and it generated a great deal of emotion in the hall. He went through the history of the Deppner family and then it was left to Stefan to describe the relevant battles and places on the Western Front, and the men who fought and died in them.

Conrad, two days before our presentation, we saw world leaders gather in

Aachen to commemorate a century since the armistice was signed on 11 November 1918. However, our way of showing respect for this momentous occasion was not to talk about the impact of the Great War on Europe but instead, to pay homage to a young Tasmanian who also died in this terrible war. Fortunately, for that purpose, you had sent us pictures of the newly erected Soldiers' Avenue of Honour and Armistice Memorial on your nearby Waverley Hill.

The photo of the commemorative plaque, with the name of a young soldier who died from wounds suffered in the Battle of Amiens, was a fitting image to close our presentation. It left the audience speechless.

We hope this report will inspire you to finally start searching for the other Tasmanian soldier who somehow came in contact with our Otto on that fateful day. Although this was so long ago, your research on the letter has brought everything back to our hearts and minds. However, one remaining piece of the puzzle is the identity of this soldier. We look forward to hearing about your success in finding him!

One last thing, Conrad. You address your emails as 'Dear quartet'. We are honoured by this title, but believe it is incorrect. With you, we are a group of five! From now on, please address your emails—'Dear friends in the quintet'.

Yours,
Willi Deppner

Conrad felt a sense of guilt that he was yet to commit to searching for the Tasmanian soldier. Willi's latest appeal was the inspiration Conrad needed to start the research. He felt a renewed sense of excitement, reminiscent of the excitement he felt when searching for Wolf's family.

He looked over the presentation slides and Willi's detailed speaker's notes and was privileged to read a short profile on him: Conrad Bentley, born in England; married with three children and six grandchildren; retired with hobbies. The text framed the photo he had sent them of Clifton Beach, an outer suburb where one of his siblings resided. The shot had been captured during a Bentley family gathering on a chilly, late-winter's day. Long and spectacular shadows of Conrad and his son were cast across the sand, and Conrad had little doubt that the audience would have been impressed by the vivid colour of the water. He recalled his German pen friend had once queried whether his shots of the Tasmanian landscape were photo edited, manipulated to enrich the blue colour of the water and sky as they often appeared abnormally vibrant.

Conrad noticed the 1914 photo of the three Deppners had been cropped for the presentation and only showed Wolf. Without the contrast of the serious faces of Otto and Ernst beside him, Conrad was now convinced Wolf's expression, once a baffling grin, looked more like genuine smile, perhaps a look of pleasure, pride.

A picture of several hundred, if not a thousand German prisoners of war, taken sometime in August 1918, captured Conrad's attention. He wondered whether the face of Otto Deppner would ever be found among the array of desperate, angry and relieved faces.

Conrad was pleased to see information on Lieutenant Preiser had been included in the presentation, a figure from the past who, Conrad felt, would have played a significant role during Wolf's last moments. A picture of a solid stone cross, erected in a field of similar crosses at the German Soldier's Cemetery at Belleau in France, with a brief epitaph of the lieutenant's name and the date, '6 June 1918', was a poignant reminder of the futility of war. In an earlier email, Stefan Busch had reported how he had fortuitously stumbled upon the stone cross when he and his family had visited their French relatives and later accompanied the local historian on a tour around the key sites mentioned in the letter of fate. Stefan also described his excitement in discovering the ruins of a former farmhouse buried under thick vegetation on the slopes of a hill beside Bussiares:

> *Once again, Conrad, your research of Mahlmann's book on RIR 273 helped us confirm that these ruins lie on the slopes of Hill 165, approximately 50 metres behind the line of battle. Therefore, it matches the place where Wolf fell, as described in his father's letter.*
>
> *Our French military expert explained many similar ruins have remained forgotten since the war, or deliberately left alone, buried under dirt and undergrowth. You can imagine our excitement when we uncovered this one!*
>
> *But there is more. With the help of metal detectors and spades we uncovered a WW1 German mess kit and various French and German cartridges scattered around the site. Yes! Such discoveries still occur a century later!*
>
> *Then there's a cellar that's been covered over with a concrete slab. We dug*

away at one edge, enough to see that the cellar appears undamaged. Conrad, I don't need to tell you that this discovery has raised speculation, and further excitement, that it has relevance to Wolf's fate…

Conrad imagined Stefan scratching the dirt around the concrete slab, enough to expose the cellar, a rush of air escaping after being trapped for one hundred years. He was touched to receive an invitation to join them for a second visit to Hill 165, sometime in the near future: Conrad! The Clignon area is just under 90 kilometres from Paris. You and Gretel can enjoy a second honeymoon there before meeting us in Bussiares! With permission from the landowner, they planned to explore the cellar and also commemorate, in some way, the fallen Wolf.

Conrad took a few breaths before he looked over the remaining presentation slides: photos of Piet's Dutch dairy farm and Conrad's visit to Duisburg, posing with Willi, Piet, Stefan and Franz, as they waved the international flags.

He sat back and closed his eyes. He visualised his four friends on stage as they pointed to the empty chair, praising the beauty of the Tasmanian landscape and enthusiastically handing the baton to each other throughout the presentation.

Conrad entertained the thought that Wolf Deppner had been standing at the back of the hall during their presentation, dressed in his smart uniform and hidden behind the intrigued faces of the audience. He ignored his mocking inner voice and convinced himself that Wolf had been there. He imagined Wolf smiling as his story was brought to life and his heart skipping a beat on learning his courageous lieutenant, Lieutenant Preiser, had also met his own fate in France.

Conrad searched for the sound of Wolf's familiar voice. He heard it. It was faint, but undeniably Wolf's voice: I applauded their efforts, Mr Bentley. They did a fine job, and I was very touched when the audience rose to their feet.

Conrad turned back to the last slide—the memorial plaque of a young Tasmanian who never made it home from France. He agreed with Willi that this was a suitable image to end their presentation.

He was heartened and challenged by Willi's footnote:

What can we do ourselves for the preservation of peace?

Chapter 17

1919
The Tasmanian Soldiers Return Home

Not until the end of February 1919, with its heavy snowfalls and the threat of scabies and flu, did the remaining men of the 40th Battalion leave France for England. After a surprisingly smooth channel crossing, they headed north to a holding camp in Wiltshire.

'Bad news, men!' announced Lieutenant Brown. 'We won't be getting our ship home for a few months, so I suggest you make the most of bonnie old England while you can!'

'What's there to do here in the middle of winter, Sir?' complained a frustrated soldier.

'Well, we certainly won't be digging trenches! Make some day trips to London and take in the shows.' He pulled Frank aside. 'Swinton! Because you're clear of scabies, I've got you billeted with a nice couple with a few nippers. That should keep your spirits up whilst we wait for our ticket home!'

Frank was grateful, but equally disappointed by a further delay in seeing his family. Like his comrades, he had seen the short channel crossing as their first leg of an imminent voyage home, but he fought against returning to the state of despair that he had left behind in a Paris café.

In late March, Lieutenant Brown returned from his investiture at Buckingham Palace. He tried to hide behind his modesty but his excited men scrambled to get a glimpse of the Military Cross awarded for his gallantry at Morloncourt, a year earlier—'Did you get to shake the king's hand, Sir?'

As the northern spring gave hints of an early arrival, Frank warmed to the chats with his caring host family and took delight in getting to know their children. The numerous dances arranged by the townsfolk, and the now frequent concerts put on by the officers, made his last weeks in England more tolerable.

On the 1st of May, as Frank prepared to board the Karogola with his excited comrades and an assortment of friendly nurses and soldiers from other battalions, he received a letter from home:

New Town

10th April 1919

My dearest Frank, my love.

We are filled with happiness that it is finally all over and you are on your way home soon. This horrid war has taken you from us for too long.

The children are all well and cannot wait to see you. I too, cannot wait to see my Frank again—unhurt, strong and happy.

The streets of Hobart are still often filled with revellers, but it all remains a bittersweet victory. What have we achieved? So many dead, including my beloved brother. How I miss Tasman so deeply.

It will be difficult for me to forget and forgive the people who treated our family and friends from Bismarck with such disrespect. As you can see, I still have so much difficulty writing this new name of Collinsvale!

Please forgive me, my love. I should not fill my letter with such gloom. We have such fond memories of Bessie and John in Bismarck before the war, don't we? Let's remember those times instead.

John has arrived home safely with only a limp to contend with. Everyone is so thankful that he escaped the prospect of losing his leg, unlike so many other poor souls we see on the streets of Hobart on crutches or in wheelchairs. Of course, Bessie and the children are very relieved to have him back.

By the time you get home, they will be settled in Waratah. John is returning to the mine as a pay clerk, as he can no longer do manual work. I will miss them terribly.

I do hope you receive this letter before you are on the high seas!

All our love from your sweet flower and the children.

I love you.

Daisy

Frank kept the letter in his breast pocket throughout the voyage. He often took it out to read, making his homesickness more intense.

As the Karogola passed Malta, the rich-blue colour of its waters gave the returning soldiers a hint of Australia's beautiful coastlines, not seen for a long time. They were refused shore leave at Port Said in the Suez Canal after a preceding boatload of Australians caused a ruckus, but their disappointment was soon forgotten when they enjoyed a sun-filled stopover in Colombo.

A troupe of officers regularly put on stage shows to amuse, encourage and baffle their men. When Lieutenant Brown appeared on stage, convincingly dressed as Mary Pickford, the darling of the silver screen, Frank spontaneously joined his comrades in applause, cheers and fits of laughter.

The array of on-board distractions was heartening and often encouraged Frank to think of hugging his wife and children and meeting his new baby daughter. He abandoned attempts to write a second letter to John, believing written words would lack his intended sentiments. Instead, he favoured a visit to Waratah and imagined embracing John for the first time in nearly a year.

When the Karogola reached Western Australia in the middle of June, the soldiers were elated. Their elation grew as they sailed from Fremantle to Adelaide and reached its peak when the ship finally docked at Portsea in Victoria.

As he disembarked, Frank was convinced he could smell Tasmania from across the water. He surprised himself by yielding freely to the cheering crowds that had lined the streets of Melbourne in honour of their return. He caught a nod and smile from Lieutenant Brown who, in turn, was relieved that the once lost soldier appeared to be shedding the ugly yoke of the Great War.

Two weeks later, Frank crossed the Bass Strait. His tired and frayed uniform was in stark contrast to its splendour when he had lined the decks of another troop ship, with John, for the reverse crossing over two years earlier.

Frank and the other men were disgruntled by an advance notice that their first taste of home would be at the Bruny Island Quarantine Station. The threat of the Spanish flu pandemic had stirred hysteria and authorities ordered that all returning soldiers required processing and a clearance of the virus before being released to the Tasmanian mainland.

After anchoring in Barnes Bay on the western side of Bruny Island, the soldiers were marched along the pier to an inhalation chamber where they surrendered their uniforms for disinfection, bathed and underwent medicals. As they were allocated to barracks or tents, the irony of being allowed to disembark for a hero's welcome in Melbourne, but denied the same immediate reception in their home state, failed to go unnoticed. Despite attempts to relieve boredom and listlessness with sports events, film evenings and the occasional skit from the officers, the men found it frustrating to be so close to their loved ones, yet still separated from them, this time, not by oceans, but by the local waters of the D'Entrecasteaux Channel.

For Frank, the long week became less insufferable with the arrival of a surprise letter from Daisy. Her father had driven her and the children to Kettering to wave across the channel:

My dearest Frank. I couldn't bear the thought of you so close, but not being able to see you. I needed to feel you closer to me. I could not last a whole week without somehow greeting you.

It is a wonder you didn't hear our cheers of joy from the other side of the channel!

Oh, how I long to hold and kiss you! The children are so excited.

Not long now, my love...

On the eve of their discharge from quarantine, Lieutenant Brown strolled around the compound and noticed Frank was warming himself beside a campfire, smiling and pressing a letter to his chest. 'We're almost home, Swinton!'

'Yes Sir. I can't wait to see my Daisy and the kids.' Feeling happy and bold, he ventured, 'Do you have kids, Sir?'

'Not yet, Swinton, but now this damned war is over, it's my mission to make a home somewhere in the bush and find a loving lass who will put up with me. I'm thinking of having half a dozen nippers. Who knows, I might name one of them after you!'

'Frank Brown. Yes, that does have a ring to it, Sir.'

'No, you silly fool. I meant Swinton!' The two men laughed. The thought of seeing Hobart again excited them. 'Here, have a cigarette on me. Shame we can't smoke it with a beer.' They warmed their hands by the flames. 'Here's something for you, Swinton! I found out from another officer that, when the war broke out, the crew of a German cargo ship captured off southern Tasmania was interned here on Bruny Island! These German mariners probably slept in the same huts and tents as us. Something for the books, eh?'

SS Oberhausen was impounded within days after war was declared and its crew of over thirty deemed enemy subjects under the War Precautions Act 1914. The German and Austrian mariners were put to work erecting structures, felling trees and clearing land in and around the Quarantine Station and further south. They saw out the war both on Bruny Island and the mainland before repatriated to their homelands after the armistice was signed on the 11th of November 1918.

'You know Sir, my John, Private Bloom, was also arrested back then. Thank God we got him released before he ended up here on Bruny! In winter, I reckon it gets pretty cold. Daisy and I came over on our honeymoon, but it was in the spring, and the sun was out. We had a picnic here.' Frank sighed. 'That seems so long ago, now. To think people visit this island on their honeymoons and, at other times, men get locked up or disinfected here. Such strange times we live in, Sir.'

'I agree, Swinton.' The lieutenant was unsure whether Frank still harboured bizarre thoughts about John Bloom. He tested the water. 'They locked up Tasmanians with German parents, but seemed quite happy to send the same men off to fight against their German uncles and cousins.' He detected no unease. 'By the way, I had that German letter of yours translated.' Frank had forgotten about the letter, and the image of the German prisoner's beseeching face flashed before him. 'To cut a long story short, Swinton, it's about a father writing to one of his three sons who was fighting on the Western Front, telling him his brother had been killed.'

Frank's thoughts raced back to the frantic battle at Amiens. 'Sir! I remember the prisoner trying to tell me about all this. I think he said his brother's name was Wolf.'

'Yes, that's certainly one of the names written in the letter. This young Wolf got shot and killed near a small French village.'

'It's coming back to me, Sir. The prisoner also seemed to know something about Tasmania. He mentioned Bismarck, for goodness' sake!' Frank dipped his head. 'It really shook me up.'

'I remember you telling me about this when we were in Paris, Swinton. Remember? We chatted in a café near the River Seine and drank some nice French champagne and god-awful beer!'

'I do. Yes, I remember, Sir.' Frank's expression soured. 'My God, Sir. I was on the brink of madness back then.'

'I think the trenches sent us all a little mad, Swinton.'

'But all that rubbish about the town of Cleve, and John being related to the—'

'Ah, let it drop, Swinton. I can assure you there's nothing in the letter about Bloom. We couldn't make out the surname, but I guarantee you it didn't start with the letter B.'

'I was such a fool, Sir.'

'You know Swinton, families from all sides of the war were writing these sorts of letters, and lieutenants like me were writing home to parents to tell them their sons died heroic deaths.' The lieutenant struggled to fight against awful memories of the war infiltrating his thoughts, of the screams and cries of agony from his dying men, details justifiably omitted from his letters to their loved ones. He shuddered and moved his hands closer to the fire. 'Seems we were sent over there to kill Germans who weren't that much different from us, Swinton. What a strange world indeed.' He paused for reflection. 'I'm just happy it's all over!'

'Same here. What are you going to do with the letter, Sir?'

'Not exactly sure. I've got a bag full of souvenirs from the war—French, German, and even a few gifts from those feisty Americans! What does one do with a German war letter in a place like Hobart, Swinton?' He paused again, deeper in reflection. 'Maybe, when I have nippers of my own, they might show some interest in all this.'

They both sensed a shift in the conversation's tone. They relaxed and shared another cigarette.

'So, Swinton, what's the news from your mate, Bloom?'

'Ah, Sir. All good. John and Bessie moved to the Northwest, and he's doing just fine at the Mount Bischoff mine. Not mining work exactly, because of his wounds, but in the office, you know, doing the pay for the miners. The mine suffered a bit during the war but I think things are picking up now. John earns a good wage.'

'Good on him! His wife's name is Bessie, you say? I like that name too.'

'Yes. She's my Daisy's twin sister.'

'Ah yes, I remember now. All coming back to me through the fog of war, Swinton!'

There was a natural pause. Each of them looked at their hands silhouetted against the bright orange glow of the campfire. Frank noticed Lieutenant Brown was gently moving his fingers as if he were playing the piano. The flames not only warmed their hands, but also their hearts.

'You know, Sir, I feel closer to John now we've arrived back in Tassie.'

'Splendid, Swinton. That's music to my ears!'

'We worked together at the Bischoff mine, way back before we got married. When I get settled, I'll visit him.'

'Good on you, Swinton! Buy him a beer from me!'

The lieutenant stood to leave. He looked at Frank and smiled. He held out his hand and Frank took it. Frank felt the lieutenant's warm hand. He knew it was not only warmth from the flames. He knew Lieutenant Brown had a caring heart that was forever present beneath his officer's uniform.

'Thank you, Sir. I was lost out there for a while.'

'I know, I know. The war has done damage to us all. I look forward to the day when I can get rid of this cough. Damn that chlorine gas, eh?'

'Good luck with that, Sir.'

The lieutenant lowered his voice. 'The next year or so won't be easy for any of us, Swinton. It might take us a while to settle back into Hobart, and Hobart itself might also bear some scars from the war, but keep your chin up. Make sure I see you back on the footy field, or at least yelling from the sidelines, eh?' Lieutenant Brown saw Frank's smile widen and knew he had well and truly won his last battle in bringing Frank back from the war, from madness. He explained that he and some of the other officers planned to put on an annual sports day, a type of annual reunion for the 40th Battalion. 'Make sure you get to them, Swinton. And make sure you bring your mate, Bloom. Understood?'

'Understood, Sir.'

The lieutenant's kind words resonated with Frank as he watched him move away and receive slaps on the back from fellow officers.

The next morning, on the last short leg of their long journey home, the brisk winter air was no deterrent for the soldiers as they assembled on deck. As the ship slowly edged closer to Hobart's waterfront, they began to recognise the more familiar contours of the Derwent River. It comforted them.

Frank saw Mount Wellington slowly take on its familiar shape and characteristics. Beside him, a soldier pointed inquisitively to a craggy peak. 'That's Cathedral Rock, mate,' said Frank with a smile. 'We city folks don't usually get to see it because the mountain hides it from us.' Frank noticed the other soldier grip the railing to stem a shaking hand. 'Don't worry, mate. It will ease up in good time.'

'I bloody hope so. It's a toss-up, what's worse—a shaking hand or the god-awful ringing in my ears!'

As the ship rounded the southern end of Sandy Bay, Frank saw a single figure taking a dog for a brisk, mid-winter walk along the beach. His excitement grew. He made a valiant attempt to close the dark curtains of war and open his heart to a brighter future. His mind transported him to a sunny day, in the near future, as he imagined he and John breathlessly reaching the summit of Cathedral Rock. A pact they had made on their way to the fight in the Great War. *We made it, John! We're on top of the world!*

Frank opened his eyes. He gasped as Mount Wellington finally revealed its true, reassuring form—a lioness as sentinel, diligently guarding her harbour city. He gasped again, this time in unison with the soldiers on either side of him. Lining the wharf, they saw their loved ones waving hats, scarves and flags. A joyous salute to their return.

Frank was brought to tears.

As he watched his men disembark, Lieutenant Brown smiled at the scenes of families hugging and kissing. He made out Private Frank Swinton swamp his family with affectionate kisses and rescue his wife as her knees buckled from under her. He saw him, a joyous, tear-filled father, greet his youngest child for the first time.

When it was his turn to leave the ship, the lieutenant was saddened to see a handful of widows left scattered along the pier, pitiful figures in dark coats. They had embedded themselves within the cheering crowd of wives, mothers, fathers, sisters and girlfriends, hoping to experience, vicariously, the same elation of falling into the arms of a loved one returning from the war, all the while pretending that their tears of grief were tears of joy.

Months earlier, Bessie had stood with Daisy on the same pier to welcome home John, suppressing their deep sadness that a bullet at Gallipoli had robbed their brother, Private Tasman Webb, of a similar jubilant reception.

Later that night, after being warmly welcomed home by his extended family and friends, but now alone and unable to sleep, Lieutenant Brown allowed himself to recollect the horrors of the Western Front. He got drunk to help convince himself of his good fortune to return unscathed, as some had told him, but he knew his immediate future was uncertain.

He opened his field diary, his constant companion for nearly two years, and the German letter, the letter that had caused Private Swinton so much torment, fell to the ground. *What on earth am I going to do with this damned thing?*

He put the letter aside and wrote:

30th June 1919. Left Barnes Bay at 8.30am and arrived in Hobart at 10.30am. Home at 11.30am, at last!

Under a year later, Daisy delighted in the birth of a post-war baby. 'Look at his face, Frank. I see my brother in him.'

Frank picked up his newborn and studied his features. 'You are right! He looks just like your brother. We must name him Tasman. Our little Tassie!'

'Bessie has always been beside me when our babies were born. This is the first baby she is yet to see. I miss Bessie and John since they moved to Waratah.'

'I miss them too, my sweet flower.'

Daisy knew Frank had battled with his initial plan to visit John, even write to him. The longer he had left it, the more it faded into the background as he tried hard to settle back into civilian life and keep down a steady job. As she watched Frank gently stroke Tasman's face, she felt now was the best time to test the water. 'Frank, my love, I must give you some news. Bessie wrote to me to say there is work for the taking in Waratah. John can easily find you a job at the Mount Bischoff mine, if you…'

Frank looked up with a tender smile. Daisy was somewhat surprised but equally delighted by his response. 'I see you and Bessie have been scheming behind my back!' Coyly, Daisy dipped her head. 'Well, my sweet flower, only a fool would ignore a job offer in Waratah. We shall move there, and without delay. I've put off seeing John for too long and you can introduce our baby Tassie to his adorable Aunt Bessie.'

Toward the end of 1920, with their four children and whatever household items they could fit into a truck, Frank and Daisy drove into the main street of Waratah to a joyful welcome from John, Bessie and their two children, all eager to show off the waterfall that flowed through the town centre. The commotion encouraged inquisitive townsfolk out from their homes and shops.

At the sight of his best friend, Frank immediately fell into John's arms. 'It's so good to see you, mate.'

Daisy and Bessie gathered up the children and demanded their husbands visit the local pub, the Bischoff Hotel, to talk over old times and mend their bruised friendship...

As they sauntered into the bustling hotel, Frank could not ignore John's limp and he fought hard against images of the Western Front that were trying to infiltrate and tarnish their reunion, all the while accepting that such intrusions were likely.

'Another beer, Frank?'

'Of course, mate!'

'The publican wants to shout us the next round. He's a good bloke. He fought at Gallipoli.'

Frank was overcome. Tears welled up in his eyes. 'John, I don't deserve you as a friend. You stuck by me, even though I shoved you aside and spoke ill of you. Please forgive me, mate.'

'Don't be a fool, Frank. That was the war talking. Not you.'

They observed other men in the Bischoff Hotel sharing similar stories. The absence of their uniforms had not dampened their camaraderie. They slapped each other on the back or playfully punched each other's arms, all the while wishing that they could embrace each other to test whether the unique bond of Australian mateship was still as strong as it had been on the battlefield. Like Frank and John, the other men had been lured to the mining towns with the promise of post-war work and a happier future. The two friends warmed to the atmosphere and let down their guard.

Frank talked about his delay in England before the long voyage home. 'Ha! That quarantine station on Bruny Island was something for the books, eh? Did you have to spend a week there too, even though you had a busted leg?'

'Yes. But I don't remember much about it. They still had me on painkillers. Still, I was one of the lucky ones, Frank.'

'Ah, those poor diggers who dodged all the bullets only to be snuffed out by the blasted Spanish flu.'

'Talking of Bruny Island, Frank, you saved me from the internment camp there, when the war broke out.' John's eyes now filled with tears. 'I don't think I ever thanked you enough for that.'

'Rubbish, John.' Frank paused. He dipped his head. 'It's me who should thank you for getting me out of the war in one piece.' Frank stuttered. His emotions were raging inside his stomach. 'You need to know, I wrote you a letter from France, but you were shipped back before you got it. I wrote to thank you for sticking by me. John. Oh John, I…'

'I hated leaving you behind Frank, but that damned German shell had the last word!'

The third beer soothed them. John reached across the table and desperately grabbed hold of Frank's hands. They instantly felt their spark of friendship had not been completely lost to damp trenches and the sound of whistling bullets. They were reluctant to release their grip until inquisitive looks from inebriated miners forced them to convert their hold into a vigorous handshake.

'Frank, the job in the mine is all set up for you to start on Monday.'

Within no time, the pleasure of small-town life in Waratah was the tonic the two friends needed to fully restore their bond. After a couple of years, Frank shifted his skills from the mine to the Bischoff Hotel, where he soon gained the reputation as the man who knew everyone and everything in the area.

Each couple took delight in co-nurturing their respective children and both families periodically returned to Hobart, in convoy, to visit the grandparents. Daisy and Bessie thrived in their new community and took pride in introducing some of the fineries of the city and assisting in the classroom.

Frank and John watched their children grow with pride and boasted about their wives' achievements to anyone who stopped for a chat on the main street or in the pub. Whenever they could, the two friends stole away for bushwalks, as they had done so many years earlier as boys on the threshold of manhood. They gained a renewed appreciation for the Tasmanian landscape. Frank congratulated John whenever he limped to the crest of a hill or successfully crossed a swollen creek.

They sidestepped talk of the war, yet whenever it inched its way into their conversations they tethered themselves to the life raft of mateship. Frank revealed that his hand tremor resurfaced now and again, but resisted telling John about his persistent nightmares of trying to outrun the plumes of chlorine gas, falling over in a trench and desperately looking around, in vain, for his best mate to help him. John preferred to conceal his numerous shrapnel scars, but told Frank how lucky he felt that he avoided leg amputation.

As with all returned soldiers, they came to accept that their psychological wounds would take longer to heal.

Chapter 18

1934
Germany

'Wittmann!', Felix turned around to see his retired teacher hurrying across the street to greet him. 'My dear boy! How nice it is to see you after all this time. You look no older. How long has it been? Fifteen years?' He was relieved to see that the bruised soldier he had found weeping on the street back in 1919, who was riddled with guilt and remorse, had fought back and reclaimed some of his former cheerful disposition. 'How is the family, Wittmann?'

'My Lina is lovelier than ever, Sir.'

'And the children?'

'We have three now. I think the last time I saw you, before you left for Cologne, Lina and I were newlyweds.'

'Yes. All of Cleve rejoiced at your wedding and then the arrival of your firstborn. We were all blessed to have something of joy to celebrate so soon after the war ended.'

'I think you will be proud, Sir. My children are all doing well at school.'

'That's wonderful news, Wittmann. We must talk more. My favourite coffeehouse still stands after all this time. Come…'

As Herr Stummhofer perused the menu, Felix looked at his former teacher from across the table. He saw an older man, but the same man with a compassionate expression on his face. He felt comforted that Herr Stummhofer's voice had not lost its calming tone, and it briefly encouraged him to reflect on happy times—of the quartet parading around the school, making pacts of friendship and racing each other through the fields. He was surprised at how easily the vibrant colours of his youth returned. He smiled to himself as he recalled the delight on Erich's face when Frieda Graf had first kissed him, but sensed the images of Wolf's death and the pain of Bruno's inexplicable disappearance were trying to push through. He fought hard to hold them at bay.

As they waited for their order, Herr Stummhofer observed Felix deep in thought and chose not to interrupt, hoping his reverie was of happier times. His own thoughts returned to his classroom and the charm of the quartet. He laughed to himself that Felix Wittmann had always used charisma and wit as a smokescreen for his slow academic progress. He thought of Wolf Deppner's cheerful temperament, and Bruno Klug's steady character and unbreakable loyalty to the quartet. Bruno, my dear boy. What was your fate in France? Why did you not return? He recalled Erich Wiese's fascination with exotic flora and persistent questions about Australia and Canada. His thoughts wandered to Marie Bloom, his sister in Tasmania, and the concern he had felt when her regular correspondence ceased during the war. Only recently had her letters returned to some of their former cheer:

Collinsvale

3rd July 1934

My dearest brother, Günter.

I send you warm greetings and I am pleased to hear you continue to enjoy your retirement in Cologne. I have faint memories of our parents taking us there as children, of seeing the cathedral and picnicking beside the Rhine. Please send me some photographs.

Do you miss Cleve, Günter? It is doubtful I will recognise our German hometown anymore, given I left so long ago now. I confess, I will find it difficult to adjust to the new spelling of 'Kleve', should the proposed spelling changes be allowed.

The world is changing fast, my dear brother. And after all these years, I still think of my Tasmanian hometown as Bismarck. We are advised to forget the past and dwell more on the present, but I must confess, thoughts of the past often come to the forefront of my mind.

I have good news. Although John and his family enjoyed their time in Waratah, they are returning to Hobart. Bessie's parents have bequeathed them a large house in the Hobart suburb of New Town and Frank, John's brother-in-law, has found John a clerical position with a local newspaper.

Many times I have written to you about the charming Frank Swinton. He has always been a good friend to John and has helped with odd work around our property.

We are so proud of John's children. His daughter is now over twenty and wishes to pursue a career in nursing. She has blossomed into a beautiful woman and looks like her mother. Our grandson has John's gentle nature and blond hair, a feature certainly passed down through the Stummhofer side of the family! He plans to start an apprenticeship in carpentry next year. He is skilled with his hands and extremely athletic, like his father was before the war.

I have enclosed photographs of us all, but I feel such static prints often fail to show the true spirit of a person's character.

John's wife, our dear Bessie, has always been like another daughter to us. John was lucky to have such a devoted wife who fought hard to cheer and motivate him after the war, all those years ago now. Daisy, her twin sister, did the same for Frank. I got so much pleasure in seeing these sisters nurse their husbands back to full health. Dare I say, it fell on us women to bring everything back to some semblance of order after those troubling times.

My dear Günter, for so long you had plans to visit us, plans that were dashed by a war that spread its mean tentacles over the entire world. They say it was the war to end all wars. I pray that is the case.

Your last letter spoke of your sorrow over the loss of your beloved Weimar Republic. It pains me to know you concern yourself so greatly with these matters. I remember you as a proud man reared in a country that had an *abundance of kings, princes and princesses. Such a far cry from the Germany of today, therefore I share your unease.*

Our newspapers describe the German National Socialists making sweeping changes whilst your revered ex-president, Paul von Hindenburg, lies on his deathbed.

Remain strong, my dear brother.

Your devoted and loving sister,

Marie

A group of uniformed men burst into the café and interrupted both Herr Stummhofer and Felix who were deep in thought.

Felix politely waited for Herr Stummhofer to speak first.

'Tell me more, Wittmann. What news from Cleve? I hear Johannes Graf, the son of Cleve's Foundry Manager, has become a respected and well-liked teacher at my old school.'

'Yes, Sir. Our oldest boy enjoys his geography classes very much.'

'It is good to know young Graf picked himself up after the war, despite losing a leg. I predicted he would make an excellent teacher. Does your wife still communicate with his sister, Frieda? They were good friends, were they not?'

Felix was thrown by the mention of Frieda's name, now seldom uttered between him and Lina. After Frieda crossed the English Channel so many years ago, whatever fragile thread remained between the two friends had further weakened. 'My Lina did try very hard to keep in contact, but to no avail, Sir.' Tactfully, Felix added he suspected their letters were censored for a long time after the war and, as a result, all communication ceased.

'I sincerely hope the young lady managed to find peace in a post-war England.' There was a brief pause as the two men gathered their thoughts. 'How is your work at the Klugshof Brewery?'

'I finished work there two years ago, Sir. Do you remember Herr Welle? He's been training me in plumbing and radiator installation. I will be forever grateful to Bruno's uncle for giving me work after the war, but the promise of better wages with Herr Welle came at a good time. Lina and I are saving up to purchase the Winkler house, the one with the large field beside it. Do you remember it, Sir?'

'I certainly do! The late Herr Winkler and I were well acquainted. I'm happy for you, Wittmann.'

'My new boss, Herr Welle, secured the tender to install radiators in the military training school under construction in the Eifel. He's taking me with him. I'll be away for few months and will certainly miss the family, but I will earn enough to finally purchase the house.'

'What a splendid opportunity for you, Wittmann. I've read that our economy is improving.'

'We must thank our Führer for that, Sir!'

The mention of the new chancellor's preferred autocratic title forced Herr Stummhofer to shift in his chair. Earlier that morning, he had arrived from Cologne to attend one of many memorial services held across Germany for the former president and statesman, Paul von Hindenburg. Herr Stummhofer attempted to ignore the outrageous number of flags displayed in shopfronts and lining every street, but he flinched when he saw an oversized swastika flapping in the wind and obscuring the large Hindenburg portrait hung above the portico of the Cleve Town Hall. He lamented the demise of the Weimar Republic and the loss of its tricolour flag, but to avoid censure, he had learned to choose his words carefully when discussing the new regime. 'Yes, Wittmann. Undeniably, Germany's new government has generated some prosperity after the stock market collapse and the fall of the republic.'

'And our Führer has freed us from the shackles that bound us to the dreadful Treaty of Versailles.'

Herr Stummhofer suspected Felix would quote the words of others rather than champion political opinions of his own. He forgave Felix's naivety and declined to respond, instead allowing his mind to travel back to the golden period in the 1920s, when life pulsated with the promise of art, music, dance and prosperity. He accepted that Felix, like many of his generation, was being carried along in the fast-flowing stream of optimism that their new leader had inspired. The front page of a morning newspaper, left behind on the seat of his train carriage, displayed an article and photographs of Ordensburg Vogelsang, the construction site of which Felix spoke. Although Herr Stummhofer was aware four elite training schools had been planned throughout the Third Reich, he was stunned by the scale and ostentation of the Eifel project. Workers' unions had recruited hundreds of labourers for its hasty construction, many of whom had been unemployed for a long time. The photographs showed the workers posing on tall scaffolding, their faces aglow with renewed patriotism.

Felix disregarded Herr Stummhofer's apparent ill-ease and noticed that he, along with other members of his generation, often struggled to utter the title of their new leader. As if by rote, he praised the Führer for being the Germany's saviour. 'Thanks to our Führer, Germany is rising like a phoenix from the ashes!'

With that, Herr Stummhofer's self-control all but disappeared. He fought against crashing both fists on the table, but his voice, normally calm and controlled, could not hide his indignation. 'Wittmann! Let me give you some words of advice. Be careful with broad terms and slogans. One must be sure to educate oneself about the complexities of politics before espousing them.' Herr Stummhofer became aware his loud voice had reached patrons seated at adjoining tables, and he saw Felix's puzzled expression had turned to displeasure. He lowered his voice. 'Please listen to me, Wittmann. One man alone cannot make a country prosperous and influential without a good government and advisers to guide and steady him. However, one man, who wears a uniform and acts mostly alone, can easily cause harm and chaos.' He withheld—the world does not need another war.

'But Sir, the Führer has given me the opportunity to better my life. To make a better life for my children. I must be grateful for that.'

Through the window, Herr Stummhofer saw a swastika flapping wildly on a lamppost. He felt overpowered by the zeal of youth and the growing tide of misplaced patriotism. 'Wittmann, my dear boy. Please be assured, you have my support to make a better life for you and your family.'

'Thank you, Sir.'

The other patrons relaxed.

'Will you visit Erich Wiese whilst working in the Eifel?'

'That's my plan, Sir. I hope to get a weekend free to make the trip from the construction site to Heimbach. It's been such a long time since I've seen Erich. I've been told he may go under a new name and has become an artist.'

'That does not surprise me in the least. Wiese always had an eye for fine art. I would appreciate a report of your meeting with him, Wittmann.'

The door swung open and a band of Hitler Youth, fresh from their dress rehearsal for the von Hindenburg Memorial Parade, entered and discourteously left the door ajar. The cold air reached Felix. He shivered and frowned. His thoughts were fast returning to the battlefields and agonies that were still trapped in his mind after so much time.

More soldiers entered the café, and Herr Stummhofer struggled to hide his displeasure. 'I have enjoyed talking with you, Wittmann, but I must take my leave to attend our former president's public farewell. Please pass on my regards to Wiese when you see him.'

'I will, Herr Stummhofer. Farewell.'

As he left the café, the retired teacher again averted his eyes from the line of swastikas, but the noise of the flags flapping above his head followed him with every step. He thought of the quartet again, the four boys who had given him so much joy. He remembered them as recruits, parading around in their new uniforms in the Graf courtyard and posing for the camera, oblivious to the miseries war would bring them. Abruptly, the image of the four was replaced by an image of a single soldier—Sergeant Felix Wittmann, pledging his sole allegiance to the Führer.

He shook off the image. It was much too painful. Felix, my dear boy. Please take care.

Chapter 19

2018. December
Tasmania

'Wally!' called Conrad.

'Geez, Conrad. You look like you're gonna wet your pants! What is it this time?'

The two were now accustomed to talking to each other in the absence of the boundary fence. The French builder, whose accent made their wives swoon, had only succeeded in dismantling it and erecting the galvanised uprights before he flew to Europe to deal with a family matter. He had asked Gretel and Patricia if they wanted him to arrange a substitute fencer to finish the job, but they declined, joking that it would be nice to see their husbands get to know each more intimately without a barrier between them. At first, even the conspiratorial wives were shocked at how open and exposed they felt if they ventured into the garden, but it took longer for

Conrad and Wally to adjust. After a while, they gave up trying to partially conceal themselves behind bushes.

'Wally! How do I know the name Joe Furlani?'

'Joe? Well, for starters, your Gretel worked with Joe's wife years ago at the school. And Joe crewed way back with me and Baz on King Will, with Baz's dad at the helm. I've probably mentioned Joe a few times. Why?'

'Look at this photo.'

In an attempt to match the handwriting of the English inscription in the war letter, Conrad had tirelessly searched the internet for scanned copies of war diaries, diaries of Tasmanian soldiers who had fought at the Battle of Amiens. His efforts led him to Lieutenant Alfred Percival Brown and a photo of the retired lieutenant imitating drill lessons with his grandchildren. Conrad immediately recognised Joe Furlani's name in the footnote.

'Yeah. That looks like Joe as a youngster, with his sister. And I recognise his granddad. I met him once or twice. I don't get it, Conrad.'

'Well, you know how the Deppners asked me to find the face of the Tassie soldier...'

Wally looked up to see Conrad's wide smile. 'Bloody hell, Conrad! No way!'

'Yes!'

'How do you know it's him?'

'I waded through all the soldiers' diaries on the internet until I got a close match with his handwriting.'

'Unbelievable! You're frickin'... tenacious, mate!'

'This Lieutenant Brown wrote about fighting at Amiens on the same day Otto Deppner was taken prisoner, but I couldn't see any entries about him taking the letter as a souvenir.'

'Well, that's understandable, mate. Not much time to write about finding letters when you're fightin' for your life, eh?'

'I need Joe Furlani to verify the handwriting.'

'You can do better than that, mate. Joe's mum, Bessie Furlani, lives just around the corner from us. I saw her at the supermarket only a few weeks ago. She's in her nineties, but believe me, she's still got her wits about her!'

'Really? Can you call her for me, Wally?'

'Why? You think she might get freaked out if a madman turned up on her doorstep waving a letter from the First World War?'

'Yep!'

'I'll call Joe first and see what he thinks.'

'Can you call him now?'

'Nope. Later. I want to see how patient you can be! How's the broken arm?'

'Getting there. I'm being... patient with it.'

'Good to hear!'

'But I'm a little... impatient to get back to my violin playing.'

'No doubt. And the bushwalks?'

'I'll get back on the track soon, but I suppose I need to be...'

'Yeah, yeah. I get the message. Talkin' about being patient, has your Captain Baz found a new boat yet?'

'He's still looking around. He says there's no rush with two of his crew down.'

'Oh, yeah. I heard your mate, what's his name?'

'Martin.'

'I heard the boat crash really put the jeepers up this Martin bloke, and he's gonna give up sailing for a while.'

Conrad resisted pressing Wally to take his place in the crew.

Wally's son appeared. 'Hi, Conrad. How's it going with the broken arm?'

'Getting there, but I'm a patient man. How are you, Andrew?'

'Getting there.'

Andrew's rescue from Melbourne had not been without difficulty as he initially resented interference from his parents and was pressured by his right-wing associates to ignore their pleas to return to Tasmania. Wally would not give up. He seized an opportunity to have a frank father-to-son talk over a beer in a pub.

'Andy, mate. We love you. You are our precious boy. I know that deep down in your heart, all this shit that's happened in Melbourne is not what you want. It's not what you really believe in.' Wally looked intently at Andrew who was fumbling with his glass, and resolved, I will not leave

Melbourne without my son! Wally persisted doggedly, but with a gentleness that was effective. Andrew eventually yielded and looked up into his father's eyes. He wept. Wally leaned over the table and reached for his son's hands. I've got him back!

On the ferry trip home, Andrew was left alone to look out across the waters of the Bass Strait, toward Tasmania. He was exhausted, confused and embarrassed, but with every swell and spray of salt water on his cheeks, he felt the grip of his troubled time on the mainland loosen, and he was surprised by how much he longed for home. Later, he fell into a deep sleep, comforted by the rolling sea and the knowledge that his parents had rescued him.

Wally and Patricia came to accept that any logical explanation for the events in Melbourne would forever elude them. Andrew's own attempts at justification were similarly unconvincing, but he reclaimed respect at the same pace as his hair regrowth.

Weeks later, as Andrew jostled into place where the boundary fence once stood, Wally announced: 'Andy's got something to say, Conrad.'

'I... I umm. Well, I'm sorry for all that neo-Nazi shit in Melbourne, Conrad. I didn't mean to insult you and Gretel, you know, with all your German connections and stuff. I got mixed up with an idiot crowd and did some idiot things. Dad tells me that's 'Dummkopf' in your language, Conrad.' Andrew conceded he was on shaky ground to try and blame others for his poor behaviour, or alcohol and drugs, but explained that the far right group had cunning methods to recruit new members who showed vulnerability. 'I want you to know, Conrad, that deep down, I don't support what that mob stands for. I'm really sorry.'

'I know, Andrew. We got a shock when we saw it on TV, but I'm just glad you're back safe and sound in Tassie. And we're so relieved no charges were laid, aren't we Wally?'

'Bloody oath, mate.'

Conrad and Gretel had met with Wally and Patricia on a few occasions, nights of agonising debate over how someone like Andrew, raised in a respectful and caring family, could be fooled and manipulated so quickly and easily by a radical group. 'It's like your war letter stuff, mate. We won't get all the answers.' The troubling and bizarre events in Melbourne would hover over them, unresolved.

Andrew's apology was fitting, soothing. The three men relaxed. They looked at the ground and gently kicked at the soil.

'Shit, Dad. Your mulch is invading Conrad's garden! When's the new fence going up?'

Conrad and Wally smiled at each other.

As Andrew moved off, Wally gave Conrad a knowing look. 'He meant it, Conrad. He's not a bad kid.'

'I know, Wally. I know.'

Wally let out a faint sigh of relief. 'By the way, mate, Trish has organised for you and Gretel to join us up at the shack for New Year's Eve! We've finished the renos and now ready to entertain royal guests.'

'What can I say?'

'Thank you, would be good.'

'Love to, Wally.'

They turned to the sound of Gretel calling from the back door. 'I'm off to art class now, Conrad. Hi, Wally! Did Trish tell you she's coming with me? Looks like we've got another budding artist in the neighbourhood!' The two men grinned at each other. The news that both their wives would be absent one night a week meant an opportunity to share a beer and chat. 'Don't miss me, sweetie. Oh, I nearly forgot. You've got a parcel from Heimbach. It's on the kitchen bench.'

Conrad looked at Wally with a surprised expression. 'It's a bit early for my birthday. I wonder what Anke and Pascal are up to? Come and have a look, Wally.'

'Nah, sorry mate. I've gotta mow the lawns. Tell me about it later.'

Inside, Conrad discovered an item protected by layers of bubble wrap with a charming gift card of Heimbach's 11th Century castle. He was relieved to see Pascal had written in the card. Although he looked forward to Anke's emails, Conrad had often struggled to decipher her self-proclaimed, messy handwriting:

Hello Bentleys of Hobart! Greetings from Heimbach!

We loved having you stay with us again and Anke's parents send their greetings. They have fond memories of the garden concert, with you on violin and Anke on viola, and ask to see a replay of the videos whenever we meet.

Thank you for your latest, very lengthy email. Anke will reply with corrections to your German when she finds a free moment.

The boat crash on the river sounded very dramatic! We hope your arm recovers quickly as you must be missing the violin playing.

I've just started a new programming job, conveniently working from home, and Anke is enjoying her work in Bonn—Beethoven's birthplace, Conrad!

It's a pity we didn't get to a performance of his Ninth during your visit, but better luck next time!

Now, to our special gift. Anke found it amongst the usual junk at a local car boot sale. Given Gretel's flair for painting flowers and landscapes, it caught Anke's eye. It wasn't until we got it home and removed the false backing that we noticed the inscription and realised its significance.

Anke talked to her friend at the Heimbach International Art Academy (remember our visit there?) who did some research on the artist. We've enclosed a very interesting newspaper article about him, written in the 1950s.

When you've had the time to take all this in, please email us, or better still, call us on Skype. We want to share in your excitement!

Regards,

Pascal and Anke

As he struggled to release the gift from its wrapping, Conrad's excitement and curiosity intensified. At first, he was disappointed when he saw a painting on what appeared to be a strip of timber—a limewashed house set as a foreground to a seemingly faded landscape. On closer examination he noticed most flowers, some possible clumps of sage, had been painted with a blue pigment, and it was this colour that had retained its radiance, a hint to the work's original palette. He turned it over and noticed an inscription:

THE WILDFLOWERS OF BUSSIARES

Remembering four friends from Cleve who fought together in France:

Wolf Deppner
Felix Wittmann
Bruno Klug
Erich Wiese

Known as the quartet.

Erik Weide
1922

Conrad was stunned. His mind raced. It's the quartet! Wolf's quartet! He caught his breath. Who was this artist, Erik Weide?

Surprisingly, his normally disparaging inner voice offered good advice. Read the newspaper article, you fool, Bentley!

PERSONALITIES FROM HEIMBACH

ERIK WEIDE—ARTIST IN RESIDENCE DIES AT AGE 62

by Ingrid Trust, Art Editor. 10th of June 1955.

Erik Weide, born Erich Wiese 1892 in Kleve, affectionately known as 'Heimbach's artist in residence', died on the 3rd of June of natural causes, according to police.

Weide is best known for his 1925 exhibition 'The Paling Series'. A review of that exhibition described how he used fence palings, most cut into 10 by 20cm lengths, as his canvases. The timber came from beech trees felled in the Eifel Forest—a common resource for house construction and fencing in the 1800s. Weide said he used the timber because he saw little need for a boundary between him and nature. The artist chose to leave some of the palings in their weathered form, painting flowers that appear to germinate from the grains, gnarls and imperfections. 'I wanted to show the beauty of the flowers escaping from the decay in the timber,' Weide said. Other paintings were more representative of events rather than moods. For that, he sanded back the palings and painted on cleaner surfaces. For his inspiration, Weide spoke of life and loss.

Research on Weide shows he had a brief association with a group of progressive painters, writers, sculptors and intellectuals, primarily from Cologne, who had turned to the constructionist trend of the early 1920s. They founded the 'Experiment Kalltalgemeinschaft' in Simonskall, fifteen kilometres from Heimbach. This rural art society had invited Weide to a number of its meetings, and a founding member, a woodcarver, inspired him to look upon timber as nature's material for artistic expression.

Research has also uncovered traditional larger works—oil on canvas— most completed in 1935, including four portraits of WW1 German soldiers, one a self-portrait. In a rare interview in 1937, the normally reclusive Weide said two of the portraits were of his comrades who died in France, the third visited him in Heimbach in 1934. 'This visit compelled me to paint, to honour the lives of my three best friends.' He went on to say, candidly, that fleeing his hometown of Kleve was an attempt to put the trauma of war behind him. 'By running away, I was able to forget the war for a while but, at the same time, I failed to fully heal because I had left behind people I loved so dearly, including my only surviving friend. I didn't realise how much I missed his friendship until, years later, he did some construction work near Heimbach and paid me a visit.'

Art critics of the time commented on Weide's ability to capture the soldiers' joyous expressions in the four portraits, contrasted with their blemished uniforms which symbolised their struggles in combat. A few less discerning critics interpreted the soldiers' smiles as defiance or disrespect for the sacrifices other soldiers made in the war— interpretations Weide rejected. He said the paradox between the beauty and ugliness of war was deliberate and sincere. 'My time in France and Belgium was not spent entirely in trenches or on scarred battlefields. I still saw some glimpses of the beautiful countryside, and it is those visions that stayed with me as a testament to my friends.' The current whereabouts of the soldier portraits remains unknown.

Weide's distinct style was recognised throughout the Eifel in the 1920s and 30s and a revived interest in his works followed his benevolent deeds after World War II. He donated most of his palings to those residents who were rebuilding their homes after Heimbach was bombed by the Allies. 'I wished to offer some cheer to the freshly painted walls as I too have experienced the struggle of rebuilding a life after war,' Weide said.

According to the authorities, Weide has no surviving relatives. His appointed Estate Attorney released information that any profits from the sale of Weide's property and meagre assets are to be bequeathed to the Heimbach Grammar School to finance the expansion of its art curriculum.

It is noted, two large scale paintings were found on his premises. The first, a profile of a raven-haired young woman wearing a blue dress, gazing across a body of water—an inscription on the backing reads, 'I will never forget you, Frieda G.'—and the second, a near-completed portrait of an unidentified officer clutching a chest wound, titled 'The Fallen Lieutenant'. The red pigment of the wound is dramatically smeared across the canvas in a wide brush stroke. The reason for such apparent defacement is speculative.

Although the pieces from Weide's 'Paling Series' have been scattered, mislaid or forgotten with the passage of time and changing tastes, such was the quantity of this work that it is conceivable some may reappear here and there, or be re-discovered by future generations.

Many of Heimbach's residents will be unaware that Weide's painting, 'The graceful river that flows through Heimbach', was donated anonymously to the Town Hall in the late 1940s, where it remains on public display.

Heimbach remembers its artist in residence—Erich Wiese, later known as Erik Weide, 1892-1955.

*

Conrad sat in silence, trembling slightly. It took him a moment to gather his thoughts. He realised it was an inconvenient time to make a Skype call to Germany.

He anticipated Gretel's return and her shared excitement in the discovery. With the sound of Wally's mower whirring outside, he typed:

Dear friends in the quintet—my dear Willi, Piet, Stefan and Franz.
I am overcome with emotion. In English, we can also say 'My emotions are overflowing!'

Another incredible coincidence has occurred in this ongoing story of the letter of fate. Fate has played its hand once more!

My friends from Heimbach have sent me a gift…

Satisfied enough with his hasty German, he rushed out to garden.

Wally looked up to see his neighbour waving something in the air. He cut the motor and removed his gloves. 'Bring it over, mate.' Conrad did not hesitate and edged between the bushes. 'Welcome to the Archer's garden, Mr Bentley! What have you got there?'

'Another piece of the puzzle!'

Chapter 20

1934
Tasmania

After winning his feature race at the ANZAC Sports Day at Franklin in the Huon Valley, Lieutenant Brown had spotted Frank in the crowd and excitedly rushed over to him. 'Swinton, you look as young as ever. What's it been now? Fifteen years?'

Frank had read that his lieutenant continued to organise the event, and he made the effort to put aside money for petrol to make the journey with Daisy and Tasman, their teenage son. Following a church service and street parade, they gathered at the sports grounds with the locals and other visitors for the various races and fun events.

'Did you just see me lead the charge over the line to win the Australian Imperial Force's sprint, Swinton?'

'I did, Sir. And in gumboots!'

'You've got to have a bit of fun. Make people laugh, don't you think?'

Frank remembered his lieutenant doing just that on makeshift stages on the Western Front. 'This is my wife, Phoebe. We're expecting our ninth nipper anytime now.'

'Nine! My word, Sir. Congratulations. I'm pleased to meet you, Mrs Brown.'

'Please call me Phoebe. No need for formalities down here!'

'This is my sweet flower, Daisy.'

The four exchanged smiles and courteous handshakes. Daisy could not resist. 'It's so nice to finally meet you, Lieutenant Brown. Frank has spoken of you many times.'

'With kind words I hope, Daisy!' They laughed, and Daisy observed an almost constant smile on the lieutenant's face. 'I remember your husband was always keen to talk about you and your children. Ha! If my memory serves me correctly, even when the bombs were going off!' He gave Frank a wink. 'So, what news with you, Swinton?'

'We have four children now. Tasman is our youngest—we call him Tassie. He turns fifteen this year, so he's knocking on the door of manhood.'

'Where is he? He's welcome to race if he wishes.'

A vivacious girl skipped across the sports ground and tugged at Lieutenant Brown's arm. 'Daddy, did you see me win my race?'

'Of course I did, my little Bessie.' At the mention of the name, Frank and Daisy looked at each other and smiled. 'Yes, Swinton! I remember you telling me the names of all your family members and I stole this one!'

'Who are you talking to, Daddy?'

'This is Mr and Mrs Swinton. Say hello to them, Bessie.'

The little girl repeated the name 'Swinton' and giggled.

Daisy knelt and took her hand. 'I have a sister called Bessie, and she's just as pretty as you. How old are you, Bessie?'

'I'm seven.'

'Bessie, darling. Please go and fetch your little brother. I want him to meet Mr and Mrs Swinton.' Again, Bessie giggled. 'He's over there with the other nippers.'

Frank turned to his lieutenant. 'She's lovely, Sir.'

'Swinton, as my wife pointed out, there's no need for formalities down here. I'm not sure how it came about, but since I was in my early twenties, even before I was in uniform, everyone called me Gus. So, you're free to address me as such.'

'I don't think I can do that, Sir.'

'Really? Then what about, Sir Gus?'

'No, Sir. You are my lieutenant!'

With a tilt of the head and another wink, 'Okay, as you wish… Private Swinton.'

'Daddy! Here's Swinton.'

Frank turned with his mouth agape.

'Mr Frank Swinton, meet our son, Swinton Brown. See! I kept my word!'

With curiosity, young Swinton Brown looked up at the stranger as his sister tried to push him closer. 'This man's got your name, Swinton!'

The two children glanced at each other with surprised expressions and could not contain their amusement.

Frank knelt. 'I'm pleased to meet you, Swinton.'

The bashful younger Swinton tried to hide behind his father.

'Mummy, can we have some ice cream?' sang Bessie.

'Of course, darling. We'll leave your father and Mr Swinton to talk while we go off in search of the ice cream stall.'

'I know where it is, Mummy. Just follow me!'

Phoebe Brown placed a loving hand on her husband's cheek. 'Off you go, darling. Like you and Frank, Daisy and I have much to talk about.'

The two men hurried off to the ANZAC beer tent…

As they squeezed into in the large marquee, surrounded by boisterous patrons and protecting their beers from being spilled, Lieutenant Brown and Frank smiled at each other. Frank waited for his lieutenant to speak first.

'The last I heard you were on the Northwest, weren't you Swinton?'

'Yes, in Waratah. We moved back to Hobart a few years back so young Tassie could go to high school. It's the first time he's seen the Huon Valley.'

'Am I safe to assume this Tasman of yours takes after his father and plays footy?'

'Yes. But he's a much better player than I was, and much faster on the field than his Uncle John!'

'Then he must race today. Let's see if he can beat us country folk!'

'I'm sure my Tassie will be up for that, Sir.'

'You were in Waratah with Bloom?'

'Yes, Sir.'

'How is he?'

'He's doing fine. John and Bessie are moving back to Hobart too. Their daughter plans to go to university and their son will start an apprenticeship down here.'

'Splendid.'

'John wanted more children, but the German shell put a stop to that.' Both men dipped their heads as they recalled the deadly battle at Morlancourt on the River Somme, so many years earlier. 'John always spoke fondly of you, Sir. How you looked after him in the war and all.'

'Bloom was always a good judge of character!'

Frank's words spilled out. 'I was so lucky John didn't give up on me. All that rubbish in my head about him being a German spy. The terrible things I said about him. It makes me feel so foolish now.'

'The war was to blame, Swinton. All done and dusted.'

The lieutenant noticed Frank still suffered from hand tremors and, at times, the twitching extended the length of his arms. His mind flashed back to the last stages of the war. He recalled Frank's slide into madness and his paranoid thoughts about his best friend, but the details had become blurred.

Over the years, the lieutenant had made great effort to replace the horror of those times with the enjoyment of civilian life, marriage, work and the delight of fatherhood. He tried desperately to put aside the responsibilities and pressures he faced as a young officer, but they had taken their toll, more than he had realised. For a while, he had drifted in and out of Hobart and happiness before meeting his beloved Phoebe. Under the starched surface expected of an ex-officer, she immediately saw gentleness and humour—'My proud lieutenant. My dearest Gus. How could anyone resist marrying you?'

Marriage and the arrival of many children helped him build a new life, a contented life for which he had yearned. For the most part, he managed to push aside thoughts of the war, but his persistent morning cough often served as an irksome reminder…

The mood in the ANZAC beer tent was jovial and infectious. Frank and the lieutenant warmed to the camaraderie of the other returned soldiers and listened to them brag about beating their rivals in the races, or lamenting their losses.

'Have another beer, Swinton. Tell me about your nippers.'

'All grown up now, Sir. My two oldest children are both married and on the mainland. My youngest daughter runs her own flower shop in the city. She has heaps of admirers knocking at the door, but she won't settle for any Joe Blow. When you get to meet our Tassie, you'll see he is a bonzer lad.'

'You must be proud, Swinton.'

'I am, Sir.'

The lieutenant impressed Frank by reeling off the names and ages of his eight children, from youngest to oldest, and then in reverse, and how he also expected them, in years to come, to move from the valley and start their own lives in Hobart, or beyond.

'What work do you do down here, Sir?'

'I'm what they call a 'jack of all trades'. I did a bit of orchard work for a while. I had a transport business, did some other odd jobs here and there, building fences and the like, but now I run a petrol station. I try to spend the rest of my spare time, when I can get it, with the family—picnics and walks, that sort of thing.'

Frank mentioned the prominent peak he had observed on their drive down and explained he wished to climb it one day.

'I reckon you mean Cathedral Rock, Swinton. Why have you got your sights set on it?'

'It's been in the back of my mind for years, Sir, nagging at me like a loose end from the… from the war. I just need to climb it. With John.'

'With his gammy leg?'

'You know John, Sir. He'll make it.'

The lieutenant explained that he had climbed the peak some years back with a local bloke who knew how to find the right track. 'I can give you the directions.' The lieutenant looked around furtively and whispered, 'But you must keep them top secret!'

Frank recognised the lieutenant's theatrical expression and wondered if he still performed on stage. He imagined him dressed in his uniform and entertaining his children, or any future grandchildren, parading them around like toy soldiers. Attention! At ease!

'Thank you, Sir. Top secret directions to Cathedral Rock would be bonzer.'

They finished their beers and shook hands.

'I expect to see you down here every year, Swinton. Next time, bring Bloom with you. Understood?'

'Understood, Sir.'

The lieutenant noticed Frank's arm give a violent twitch. He was tempted to enquire. Surely after all this time the shakes can't still be from the war, he thought.

Frank sensed the lieutenant's scrutiny and nervously tugged down on his cuffs.

'Now, Swinton…senior. You need to introduce me to this bonzer lad of yours, and sooner rather than later. I hear there's a pest of a newspaper reporter scampering around and trying to hunt me down for an interview. Apparently, he wants to get a story, and a shot, of a local bloke racing in gumboots!'

※

Armed with the lieutenant's hand-drawn map, Frank settled into the return drive.

Daisy was tired from the full day of fresh air and conversation. She gently leaned her head on Frank's shoulder. 'Your lieutenant's wife is adorable, Frank. And their little Bessie acts so grown up. Did you see how she bosses young Swinton around?'

Tasman was in the back seat, admiring his race trophy. Frank and Daisy had stood beside Lieutenant Brown and Phoebe, all cheering as he was first to cross the finish line in the 100-meter dash.

In the rear-view mirror, Frank clearly recognised the features of his wife's family on his son's face. A wave of pride and happiness washed over him. His children had given him immense joy.

'Your lieutenant is a very nice man, Dad. He showed me his medals and told me you and Uncle John were two of his best soldiers.'

Frank realised he had forgotten to ask Lieutenant Brown about the

German letter, the letter from the soldier named Otto. For so long, it had remained shelved away in his mind.

'There were thousands of good men in the Great War, Tassie. We need to make sure good men are never asked to fight in another one.'

'Do you think I'd look handsome in uniform, Mum? As handsome as Uncle Tasman did when he joined up to fight in Gallipoli? It's sad I never got to meet him.' Daisy sighed at the mention of her fallen brother and looked up at Frank with a concerned expression. Tasman saw his mother's unease and tried to lighten the mood. 'I think I'm more suited to being a pilot. Do you think I'd look better in an air force uniform?'

His parents were unable to answer. Only last week, they had read about the rise of fascism in Europe. Neither of them fully understood its meaning and implications, instead they relied on the negative connotations in the newspaper article to inform them of its potential menace—'Don't worry, my sweet flower. We are far away from all that madness.'

Glimpses of Cathedral Rock appeared through gaps in the trees, flashes of a majestic steeple that emerged from the surrounding bushland. Rays from the late afternoon sun threw shafts of light on its craggy summit.

Once again, Frank's mind travelled ahead to an image of him conquering the peak, a pact made with John on the deck of a troop transport ship long ago. He saw himself giving John a helping hand to achieve the final climb. We're on top of the world, mate!

Chapter 21

2019 begins
Tasmania

'Wow! I see what you mean by laying out the red carpet!'

'Only the best for our royal guests, mate!'

For New Year's Eve, Conrad and Gretel had arrived at the Archer's shack and were immediately impressed with its luxurious interiors and elevated views across the white sands of Binalong Bay and farther out to the Tasman Sea.

'How was your trip, Gretel?' enquired Patricia. 'You don't usually drive, but I suppose with Conrad's arm still in a sling…'

'Ugh! Nearly three hours of his Beethoven blasting out through the speakers! It's the only thing that seems to make him happy lately, Trish.'

'You poor thing. Let me get you a glass of champagne before we show you around the bay. Wally, we need music, but not classical! And get Conrad a drink. Apparently he needs cheering up.'

As the four strolled along the beach, they smiled at the children frolicking in the waves, still excited with their Christmas gifts of multi-coloured inflatable turtles and unicorns.

They rounded a bluff and stumbled upon a secluded cove framed by granite boulders with a narrow channel that enticed braver swimmers into the deeper waters. The rust-coloured lichen that typically coated the East Coast rocks appeared bright orange under the late afternoon sun. The contrast with the azure of the water was enchanting. Gretel had captured similar scenes in many of her watercolours now displayed throughout the Bentley's home.

'Come on, Trish,' beckoned Gretel. 'Let's take the boys for a swim.'

'Great idea!'

Wally panicked. 'I don't have my bathers.'

'Ha! Good try!'

'Anyway, I don't think Conrad should be goin' in with his broken arm.'

'Another good try, Wally. A swim will do us all good, including my grumpy husband.'

It was Conrad's turn to panic. 'Gretel. Don't tell me you're going in—'

'Oh don't panic, Conrad. I promise not to take off my bra and knickers! Come on everyone! Last one in! Make sure you take off your sling, Conrad.'

They heard a splash. Gretel emerged with a shriek, an advanced warning to brace themselves for the shock of a cold plunge.

After a sumptuous barbeque, their skin still tingling from the invigorating coolness of the Tasman Sea, the four sipped coffee and relaxed on the Archer's new sundeck. They breathed in the agreeable, salty air and continued to admire the views. The angle of the setting sun magnified the glistening silver peaks on the swells.

'How's the arm after the swim, Conrad?' asked Patricia.

'I nearly died in the freezing water, but I guess it did my arm some good!'

Gretel reached over and lovingly took Conrad's hand. 'I know you miss your music, but it won't be long before you can get back to it.'

'And let's not forget the bushwalking,' piped in Wally.

'Actually, the Waratah Ladies are putting on a walk to the base of Cathedral Rock in a few weeks. Because they're not doing the last steep climb to the peak, I'm booking in.'

'And I suppose your broken arm doesn't stop you from talkin' German either, eh mate?'

Conrad thought of his German conversation group that had met for coffee during the post-Christmas break. Irene made a surprise appearance and looked amazingly well after her cancer surgery—'Now that's all over, I can start my six months of chemotherapy!' she had told them. Conrad sat back and observed the friendly interaction within the group, all congratulating Irene on her tenacity and resilience. Paul was lauded for passing an assessment to keep his driver's licence—'Not bad for someone in their nineties, is it Conrad?' Paul also spoke of his new project at the Army Museum, researching the original field-grey tint of a German Howitzer. In late August 1918, the French had handed over the cannon to Australian troops as a war souvenir, and it eventually ended up in Hobart where it had been repainted more than once. Conrad noted the significance of the date and wondered whether it could have been fired in the battle for Amiens.—'I'll come over next week for a proper chat, Paul. You just never know, it could be another piece of the war letter puzzle!'

Gretel pulled Conrad from his trance. 'You and Wally will be pleased to hear our French builder, Emanuel, is back from Europe,' his name deliberately emphasised with a French accent.

'Been practisin' your French, eh Gretel?'

'Oui, Monsieur Wally!'

'Impressive!' Wally's attempt to sound French by elongating the last syllable missed the mark.

'Our Emanuel's got a friend who's a painter and decorator.' Gretel knew this would get Conrad's full attention. 'You're off the hook, sweetie. I'm paying him to repaint the balcony railing for you.'

Conrad could not hide his glee.

Wally noticed their wives were exchanging grins like a couple of naughty schoolgirls. 'Out with it, Trish!'

'Well, as a surprise,' smiled Patricia, 'we've asked Emanuel to install a gate in the fence!' Conrad and Wally coughed and spluttered as they struggled to comprehend such a pointless feature. Patricia could not prolong the ruse and burst into laugher. 'You poor things, we're only pulling your legs.' Silence, then more grunts and coughs. 'You should have seen your faces!'

'You little devils!'

'Well, to be honest,' added Gretel, 'we mentioned this idea to our lovely Emanuel, but he put us off. He said gates on a fence line are a thing of the past.'

Wally let out an audible sigh. 'Good on ya, Emmanuel!'

'You need to practise your French a bit more, Monsieur Wallee!' quipped Conrad.

'Wee!'

The four laughed. The cheerful atmosphere on the sundeck was infectious.

'I need a beer! You two naughty devils can get your own drinks for scarin' us like that! One for you, Conrad?'

'Wee. Merci!'

Conrad sat back and smiled. After weeks of inactivity and frustration, he began to feel joyful. He heard waves breaking in the distance and looked forward to seeing the sun rise over the water.

'What's the latest with your letter research?' asked Patricia. 'Have you met Bessie Furlani yet?'

Wally cut in, 'He's talked to her on the phone and seeing her next week, aren't you, mate?'

'Wee!'

Conrad took a moment to recall his delightful phone call with Bessie. Among other things, she looked forward to showing Conrad her father's medals; a studio portrait taken on the eve of his deployment, looking dashing in his new uniform and slouch hat; photos he took in England and France during and after the war; and a newspaper clipping from an ANZAC Sports Day at Franklin. 'I think it was 1934, Mr Bentley. You'll laugh when you see a photo of him with sleeves rolled up and racing in gumboots!' She described her father as a bit of a larrikin, seldom without a smile on his face and that he loved to dress up and put on shows for his troops. 'A German letter written in 1918, you say Mr Bentley. How very intriguing…'

Conrad frowned. 'I don't think Bessie had much recollection of the war letter.'

Gretel tried to make light of it. 'Well, that's understandable. Not everyone would be as passionate about the letter as you are, Conrad!'

'The thing is, Lieutenant Brown's diaries, his letters and the souvenirs he brought back from the war, had all been stored together in the museum archives, so it's a bit of a mystery how the letter of fate got separated from the other stuff.'

'Geez, mate. You're overthinking things again! You won't always get the answers, you know.'

'And there's something else that's been bugging me. Like Franz Deppner said, it's a common practice to frisk all prisoners of war and take their possessions, so that's probably why Otto Deppner handed over the letter.'

'What's your point, mate?'

'Well, I doubt an officer would have done the frisking. You know, surely that sort of thing would have been delegated to the foot soldiers? So, if I'm right, how did Bessie's father, Lieutenant Brown, get hold of the letter?' Conrad heard a quick shot fired by his inner voice. *You're never satisfied, Bentley!*

Wally's voice was next. 'Gretel! Tell your husband to stop overthinking everything and be satisfied with what he's done with all this letter stuff.'

'Sweetie! Wally's right. Enough is enough. We know you don't like giving up on things. You like to fill in the gaps and solve everything,'—she resisted adding the description tenacious—'but you have to be satisfied with what you've achieved and accept that after one hundred years you're not going to find all the missing pieces of the puzzle you keep talking about.'

Conrad bit his lip. 'I have a wise wife!'

'Oh, Conrad!' cried Patricia. 'Speaking of pieces of the puzzle, did Gretel tell you we took the painting you got from Heimbach to our art class? We told them the whole story about your research on the letter and finding the Deppners, and about the painting dedicated to Wolf's quartet turning up years later. They were fascinated. Gretel said she was very proud of you.'

'Really? She said that?'

'I bet Wolf's relatives were fascinated to hear about the painting too.'

Again, Wally jumped in. 'They were over the moon about it! Conrad says the painting belongs to them, so he's sending it back.'

'It's such an amazing story, Conrad,' said Patricia sincerely. 'You should write a book about it!'

'Oh, God no! I'm no good at writing. Just ask Gretel! Besides, I couldn't do this story any justice. There's too many gaps to fill. The Deppner family wouldn't like it if I made up stuff, you know, let my imagination run wild and reconstruct the past. I'd need to change their names to respect their privacy. It just wouldn't work.'

'But I remember you said from the start that you wanted to give these soldiers a voice. You've got to finish with the letter somehow, Conrad.'

'I agree Patricia, but not with a book.'

'What about your music?'

Conrad looked puzzled.

Wally leaned over. 'Trish means you should write some music about all this stuff, mate.'

'Yes, Conrad. That's exactly what I mean. Can't you compose something in honour of these soldiers? A string quartet, maybe. Has that ever been done before?'

The suggestion struck Conrad with force, and sounds began to whirl around in his head. He heard a strident chord, silence, then a faint hint of a melody from a cello…

Gretel saw Conrad's mind was awash with the suggestion. 'Wally, while Conrad drifts off into his fantasy world of music, you need to refill our glasses.'

In the fifteen minutes prior to 2019 making its appearance, Conrad struggled to join in with the small talk, but the others were not perturbed by his inattention. He felt anxious to give this seed of a string quartet a chance to germinate and grow.

He imagined the three nonagenarians, Bessie Furlani, Franz Deppner and his friend Paul, make the same appeal: Don't delay, Conrad. We want to hear this masterpiece before any of us fall off the perch!

His quartet leader's rational counterargument was next: It will be a difficult task. Composing quartets cannot be rushed, Conrad.

And from Wally: So, mate. Tell me. When's your violin band off to Carnegie Hall to perform this quartet of yours?

As minutes passed, Conrad's head flooded with the sound of blended strings…

'Happy New Year, mate!'

Patricia raised her glass. 'Happy New Year, my lovely neighbours!'

'Happy New Year, sweetie!'

The sea below had taken on the appearance of black silk. It acted like a sounding board that reflected a blend of sounds from the neighbours' yards and parties on the beach—whistles, bells, cheers, music, sirens and dog barks. The sounds added to the jubilation on the Archer's sundeck.

Conrad smiled as he heard a radio broadcast of the fourth movement from Beethoven's Ninth Symphony, the choir in full voice but competing with the sounds of Love is in the Air from another party. 'Can you hear the Beethoven?'

'How can we miss it, mate!'

'Come on! You must admit it's a fitting sound to welcome in a New Year!'

Conrad's smile lingered. He thought Beethoven's music matched the mood of togetherness, of joy, maybe even of peace, not only on the sundeck but also spreading across the bay. His smile widened as Schiller's words about unity and triumph against war came to life—All men shall become brothers.

The four embraced as the nearby celebrations reached their crescendos and filled everyone with promise. There was no compulsion to talk. They simply sat and smiled at each other for a while, allowing the festivities to run their course.

Before long, Gretel and Patricia retired, allowing the men to quickly claim the comfortable sun lounges.

'It feels good up here, Wally. Thanks for inviting us.'

'My pleasure, mate.'

'You're grinning like a naughty schoolboy. Don't tell me you're up to something too!'

'I've got some news for you, Conrad…'

'I'm waiting.'

'I met your sailing mate, Chris. He's a nice bloke.'

'I'm not following.'

'Our Captain Baz introduced me to Chris. The three of us met for... cafe lattes and had a good old chat. When Baz gets his new boat, I've agreed to crew instead of the other bloke, Martin.'

'What?'

'Yep! I'm gonna take Wednesday afternoons off work for sailing.'

'Oh, Wally.'

'Orders from Trish. What did she call it? Transition to retirement. Apparently, I need to start enjoying myself and what better way than out on the Derwent River, eh mate?' Conrad was unable to respond. He was touched. 'Anyway, there's no rush. You need to get your arm workin' again.'

The two sank further into the sun lounges. The sounds of the New Year celebrations had faded, but the murmurs of the sea continued.

The effect of the beer encouraged Wally to venture into somewhat foreign territory. 'So, mate. I've been thinking. If I'm gonna put my life on the line and join you on the river, I need to know a bit more about the real Mr Bentley. You know, so I can feel safe as one of your crew members.'

'What are you talking about, Wally! You know all about me. How many years have we been talking over the fence?'

'Ten bloody years! But that's ten years of you talking about your projects. Things you're doin', or things you're doin' with other people, and stuff. You don't really talk about yourself.'

'Rubbish. I talk about myself all the time. Just ask Gretel!'

'Rubbish. You have a knack of avoiding talkin' about what makes you really tick.'

'Are you sure about that? Try learning German, violin band, as you call it, my Beethoven craze, having chats over the fence—when there is a fence—with my self-proclaimed, good-looking neighbour, bushwalking, the sailing—when I don't have a broken arm—all the fun with the grandkids ... shall I go on?'

'Yeah, yeah. All good things. Especially the bit about your good-lookin' neighbour. I hear he's a great bloke. But come on Conrad, tell me something I don't know for a change.'

Conrad felt a significant shift in the tone of their conversation. He was intrigued. 'So, you want me to tell you my deepest, darkest secrets.'

'Shit no! Just one!'

Conrad looked out over the water and noticed the clouds had released the moon. Its reflection left a glistening streak of light on the ebony water. 'Okay then, Mr Archer. You asked for it. I haven't even told Gretel about this…'

'I'm waiting.'

Conrad took a gulp of his beer. 'I've felt the presence of a young soldier. Right from the start, when I got the war letter.' He paused. 'It's Wolf Deppner.'

'Shit! Why did I ask?'

'I hear his voice, Wally. I've… I've seen him.'

'Bloody hell.'

'Do you think I'm going mad?'

'I think you've always been mad!'

Conrad looked closely at Wally and saw sincerity in his smile. Lately, their conversations in the absence of a fence had seemed awkward, stilted. Yet now, looking over the peaceful water, Conrad felt a sense of release in his disclosure. He heard a shout and raucous laughter coming from the beach. He wavered. 'It's just all in my head, Wally. You know, in my subconscious.'

'Rubbish, mate! I'm not lettin' you back out on me now!' Conrad was unsure how to respond. Wally helped out. 'I'm pleased to meet the real Mr Bentley.'

'You mean the madman?'

'Yep. The crazy man who sees the ghost of a German soldier who died one hundred years ago.' Wally's voice shifted to a more serious tone. 'Surely by now, mate, you would know that it's all been fate that's led you to this letter.'

'That's what dear old Franz Deppner said to me!'

'I'm not gonna pretend I understand all this, Conrad. I'm not into spirits and ghosts, and all that shit, but I know you're a deep thinker, an overthinker, so…'

'I think Wolf's gone! I haven't felt his presence for a few weeks.'

'It's simple, mate. You've completed your mission.'

'You think so?'

'By finding his family, you've given young Wolf a voice—what you set out to do from the start. A voice for all those poor bastards who got killed in that frickin' war to end all wars.' Wally paused. 'Wolf's given you the thumbs up, mate. There's no more for you to do.'

'But I still feel like there's a loose end.'

Wally closed his eyes for a few seconds and considered his response. 'Well, it looks like my Trish has given you the answer, mate.'

'You mean music? A string quartet?'

'Yep.'

Conrad felt himself sliding into a sea of emotion, a sea of relief. He fought back tears. He leaned back his head and peered up into the night sky. The full moon was breathtakingly bright. Parties around the bay were coming to a natural close as the revellers calmed down, reflected on their New Year's resolutions or sought out comfortable beds.

Moments passed in silence…

'Are you falling asleep, Wally?'

'No, but it won't be long. But please, keep goin', mate. Tell me more about the real Conrad Bentley.'

Conrad accepted the invitation. In a slow and confident voice he revealed stories from his childhood in England, memories of clambering on his father's knee while the family celebrated birthdays, admiring his parents for their adventurous spirit in moving to the other side of the world, and growing to love Hobart, their new home with its attractive mountain and river harbour. Conrad explained that his sister, through researching the family tree, had uncovered a previously unknown branch of the Bentley family in America.

'Wally?'

'Still here, mate.'

'Apparently, we've got a skeleton in the closet! My great-grandfather abandoned his family in England and ran off to America with his mistress who was German, or maybe Scandinavian. The trail's gone cold because the mistress probably used a false passport to get to England after the First World War.'

Conrad continued. He surprised himself with his train of thought and candour. The colours of his youth revealed themselves—meeting Gretel, marrying at a young age and both learning how to navigate the path to adulthood as young parents. He expressed pride in his three children and the distinct personalities and quirks of his grandchildren.

Wally's breathing slowed. He shifted position and was close to falling asleep, but managed, 'I'm still listening, mate.'

Conrad talked about music as his constant companion, and of his pleasure in taking up the violin at a relatively mature age. 'Did I tell you I used to play the oboe in the Army Reserve Band, before I switched to the violin?' He described his time as a military bandsman and thought back to when Alan, his quartet leader, had shown him a picture of Paul Hindemith, the German composer and violist, posing as a member of a wartime string quartet. Conrad recalled feeling somewhat uneasy, but equally fascinated by the image of four elegant, highly polished instruments shining bright against dull German uniforms. 'I researched this Hindemith bloke, Wally. Before he faced combat on the Western Front, his music-loving commander instructed him to set up a quartet to perform for military personnel. Imagine that! The top brass listening to the sweet sounds of Haydn's Emperor with bombs exploding in the background!' Conrad thoughts turned to his English great-grandfathers who were both musicians. He knew they had also fought in the Great War and wondered if they too had been recruited to play music for officers.

Melodies, rhythms and rich, full chords began to whirl and sparkle in Conrad's mind.

'Wally, I'm warming to this idea of writing a string quartet.' He smiled to himself. Yes! That's how I can pay tribute to the soldiers—to Wolf.

'Wally…?'

This time there were only faint snores in reply. Conrad shut his eyes. In a soft voice, almost a whisper, he continued to talk to his best friend. 'I think a quartet just might work. Music for strings can express the horror of war and the tragic death of young, idealistic men.' He stopped to consider his statement. 'Do you think death is what it's all about?' Wally gave no answer. He looked peaceful in his slumber. Conrad's mind travelled back to kneeling beside his father as he lay dying, peacefully, in his own home, held by his family who cared for him so dearly. Conrad's recollection was vivid—his mother tenderly cradling his father's head in her lap and gently caressing his cheeks. His siblings gathered around in a circle, reaching out, crying softly and saying their farewells. 'It's a strange thing to say Wally, but it was beautiful to see. It was like looking at a painting.' Conrad recalled his father reaching for his hand. He saw no pain in his father's eyes, just something like acceptance, maybe happiness. Conrad's tears fell. Oh Dad, I wish you could have heard my Sage Quartet at its best.

Conrad missed the camaraderie and banter of his quartet. Sounds of the music that they had rehearsed and performed floated in and out of his thoughts. He felt a wave of exhilaration wash over him as he contemplated music for his own soldier's quartet, motifs that would not only express the despair of combat but also comradeship, a voice for those who made it home. His thoughts turned to Lieutenant Brown. He looked forward to more talks with Bessie Furlani and learning how her father survived the Great War.

He paused. The joyous sounds in his head turned melancholic as he thought of those countless soldiers who had not returned—of Wolf Deppner, Bruno Klug, their lieutenant and so many more.

The distraction made him feel anxious. His thoughts raced. There's an ocean of good string quartets out there. How can I ensure my soldier's quartet is not derivative? How many movements? A major or minor key? What type of harmonies? What cadence for the final bar? A resolution. Or should the quartet leave the listener anticipating more? An unresolved war…

Conrad closed his eyes as the sounds of his quartet faded behind sniggers and insults from his inner voice. You fool, Bentley! This is a ridiculous idea. You don't have it in you. Give it up.

After a while, Conrad sighed and opened his eyes. Again, he noticed the splendour of the moon. It captivated him. As his doubts began to fade, he thought of the letter of fate, of its challenges, of the excitement and rewards gained from solving most of its riddles, its mysteries and deeply hidden secrets…

He smiled to himself as his thoughts turned to Gretel. He imagined her waking in the morning, demanding that they all go for another swim and then wandering off with Patricia in the late afternoon, armed with their watercolours and oil paints to capture the desired contrast of colours of the bay at twilight.

He looked around and was drawn to a gentle glow of light shining through the glass of the sliding doors. Patricia had thoughtfully left on a lamp in anticipation of their inebriated retreat to sleep. The soft light enhanced the beauty of a vase of vibrant blue flowers.

His breathing slowed. There were sounds of insects. He could just make out the sound of waves lapping against the granite boulders in the cove. He heard faint sounds of other swimmers taking a night swim, their first for the New Year, the effect of celebratory champagne a buffer against the cool water.

The moon appeared closer, incredibly brighter.

Conrad sensed another presence. A soldier. There was no odour of dirt or dampness.

Wolf's uniform was crisp, spotless…

'Thank you for finding me, Mr Bentley.'

Conrad's inner voice of doubt conceded defeat. 'Wolf, I'm planning to compose a soldier's quartet.'

'That sounds splendid. What better way to give a voice to fallen soldiers than through music. I applaud your plan, Mr Bentley.'

Wolf turned and gazed out over the Tasman Sea. He looked young and handsome.

Moments passed in silence…

Conrad closed his eyes. A gentle breeze caressed his cheek. He felt reassured, happy.

'Wolf?'

The moon slowly drifted back behind her protective shield of clouds.

'Farewell, Mr Bentley.'

Acknowledgements:

Patricia Baldwin, Grant Bewick, Steve Brown, Robyn Colman, Col. Mario Cremer, Anke Frank, Joe Furlani, Tony Hickey, Pascal Hirsch, Irene Jepson, Michael Knieper, Gilles Lagin, Jo St Leon, Maj. Chris Talbot, members of my German conversation group and local bush walking club

To Bessie Furlani and Paul Thost, two nonagenarians with strong links to this story, whose vitality has been a great inspiration to me.

I thank the Europeans who are also at the centre of this narrative:

Willi Deppner, Stefan Busch and Piet Janssen (pseudonyms).

In memory of Franz Deppner, the third inspiring nonagenarian.

This book resonates with the voice of Wolf Deppner who, like too many others of his generation, died in the war to end all wars. Wolf spoke to me, loudly…

Dr Rosie Dub: https://centreforstory.com/rosub/

The following people responded to my persistent emails and, in turn, helped shape the storyline:

Ilka Borowski, https://www.volksbund.de/home.html

Kathy Duncombe, http://www.bica.org.au/brunyquarantinestation/

Andreas Kitz, http://www.reserve-infanterie-regiment-68.de/

Klaus-Dieter Stellmacher, https://www.fraktur.com/

Philipp Steinhoff, www.erbenermittlung-freiburg.de

In addition:

Army Museum of Tasmanian

Archives Office of the Anglican Diocese of Melbourne

Bellerive Yacht Club

Centre for City History, City Archives (Zentrum für Stadtgeschichte – Stadtarchiv), Bochum, Germany

Derwent Symphony Orchestra

Federal Archives Department (Bundesarchiv Abteilung Militärarchiv), Freiburg, Germany

Libraries Tasmania

Mayor of Bussiares, Monsieur Fraeyman

Mayor of Licy-Clignon, Monsieur Julliet

Municipal Clerk, Madame Guilmain

Wesley Hobart Museum and Heritage Centre

It was not possible to devote the time needed to write this book without the love and encouragement from my wife and immediate family.

Shawline Publishing Group Pty Ltd
www.shawlinepublishing.com.au

SLP
SHAWLINE
PUBLISHING
GROUP